The Hanging at the Hollow Tree

A JOURNAL THROUGH TIME MYSTERY

SARAH M STEPHEN

WZE PRESS

Copyright © 2022 by Sarah M Stephen

All rights reserved. No portion of this book may be reproduced in any form without written permission from the publisher or author, except as permitted by copyright law.

WZE Press
Vancouver, B.C.
https://wzepress.ca

Edited by Janet Fretter
Cover by ebooklaunch.com

Library and Archives Canada Cataloguing in Publication
The Hanging at the Hollow Tree / by Sarah M Stephen
ISBN: 978-1-7778330-4-6 (paperback)
ISBN: 978-1-7778330-3-9 (digital)

This is a work of fiction. Names, characters, places, and incidents are of the author's imagination and used fictitiously.

To my parents. Thank you for everything.

A Note about Language

This book is set in Canada and written in Canadian English (which is very similar to British English). If you're unfamiliar with the differences, we use *our* instead of *or* in "colour," "favour," and "neighbour" and double the *l* in "travelled."

CHAPTER 1

Jack (1897)

DETECTIVE JACK WINSTON pinched the bridge of his nose and blinked, but it was no good. The lines of his journal still swam, thanks to the whisky he had enjoyed the night before. He rested his hand on the book. It was probably for the best. He should save the remaining pages for when he needed Riley's help, not just to recount how his uncle had been overly generous at dinner the night before—the cause of his current state. Still, writing to Riley always picked up his spirits. He would keep it brief.

Just as Winston picked up his pencil, Constable Thomas Miller entered the room. "Sir, there's a body. In Stanley Park. Young stable-boy reported it, poor lad." Miller fiddled with a button on his cuff. "Found the body hanging near the Hollow Tree."

Winston rose. The fresh air of the park would help clear his head. He would preserve the journal for more pressing issues. "Call for the carriage, Thomas. We'll go at once."

THE JOSTLING OF the carriage did nothing to help Winston's head, but as soon as they crossed into the park, he sat forward and inhaled deeply. The air was so pure among the trees the fogginess in his head began to clear. Winston had felt the same on his first visit to the park. He had recently arrived in the city and his uncle had taken him on a tour. Private coaches and hansom cabs had lined the park roadway as they approached the Hollow Tree, the eager passengers waiting their turn to see if their carriages could really fit inside its trunk.

Miller's voice brought Winston back to the present moment. "The poor boy was breathless when he got to the station. He couldn't find the park groundskeeper and thought it best to tell us right away."

Winston nodded.

"And I notified Evans. He'll meet us there."

As the carriage slowed, Winston saw that rather than a lineup of tourists, a lone horse was tied to a rail at the road's edge. Ahead of it, a single carriage waited. He recognized it as belonging to Doctor Evans, the city's medical examiner.

Winston and Miller approached in silence, a blanket of decaying leaves cushioning the sound of their footsteps. Evans stood beside a man Winston didn't recognize. The doctor turned to nod his greeting, but the other man's focus remained on the body. Winston braced himself to examine the scene.

The body wasn't suspended from the Hollow Tree but from one nearby. The famous landmark had few branches that would be strong enough to hold a man. Still, the location, so close to such a popular destination, struck Winston as a deliberate choice. He pulled his notebook from his satchel, his fingers glancing his journal, and made a note to consider the meaning of this location.

Evans introduced the man beside him as a park groundskeeper. A sturdy fellow in workman's clothing, he met Winston's eyes and said, "I was about to climb up and cut him down when the doctor stopped me. Said you'd want to look first."

Winston didn't really want to look, truth be told, but almost immediately, he realized what Evans had wanted him to see. He motioned for Miller to look at the ground.

"What are we looking for? I don't see anything," Miller said.

"Exactly. What did he stand on?"

"Ah, I see." Miller nodded and gave his chin a rub.

"Do you have a ladder?" Winston called to the groundskeeper.

"I do, but not with me. I rode up here." He gestured toward the horse. "I can return with my cart. Do you need anything else? You can use my knife to cut the rope if you haven't your own."

Winston produced a pocket knife from his satchel. "We might reach him by standing on a carriage. Before you go in search of that ladder," he said.

Winston returned his gaze to the body and steadied himself to take in the physical details. Although he'd been training to overcome his squeamishness, it was still a work in progress.

"Could he have jumped from the branch?" Miller asked.

"Doubtful," said Evans.

Winston inhaled and raised his eyes up the body, scanning quickly past the man's horribly reddened face, to look at the branch. It looked too insubstantial for a man to have jumped from. He wasn't sure how it was even supporting the body now. He approached the tree and rubbed his hand along the trunk. Its bark was cool, and pieces flecked onto his palm. In an instant, Winston was back in his neighbourhood park in Toronto, where he had played as a child. He had stood behind a tree with his eyes shut and couldn't understand how his odler brotoher Ellis had found him in their hiding game. The trunk in front of him now would have easily hidden him from Ellis's view. He smiled at the memory, sliding his hand inside his pocket to feel for the stone Ellis had given him.

The constable's voice stirred Winston from his thoughts, and he realized he'd missed his question. "Can you repeat that, Thomas?"

Miller's brow knit in an expression of puzzlement. "I asked how would he have climbed up there? Or the groundskeeper?" He approached the tree and rubbed his hand along the trunk as if to look for what had so gripped Winston moments earlier.

Winston forced his attention back to the dead man. "That groundskeeper has probably spent more time in this park than anyone. He must know how to climb a tree."

Beside him, Miller shifted his weight as if he were about to walk toward the body. Winston held out his arm. If the hanged man had not done this to himself, they were now investigating a murder. They needed to look for signs of who had been there. "Thomas. Don't move. Do you see anything on the ground that may be of use? Footprints to suggest how many people were here? Tracks from a cart?"

Miller lowered himself to inspect the area. The ground was covered by a carpet of sodden leaves. He picked up a soggy yellow leaf by its stem and dropped it again. He stood and crushed it with his boot. After he failed to leave a mark, he frowned. "Nothing."

"Very well. Let's get this man down," Winston said. "Get the carriage. Stand on the driver's box. That should give you enough height to reach him."

Miller blanched at the request. Winston reconsidered. "We'll do it together. Evans and the groundskeeper can stand on the ground, and the driver can make sure the horses are still."

After the driver had manoeuvred the carriage close enough to the tree, Winston stepped back and steeled himself for what he was about to do. Miller was taller than he and would have a greater reach. "I'll hold his legs if you can cut the rope." He handed Miller the knife and clambered onto the front of the carriage, where the driver sat. Miller positioned himself next to him and steadied himself. Winston closed his eyes and warpped his arms around the hanged man's legs. As Miller worked beside him, Winston concentrated on breathing in the forest air. When he felt the rope slacken, Winston panicked, unsure what he was supposed to do with the body.

Below him, Evans called out. "Lower yourself, Jack. Bend at the knees. We'll take the body from you."

With his eyelids still pinched tight, Winston felt the slight rock of the carriage as Miller jumped to the ground. The wool of the dead man's trousers scratched against his cheek. He felt bile rise in his throat. The driver spoke softly to his horses—"Cush, cush now,"—a welcome distraction. Winston locked his knees as the men shifted the body into their arms, and only after they had relieved him of the weight did he open his eyes and slump against the driver's seat.

The driver produced a flask and shook it at Winston. Tempting, but he declined. It was hardly past nine in the morning. And he had a murder to solve.

Winston joined Doctor Evans, who hovered over the body where it lay on the forest floor. "Will you examine him today? I would like to know what you find."

Evans nodded. "I can start as soon as I get to the station. Will you inform the man's wife?"

"The man's wife? Is he known to you? Have you found identification papers?"

"I don't need to look for his identification. He is Arthur Pierce, a local businessman. I've seen him at the Gentlemen's Club." Evans brushed a leaf from his shoulder. "I'm surprised you didn't recognize him, Detective."

Kneeling beside Evans, Winston searched the dead man's face. "Yes, I have met him. Just the once, shortly after I arrived. He looks... he looks different. My uncle introduced us at one of his dinners." Winston looked away from the face with its unnatural hue and recalled the pleasant evening and the friendly man. "Hanging is a brutal death."

"It is, Detective." Evans pulled a handkerchief from his pocket and wiped at the dead man's brow.

"You're certain this is Pierce?"

"Absolutely." Evans replaced his handkerchief. Winston made a mental note never to accept Evans' handkerchief if offered. "Jack, his death will cause a stir no matter the cause, but especially if he was murdered."

"I know. Before I speak to his wife, I will return to the station to discuss it with Chief Constable Philpott." Winston stood, brushing his palms on his legs.

"If I'm not mistaken, he knew Pierce well," said Evans, also rising.

"Are you returning to the station now?" Winston nodded toward the doctor's carriage. He had persuaded the chief constable to provide Evans with one that could transport the dead. The idea of sharing a carriage with a corpse soured Winston's stomach. "You can ride with us, if you prefer. But we'll need to look at the scene a little more."

"I'll go with him, Jack," said Evans. "So he doesn't need to be alone."

Winston admired the doctor's compassion for the deceased. "Before you go, how long do you think this man has been dead?"

"It's hard to know. He is cold, but with today's temperature, that tells me little." Evans rubbed his hands together and blew on them as if to demonstrate his point.

"Someone would have noticed the body had it been here yesterday. Even in November, this is a popular destination." Winston nodded toward the people who had begun to gather at the edge of the roadway. The park groundskeeper was doing his best to send them along. How quickly word spread when people learned of the chance to see something macabre. They were far enough away they wouldn't have been able to identify the man, and Evans had thought to cover his face with his jacket. Winston opened his notebook to jot a reminder about furnishing Evans with some blankets. He looked up from the page to find the crowd dissipating as the body was loaded.

"I agree. This happened last night," Evans said before climbing aboard after the body.

The policemen stood in silence as the doctor's carriage began its descent. As it rounded the bend out of sight, Miller turned to Winston. "What are we looking for, sir?"

"Anything that might help us understand what happened here." Winston instructed Miller to walk in increasingly wider circles as he stared at the ground. "Let's do this methodically. Make a note of anything out of place."

They had been searching for several minutes when Miller called out. Before he approached where the constable stood, Winston bent down and positioned two twigs into a cross formation to mark where he had reached in his search. The younger man stood beside a dark piece of fabric resting on the leaves. "What is it?" Winston asked.

Miller bent to pick up the material and unfurled a glove for a left hand. He squeezed it. "It's damp, but not soaked. It rained yesterday morning and stopped just after noon. I don't think this spent any time in the rain. It would be soggy."

"Meaning it was left here in the last twenty hours or so," Winston said, checking his pocket watch. He reached for the glove. "From AP" had been embossed near the edge of the interior cuff. *AP.* Arthur Pierce. "Well found, Thomas. Let's bring it back to the station."

They continued their search for another thirty minutes until Winston was satisfied. "We should return. We've put off our next task long enough," he said. He didn't relish having to inform his uncle about the murder of his friend. Before he climbed into the waiting carriage, Winston stretched his neck to take in the height of the tree, straining to see the top. It must be fifty feet around, and from the road, its hollow core was not readily evident.

WHEN THEY ARRIVED at the station, Winston waved at the desk clerk and pointed to the chief constable's closed door. The desk clerk shrugged. Winston knocked.

His uncle, Chief Constable Lawrence Philpott, sat behind a large desk with the morning paper spread across its solid top. He smiled grimly at his nephew. "Jack. I heard there was a body in the park." Winston marvelled at how well rested his uncle appeared despite their celebration of the previous night.

"A young stableboy brought the report."

"And was there much to it?"

"The body?" Winston swallowed. "Hanged. Doctor Evans attended. He believes the dead man did not hang himself. He couldn't have managed it alone. Evans is examining the body now."

"He is efficient. A fine addition to our team, lad."

Winston forced his shoulders to relax. He needed to tell Philpott about the dead man's identity, but it was never easy to break such news. "I enjoy working with him. But Evans is not what I have come to talk to you about." Winston sat, delaying for as long as possible the next moment. "The body in the park. You know him."

"Not a scoundrel, then. Who is it?"

Winston bristled at his uncle's assumption that anyone found dead in the park was a ne'er-do-well. "Doctor Evans recognized him as Arthur Pierce. I met him at your house once."

Philpott's eyes widened and he leaned across the desk, mouth agape. He inclined an ear toward Winston as if to hear him better. "Pierce? Dead?" The chief constable blanched. "Hanged? I saw him a few days ago. He seemed well, happy."

Winston pulled his notebook from inside his jacket. "Where did you see him?"

"Are you interviewing me?"

Winston waved a pencil in the air. "Unofficially, sir. You're providing context, especially as you saw him in the days preceding his death."

Philpott licked his lips. "It was at the Vancouver Gentlemen's Club. Several of us gather for a monthly dinner."

"Who was present?"

"A selection of men. Guardians of the city, if you will."

"How so?"

"We hold influence in various spheres. Pierce was a money man. He knew who had it, where to get it. I'm the law. We have representatives from the railway, the press, shipping."

"Collins?"

Philpott formed a line with his lips. "I'd rather not share the others' names, unless it's vital."

"It may be later, but I don't need the information right now. I should speak to Pierce's wife. If her husband was influential, many will be interested when they learn of his death. It's better she hears from the police first."

"I will come with you." Philpott stood. "I've known Caroline for some time. She will appreciate hearing the news from someone familiar to her." He drew his hand over his face. "You're certain it is Arthur? You only met him once."

"Evans recognized him first. He knew him immediately. We can pass by the morgue on our way to see Mrs. Pierce if you like."

Philpott ignored the offer. "Jack," he said, extending his arm, "I'm not sure we need to tell her the circumstances."

"The circumstances? Her husband was murdered. Why spare her that?"

"If it's murder, we will investigate. Until Evans is certain, it is sufficient for her to know her husband is dead."

"I believe Evans is confident it was murder. We could lose the opportunity to find the killer if we wait to investigate."

Philpott's face darkened. "Jack. Not a word to the widow about murder until Evans has prepared his report."

"I don't understand." Why was his uncle dismissing his perspective?

"I'm not discussing this." Philpott set his jaw. "And you're not to discuss murder with Caroline Pierce until we know more."

Winston opened his mouth, and Philpott held his hand out to stop the question. "I'll handle it."

Without another word, Winston followed his uncle out of the station and into his carriage, unease simmering in his stomach.

CHAPTER 2

Riley (2017)

LEAVES CRUNCHED UNDER Riley Finch's feet as she sucked in the crisp autumn air. Despite the chilly temperature, she wore only a light long-sleeved top. Soon she would be too warm.

After a quick stretch of her legs, she ran west along Vancouver's seawall, setting an easy pace to start. Her route took her from False Creek over the Burrard Bridge. From the bridge, she could just pick out the swell and slope of Vancouver Island one hundred kilometres away. Such a rare sight on a November day. She drank in the blue sky and view, a tonic to fortify her against the inevitable weeks of rain the city would soon endure.

She picked up speed, her breaths coming faster, as she passed the beaches that lined English Bay. This morning they were populated by geese and gulls pecking at debris left by the tide. Endorphins flowing, Riley turned into Stanley Park and ran up the hill to Prospect Point. She paused to gulp water at the fountain by the visitors' stand, easing the burn in her lungs, and turned to head down the hill.

She stopped at the Hollow Tree. The city's landmark had suffered damage in a recent storm, and the stump, now reinforced with steel ribs, served as a reminder of the majestic tree that once stretched into the sky. How many stories could this tree tell? She thought of the classic photograph that tourists, even today, continue to take. Did Detective Jack Winston have a photo of himself standing in its hollow?

Jack. Although she was already warm from the run, a wave of heat washed through Riley when she thought of him. The connection they had discovered through his journal energized her, as did partnering with one of the city's first detectives.

He'd left her a note this morning, the first in a while. Riley had read it twice before leaving for her run. His message had altered her planned route.

> *Dear Riley,*
>
> *I trust this note finds you well. Today I attended the scene of a body found hanging near the Hollow Tree in Stanley Park. Does this magnificent tree still stand in your time?*
>
> *The man who died was a prominent businessman, and already I sense his death will affect many. In fact, I'm troubled by the reaction of Chief Constable Philpott. He suggested I treat the death as suicide rather than as murder, whereas Doctor Evans and I are quite certain the man did not cause his own death.*
>
> *If you have a moment, could you look into Arthur Pierce? Share only what you feel comfortable telling me.*
>
> *With thanks,*
>
> *Jack*

Pierce's name wasn't familiar to her, but the archive at the Vancouver History Museum, where Riley worked, was sure to have information about him if he'd been influential in Jack's time. Before she looked him up, she'd decided to run to the park to get a sense of where the man had died.

This note was the longest Jack had written in a while. Without explicitly agreeing, they'd been writing shorter notes as they neared the end of the blank pages in the journal. How would they continue when the book was filled? She had thought, back at the end of her first case with Jack, there'd been an answer. Johnny had given her a book he'd found in the small collection of his great-grandfather's things handed down through the family. She'd written in it and waited for Jack to confirm they'd be able to use it to continue their correspondence. He had yet to reply and hadn't written a word about it in their original journal, now running out of pages. She also couldn't bring it up. How could she explain she'd come to know his great-grandson when Jack wasn't even married yet?

No, she'd decided the book inscribed to "Riley" must have been Jack following an impulse in his later years. He had believed she'd get it someday. And he'd been right.

Thinking about the dwindling number of pages in the journal left a knot in her stomach. She pushed it from her mind, yet again.

A group of tourists crowded the tree now. Riley didn't want to linger too long and risk getting cold. She could come back another time, though exactly what she was expecting to find, she wasn't sure. She snapped a couple of photos of the area around the tree and, with a parting glance, continued down the hill.

When she got to her apartment building, she checked her phone in the elevator. Her sister had sent four texts.

Call me.

Where are you???

We need to talk.

!!!!

Riley dialled her sister's number as soon as she stepped into her apartment. As was typical, Lucy didn't answer.

When Riley checked her phone after she'd showered and changed, her sister still hadn't called her back. With only two weeks until Lucy's wedding, Riley had become accustomed to her sister's increasingly panicked texts. She would rush to respond only to learn the emergency was the blue napkins the venue had ordered didn't match the blue of the ink on the menus.

Riley settled onto the couch with her laptop and had just pulled up a search engine to type in the name of the businessman Jack had mentioned in his message when another text from Lucy arrived.

Get. Here.

Riley tried calling, and once again the call went unanswered.

Riley locked her bike to the rack outside her sister's apartment building. Throughout the twenty-minute ride across the bridge and through downtown, she'd run through different scenarios that could explain Lucy's message. Her mind raced back to when she'd received the call that their father was in the hospital following a heart attack. Lucy had answered the phone immediately that day, so it couldn't be as bad as that. And knowing Lucy, it was another napkin-like emergency. Still, Riley had pedalled a little faster than usual.

She missed living with her sister but couldn't blame Lucy for wanting to live with Alex, her fiancé, even if it was in his cramped Coal Harbour apartment. His view of Burrard Inlet and the mountains to the north made up for the lack of space.

She knocked on the door to their apartment and Lucy flung it open, eyes wide with panic, and pulled Riley into the apartment.

Riley grasped her sister's arms, holding her still. "What's going on?" Over Lucy's shoulder, Riley couldn't see anything out the large balcony windows. They were covered in paper. A pile of fabric sat heaped in the middle of the room. The place was a cluttered mess. "Where's Alex? What's with the windows? And the fabric?"

Lucy shrugged out of Riley's grip and threw her arms around her. "I'm so glad you're here! I don't know what to do."

"With what?" Riley scanned the room. At the best of times, she described Lucy as mildly organized. This chaos was next level. With a toe, she pushed aside a pile of cloth at her feet to reveal tails of string tied to forks and spoons. She held her sister at arm's length again. "Lucy, what's going on? Where's Alex?"

"I'm here." Lucy's fiancé stepped out from the bedroom. His mouth formed a thin line.

Riley gave him a quick hug, whispering into his ear, "Why didn't you call me? What's she doing?"

"Honestly, I'm not entirely sure. This morning she woke up, spoke to your mother, and then did this." He pointed up. "Yesterday our place was spotless."

Overhead, half a dozen forks and knives hung from the ceiling. Riley stared at the display, bewildered. She guided her sister to the couch. "Luce. Look at me. What's going on?"

Lucy sighed. "I wanted to see if a dark theme would work." She pointed at the windows. "You know, like a magical starry night."

"And the utensils?"

"I was going to hang them from the ceiling. Since I don't have any disco balls or anything like that here."

"Seriously?"

Lucy turned to Alex. "Why don't we have any disco balls?" Her voice cracked.

"We haven't really had a need for them, I guess."

"Do you want disco balls?" Lucy asked her fiancé.

Alex looked at the ceiling and shrugged.

Riley opened her mouth to comment, but thought better of it. She got up from the couch and walked to the balcony window, peeled back a sheet of black paper, and there was that spectacular view. The low sun reflected off the water of the inlet, and the November light made the frosted tops of the mountains glow. Amazing. She turned her attention back to her sister.

Alex had his arm wrapped around Lucy. "I don't think this is really what you're concerned about, Lucy. Tell Riley."

"Tell me what?" Riley stepped toward her sister. "What's up, Lucy?"

"I just heard from Mom. She was going on about this thing she's invested in. Said she's putting in money for Alex and me as a wedding gift." Lucy stood and grabbed Riley by the shoulders, locking eyes with her. "Schools."

"Schools? I don't get it." An odd gift choice for Lucy, who had a long wish list from high-end homeware stores.

"In Africa. She's invested in some company that's building them. Focused on educating girls."

"Sounds like a thoughtful gift. What's the problem?"

Lucy looked at Alex, then at her sister. "I thought Mom would give us a gift like towels or something." She flushed. "I mean, it's great to support schools. Obviously. I just thought. . ."

As she spoke, Lucy seemed to realize how selfish she sounded. Her reaction didn't surprise Riley; Lucy had always loved fine things. She was fashionable and had translated her keen sense of style into a successful career managing a local fashion boutique. "I get you're disappointed, but it's really up to Mom, isn't it? What she gives you, I mean." Riley had spoken gently, but she felt resentment rise. Lucy's crisis wasn't so much a crisis as a tantrum. There'd been no need for her to rush over for this self-centred episode. In two weeks, her sister's "emergencies" would be Alex's problem.

"What about the decorations?" Lucy's voice had taken on a whine. "What do I do about those?" She pointed to the utensils and fabric on the floor.

Riley pulled her sister's hand and sandwiched it between her own. "It's a little late to be dreaming up new decorations. And I don't think flatware is ever going to be suitable for styling a wedding, no matter who you are."

At this, Lucy giggled. Her giggles grew louder, erupting into uncontrollable snorts of laughter. Riley bit the inside of her cheek until she couldn't help dissolving in laughter too. Alex shifted on the couch, his face betraying confusion. He'd been Lucy's boyfriend for several years but had never seen an episode of Finch Sister Hysterics, or FSH, as their mother had labelled them. As Riley found her voice again, she explained how one sister would say or do something that wouldn't be overly funny to most people and the other would break into a fit of giggles, bringing the other along until neither could remember what had set them off.

"What was I thinking?" Lucy said, trying to catch her breath. "I've already given the restaurant my instructions. It's just with the wedding two weeks away, I'm second-guessing myself."

Riley inhaled deeply. "That's completely understandable. But you've got this figured out. Mom's coming this week to see your final dress fitting, right? I'll ask her, gently, about what she's planning to get you."

"Thanks," Lucy said, pulling her sister close for an embrace. "I just want everything to go perfectly."

"I'm sure it will," Riley replied.

CHAPTER 3

Jack

After a short ride, the policemen arrived at a grand home in the West End with grounds stretching most of a city block. Both removed their hats as they approached the front door. A servant—Winston assumed it was the butler—opened it moments after Philpott knocked. Winston noted the butler didn't ask their names when his uncle asked to see Mrs. Pierce.

The servant showed Winston and Philpott into a receiving room. Philpott whispered something to the servant, who nodded before leaving them. "I've asked him to have tea prepared for Mrs. Pierce. The news we are about to deliver will shock her."

"What news?" A beautiful woman entered, skirt swishing as she walked. Her auburn hair was artfully arranged in soft swirls at the top of her head and held in place by a pearled comb. She wore a peach dress, finer than the day dresses Winston's mother wore. The soft colour contrasted against the grey sky filling the windows at the front of the room. Seeing the chief constable, the woman beamed and grasped his hands. "Lawrence, it's always so lovely to see you, but you were here only last week. And who have you brought?"

Despite the clouds, there was enough light that none of the room's electric lights had been turned on. The woman stepped back and turned toward Winston, motioning as if she were going to spin him around. Philpott stopped her with a gentle head shake and led her to a couch. He assumed the position beside her.

"Mrs. Pierce. Caroline." He exhaled. "I have some troubling news."

She blinked. "News?"

"It's Arthur." Philpott changed his position on the couch, readying himself to support Mrs. Pierce. "I'm afraid he's dead."

"Dead? I don't . . ." The woman swallowed and looked from Philpott to Winston, who sat in a chair opposite her. "I don't understand."

Philpott turned to Winston. "This is Detective Jack Winston. He has just seen Arthur. His body." Colour rose in Philpott's cheeks.

"I don't understand. Was there an accident?" The woman looked dazed. Her voice was pitched a tone higher. "He rides in the park most mornings. He's there now."

Winston leaned forward. "He was in the park, madam. I did not see a horse, but we will check." He pulled his notebook from his pocket. "Can you tell me anything about his animal?"

"Was he trampled?" Her posture stiffened and she brought a hand to her throat.

Winston looked to his uncle, who shook his head as if to quiet his nephew. "We don't yet know the cause of death. The doctor who was called to the scene, he recognized him, and I informed Chief Philpott." He paused with a pencil poised in midair. "It would be helpful to know where your husband kept his horse."

Confusion clouded the woman's face, as if she still hadn't understood what they had told her. "At. . . at the stables in the park. He has a few horses there."

Philpott placed his hand on the widow's arm. "I'm so sorry, Caroline. Who can we call for you? And who should we have come to officially identify the body? Your husband's man?"

At his touch, Mrs. Pierce slumped against Chief Constable Philpott. "Are you certain it's Arthur?" she asked in a muffled voice. "He was here. Last night. We—we have plans to visit Toronto and Montreal next month. Our son is in Toronto." She made a move as if to stand. Philpott squeezed her hand.

"Caroline, it's the worst news. Let's just sit here a moment."

A servant walked in carrying a tray of tea. She set it down on the table beside Chief Constable Philpott. "Oh, Mary, how good of you," said Mrs. Pierce as she turned to Philpott. "Did you arrange for this, Lawrence? You're ever so thoughtful."

Philpott swallowed. "Caroline. Detective Winston here—"

Caroline Pierce's head snapped in Winston's direction. "Detective? Was Arthur murdered?"

"Sir, if I may?" Winston cleared his throat. "Mrs. Pierce. My condolences for the loss of your husband. I am truly sorry to bring such distressing news. I'm afraid I have more." Winston winced against the pain he was about to cause this woman. "Your husband was hanged, Mrs. Pierce. We found him near the Hollow Tree." Beside her, his uncle's face darkened. Winston continued, keeping his focus on the woman. "Does that spot hold any significance for your husband?" Winston sensed Philpott stiffen beside Mrs. Pierce. "I know you need to grieve your husband and your loss, but if I can just ask you a few questions—"

"That's quite enough, Detective." Philpott's tone was clipped.

Tears had formed in the woman's eyes. "Oh, Arthur." A sob escaped her, and she collapsed against Philpott.

Winston nodded and kept his tongue.

Philpott wrapped an arm around the widow, then seemed to remember himself and removed it. "Caroline, I will wait with you while we find someone else to comfort you. Is your sister in the city?"

They waited as Mrs. Pierce collected herself. She looked up and smoothed an invisible wrinkle in her skirt. "Yes, her house is a few streets away."

"I remember," said Philpott, nodding. "Jack, can you fetch Mrs. Pierce's sister? She's on Bute."

"It's a blue house. Smaller than my own, of course, but her husband is not as well established as—" She wiped a tear with a handkerchief produced by Philpott. "Arthur was helping him."

WINSTON EXCUSED HIMSELF and walked the short distance to the Sawyer residence, following the instructions the Pierces' servant had given him along with the address. His uncle's assumption that everyone knew where everyone else lived in the young city reminded him of his mother, who made a point of knowing the best families and where they lived. Though she was in Toronto, he was certain she tracked the names of important Vancouver citizens and would know which of the eight houses dotting Bute Street was the Sawyer residence.

As he approached the house, Winston reflected on his uncle's reaction to the morning's events. Philpott rarely attended a crime, though perhaps his involvement today was understandable. He was more invested because he knew the victim, which perhaps explained his deeper interest in setting the direction of the case. And yet he seemed against labelling it a case at all. Winston's thoughts were interrupted when the door opened almost immediately after his sharp rap. A maid ushered him into a welcoming sitting room.

After the briefest of moments, a woman who could only be Abigail Sawyer entered. She and her sister shared the same hair colour, bright eyes, and delicate chin. Her dress was not as fine as her sister's, and, as Caroline Pierce had promised, her house was not as grand. But of the two, the woman before him was the greater beauty. Winston imagined the sisters had enjoyed their choice of suitors in their younger years.

"Mrs. Sawyer?" Winston asked.

The woman nodded her head slightly upon hearing her name. "Yes?" Her voice was low and soothing, and the word was spoken as if it were two syllables.

"My name is Detective Jack Winston, and I've just come from your sister's house."

"Caroline!" Mrs. Sawyer's hand flew to her mouth. "Is she all right?" She steadied herself against the back of a wing chair. The gesture was dramatic, though speaking to a detective about one's sister was perhaps sufficient reason for drama.

"Your sister is fine, madam. Well, she is unharmed. It's her husband. He was found dead this morning."

"Arthur? Dead?" The woman staggered. Winston offered his arm to guide her to a sofa. "What happened?"

Winston considered how to answer. She would soon hear the details from her sister. Perhaps it would be a kindness to Mrs. Pierce that he share information so she didn't have to. Winston explained about Pierce's body having been found in the park, but didn't detail the manner of death. "She's asked for you to join her at the house," he said.

The woman looked stricken for a moment, then straightened her skirt. "Of course." She swept her fingers across her head in a practised motion, tucking a stray cinnamon strand into the full knot at the top of her head. "I just need a moment." She exited the room, and he heard her footsteps as she climbed the stairs. She descended a few minutes later in a coat and boots.

"Do you mind if we walk, Detective? The carriage for such a short distance. . ."

He waved his fingers to signal he understood. "Walking will be faster, and I think it's best we get to your sister's as quickly as we can, madam. She's had the worst kind of shock."

"I can't imagine." She shuddered, the gesture taking just a little longer than necessary. She remained on the bottom step, reaching to grab Winston's arm. "This is a tragedy, you understand, Detective. Many will feel his loss, though no one will feel it as deeply as Caroline." She lowered her eyes.

Winston caught the eye of a maid who stood two steps above Mrs. Sawyer, balancing a selection of hats across her palms. The young woman flushed and dropped her gaze.

Abigail Sawyer stepped into the hall. "You said he died this morning. Accident, I assume? It is shocking how quickly people drive their carriages. I am not surprised, really. A terrible pity it's Arthur, though. He really will be missed. I should send word to my husband."

She spoke in rapid bursts as she considered the red and black hats offered by her maid. Her hand hesitated at the brim of the red one and she frowned. "Really, Bess. I hardly think red is appropriate," she muttered as she placed the black hat atop her head, pinning it with skilled fingers. Turning back to Winston, she said, "I managed myself for several years and haven't become used to someone else adjusting my hat."

Winston let Mrs. Sawyer continue her chatter while they walked the two streets to Mrs. Pierce's house. When they arrived, the grim butler opened the door, nodding at Mrs. Sawyer.

She rushed into the house without waiting for the butler to take her coat. "Caroline!" she called out upon seeing her sister. She slid out of the coat and held it behind her. The butler moved forward wordlessly and took it from her.

Abigail Sawyer collapsed onto the couch beside her sister. "I'm so sorry. Have they told you anything?" She moved with such energy that Philpott rose to give them space.

"He's. . . he's dead," Mrs. Pierce sobbed. "Lawrence says he killed himself. How will I ever look anyone in the eye again?"

Winston snapped his head to look at Chief Philpott. The chief cleared his throat. His face was unreadable. Winston felt tension building in his jaw. This wasn't what they had agreed on.

"Caroline, Detective Winston and I will leave you now. Shall I have Mrs. Philpott call on you this afternoon, or will Mrs. Sawyer stay with you today?"

Caroline Pierce dabbed at her eyes and sniffed. "You're a dear, Lawrence. There's no need for your wife to call. I'm sure my sister will stay as long as I need her." Abigail Sawyer nodded, eyes watery.

"Very well. Caroline, Mrs. Sawyer." Chief Philpott nodded at each woman in turn, and Winston followed him out of the room. When they were inside the chief's carriage, Philpott leaned to his nephew. "Make sure you keep me informed of your progress on this. I cannot imagine why Arthur killed himself, but it is important we discover the answer. The press will want to know his reasons, as will his wife." He paused.

Winston began to correct his uncle. "Doctor Evans, he said—"

Philpott cut him off. "Let's wait until he's examined the body."

Heat pricked Winston's neck. "Of course, sir," he said. He patted his jacket pocket, finding the familiar shape of the stone his brother Ellis had given him before his disappearance so many years ago. He'd kept it with him since his boyhood. Its smooth shape brought balance in moments of unease. As much as Winston disagreed with his uncle's approach, Evans would confirm the body they had seen was that of a murdered man, and then Winston could begin the investigation. He had nothing to gain by challenging his uncle over this point when it would be corrected shortly. He ventured a question. "Did you ask Mrs. Pierce if her husband's behaviour had recently changed?"

"I did not. She needs time to mourn before we ask such indelicate questions."

Winston stiffened. "That may be true, Uncle, but her memory will fade the longer we leave her. As difficult as it will be, we must ask for this information."

Philpott frowned. "You can wait a day. In fact, it may be best if I speak to her tomorrow and tell you what I learn for your report. Do you understand?"

Winston nodded as he clenched the stone in his fist.

CHAPTER 4

Riley

AFTER SETTLING HER sister and leaving Alex with a "she's your problem now" look, Riley returned home, eager to help Jack. When she opened the journal to send him a quick note confirming she would do as he had asked, she was surprised to find another message from him.

> *Dear Riley,*
>
> *Have you ever had a day where you were forced to do something you knew was wrong, yet obligations prevented you from pursuing the right course of action? I find myself facing this situation with my uncle, the chief constable. Until now, our familial relationship has not interfered with our working one.*

Riley held her hand over the page. She hadn't received two messages in one day in quite some time. A familiar thrill hummed under her skin as she read more.

> *Today, however, he drew a line he forbids me to cross. It is in relation to Arthur Pierce, the man who this morning was found hanging near the Hollow Tree in Stanley Park.*
>
> *News of this man's death will trouble many. My uncle has asked me not to investigate this as a murder. I am*

troubled by my uncle's request. My unease stems from this: The scene reveals Pierce could neither have been left hanging by accident, nor could he have hanged himself.

Despite his personal relationship with the man and his wife, my uncle insisted he speak to the widow. I was not permitted to interview her properly, yet a murder investigation means I must treat the widow as a suspect until I know for certain she is not. I am concerned my uncle has compromised the investigation because of the dead man's status in the community.

I share this with you not because I think you can do anything with the information, but because it helps to share my thoughts with you.

Your friend,

Jack

Riley tapped her pen along the side of the book while she thought of her response.

Dear Jack,

This sounds like quite a situation. How will you look into the dead man without upsetting your uncle? Meanwhile, I will see what I can find from here.

R.

PS: The Hollow Tree still stands in Stanley Park, but it suffered a fire a few years ago and stands largely supported by metal rods. I wonder if you would recognize it.

Even though she was at home, Riley had countless resources at her fingertips. She started online by typing "Arthur Pierce" into the search bar.

She found surprisingly little about the man. According to a newspaper article published around the time of his death, he had invested in many ventures and raised capital from other residents for municipal facilities such as a playhouse. Despite his business mind, several people had lost money when he died, as their money was tied to an investment that failed because he was no longer around to guide it. Riley continued searching for another hour, finding nothing more.

She pushed her laptop away from her and rubbed the back of her neck. Why wasn't there anything more? Was he not as prominent as Jack seemed to think?

CHAPTER 5

Riley

RILEY'S DAY STARTED with an email from her boss, Claire Cale, asking to see her as soon as she arrived at the museum. Claire's request meant she couldn't start the morning in the archive room as she'd planned. Jack would have to wait.

The summons had Riley's mind racing as she made her way to Claire's office. The tone of the message had struck her as urgent. Had she overlooked something? Forgotten a meeting? She knocked softly on the open door and waited for Claire to look up from her laptop. "You wanted to see me?" Riley asked.

"Yes, good morning." Claire motioned to a chair opposite her desk. "Come in, please."

Riley took a seat and leaned forward, gripping the sides of the chair. As usual, Claire's desk was spotless, an oasis of calm in a chaos of clutter. Her office was small, with books crammed onto inadequate shelves and stacked in piles on the floor. "Did we have a meeting scheduled?" Riley's voice sounded squeaky to her own ears.

Claire must have read fear on her face. She offered a reassuring smile. "Not at all. I wanted to talk to you about the next exhibit. You did a great job going through the police files for our exhibit on policing in Vancouver's early years. And Doctor Lewis speaks highly of your work with him over the last few weeks."

Riley nodded, stifling a shudder as she pictured the mountain pine beetle. Doctor Lewis had asked Riley to sort through boxes of records related to his research on the invasive insect and how its destruction of trees was changing communities and the local forest industry. As a new archivist, she was prepared to do almost anything, but staring at bugs had been a low point. "I was hoping I could work on another cultural exhibit. I mean, natural exhibits are interesting, but researching them is not really my area."

Claire's smile grew wider. "I know. I'm not sending you back to beetles." Her eyes twinkled. "I didn't know who else to ask to work with him. Everyone else here has tried to rein in his work. You accomplished something none of us has done."

Riley let her jaw drop. "Really?"

"It's true."

Pride bubbled through Riley.

"You also did a great job working with Nick earlier this year. Which is why I thought you two could look into the history of some of the successful businesses in Vancouver. It's part of a feature exhibit for early next year."

"Together? Early next year?" The timing was unusually tight.

"We had some plans fall through, and I've had this in the back of my mind for a while. I'd like the two of you to set up in the small archive room again."

Although she officially had a desk within a block of cubicles, Riley had begun to think of the small archive room as hers, thanks in part to it being where she had found Jack's journal. She wasn't keen on sharing the space again, but this assignment would allow her to help Jack with his case without raising any questions. She pulled her notebook from her bag, eager to begin. "Do you have something specific you want us to start with?"

"I've asked Nick to compile a list of companies and men to look into, including some modern-day businesses. The title I'm playing with is *From Merchants to Visionaries: Leaving Vancouver's Mark on Business.*"

Riley noted the title. "There must be some business successes from the city's early days."

Claire smiled. "Definitely. BC Sugar, Purdy's Chocolates, and Nabob Coffee all started here. And we've had some recent international successes, particularly in clothing and technology." She interlaced her fingers and rested her elbows on her desk. "Do you have enough information to begin?"

"I think so." Riley thought about Jack's investigation. "I actually came across the name of a prominent businessman the other day. I'll start by exploring him." She returned to her desk to pick up her bag and headed to the basement archive rooms. As she descended the stairs, her excitement grew with each step. Another case with Jack!

✶

NICK BLOOM LOOKED up from his laptop when Riley entered the archive. He had reclaimed his spot on the far side of the tall work counter, an indicator that he expected they'd slip back into their comfortable team roles rather than starting again with more formality. "Hey, Riley. Claire told me this morning you'd be helping me with this project. Sounds interesting, doesn't it?"

"Hi, Nick." Helping him? Riley set her bag down at the other end of the work counter and nudged a stool out with her foot. She swallowed. "Is this going to be your exhibit?" Might as well make sure they were clear on expectations from the beginning.

"As in, am I the lead researcher?" Nick tucked a lock of hair behind his ear. "Claire didn't explicitly say, but I'm the more senior of us, so I guess it's me." He shrugged with a playful grin.

Riley bit her tongue. As if graduating three years ahead of her from the same program she'd taken made him an expert. But she could probably convince Claire to give her and Nick equal credit for the exhibit. No sense challenging him now. "Okay, so how do you want to approach it? Do you have a plan?"

Nick laughed. "Not yet. Claire just asked me this morning. Maybe we could spend the morning brainstorming ideas."

"Sounds good. Should we start with a list of companies to profile?"

"Why not?" Nick turned to his laptop. After looking at the screen for a moment, he pushed it to the side. "What I've got so far is typical Vancouver. Yoga wear, social media technology, film."

"What about earlier? Like late nineteenth century? Could we show the role Vancouver-based companies had in shaping the rest of Canada?"

"Or the world. I mean, yoga wear is everywhere now."

"You're right," said Riley, looking at the subtle moon-shaped logo on Nick's shirt. "Claire mentioned a couple of successful businesses that had their start in the early days. I bet there are many companies people would be surprised to learn had history here."

"Great idea. Keep going." He made a rolling motion with his hands in encouragement. They each contributed a few more. After a lull, Nick looked up. "This is a good start. Should we split these up? Do you want to look at present-day or older companies?"

Was it going to be this easy? "I'll take the older ones, and you can start with the recent success stories."

Nick beamed. "I'm glad you said that. I'd rather focus on the modern corporate players. Maybe I'll get to meet their CEOs. Some of them are bigwigs."

Riley fought against her instinct to roll her eyes. Nick was nothing if not transparent. "Do you want me to start, or did you want to discuss your strategy?"

Nick waved his hand at her. "Let's check in a little later. I think I'm going to reach out to those CEOs now."

His ambition, however shallow, suited Riley. She could get to work on her own research while he left to make some calls. She settled into her spot at the work counter and opened Claire's email summarizing her broad vision. After thirty minutes Riley had made a few notes about influential, if not as well known, companies and individuals from throughout the city's history. The list included the coffee company, sugar refinery, railway, and, because it would help Jack, Arthur Pierce's investment company.

Her fingers tingled and heart rate picked up as she typed Pierce's name into the archive's directory. If she was lucky, the information would be digitized. If not, she'd have to sort through boxes of files, but that work appealed to her. Digging through boxes was what originally connected her to Jack. Perhaps there was something else for her to discover.

The digital gods were smiling, and Arthur Pierce's name appeared in relation to a handful of documents. She clicked her mouse and waited for them to load. The museum's equipment and digital infrastructure wasn't particularly cutting edge, or even sharp, for a public institution. Still, it worked most of the time, which was all she needed. If pages took a few extra moments to load, that was fine. She used the time to make initial notes of the parts of Pierce's life she wanted to explore.

Land records would contain lists of properties in his name. Business records would reveal other businesses affiliated with him. And newspaper articles would add richness and colour to the research. Given his prominence, there were likely photographs of the man within the museum's collection, though she would have to search through physical files to find them. Digitization of photographic records was still in early stages.

The first record contained less detail than Riley had hoped. Arthur Pierce had owned little property, it seemed. Only the house he shared with his wife. Riley wrote the address in her notebook. Had Pierce owned property elsewhere? Or had it been owned by his company? Business owners did that, didn't they? Grouped their assets under a single entity? Her friend Jules would know.

She pulled out her phone and then remembered it was nearing the end of his day in the UK. Better to wait until she had more questions so she didn't disturb Jules and his boyfriend. Maybe Johnny Winston knew a financial type who would answer her questions. She hadn't seen Jack's great-grandson since their hike a few weeks back. She held a finger over his name on her contact list and then dropped the phone back in her bag. It was too soon.

Riley moved on to business records, finding little relating to Pierce. Wouldn't a man so key to the city's growth have at least one business registered to him? Was he not as important as Jack had suggested? The newspaper article she'd read yesterday certainly seemed to think he was a man of influence. But all she'd been able to find were those few articles. She looked over at Nick. The clacking of keys from his furious typing echoed in the room. What was he writing? An essay to local business founders? Sensing her gaze, he paused.

"Found something, Riley?"

"That's the thing, Nick. I thought I would have found something about an early business leader, and there isn't much about him at all."

"Maybe his reputation is more legendary than his actual deeds."

"That's what I was wondering. Why would someone have a reputation for being a business leader, but there be virtually no record of him leading any businesses?"

CHAPTER 6

Jack

Winston knocked on the door to Mrs. Pierce's residence early on the morning after Arthur Pierce was found dead. He needed to speak to the widow alone, though he hadn't discussed his strategy with Chief Philpott. A flutter in his stomach reminded him he needed to tread carefully.

The butler opened the door, the creases on his face suggesting a frown was his regular expression. He showed Winston into the front sitting room.

Sometime following Winston's departure yesterday, the room's windows had been covered with mourning cloth. The room's electric lights did little to overcome the darkness. The fire cast a soft light, but in the small room its heat became stifling. Winston dabbed his handkerchief against a layer of sweat forming on the back of his neck. Caoroline Pierce entered as he returned it to his pocket.

"Mrs. Pierce, I am sure I am the last person you want to see, but I need to ask you some questions about your husband's final days. I find it's best to ask these questions as soon as I can, as difficult as they are."

"What do his final days matter? He's dead." She sat in the centre of a couch, spreading the skirts of her dark dress. Puffiness around her eyes betrayed her recent tears. Still, her voice was strong and clear. This woman deserved to know the truth, yet Philpott's warning rang in Winston's ears. Doctor Evans had not yet submitted his final report, and Winston had promised to avoid referring to the death as a murder.

"It's because he died in a public place. The medical examiner has not finished his report. While he does his work, I want to understand your husband. Would you mind speaking to me now?"

"Did Lawrence send you?"

Winston looked away as he searched for a response. "He mentioned he would likely check on you later today." The flutters tightened into a knot in his stomach. His answer was accurate, but evasive. Was it enough? Why had Philpott placed him in such a position?

She pulled a handkerchief from a pocket of her dress and twisted it in her hands. "You said you have some questions?"

Winston edged forward in his chair. "Did you notice your husband's mood had been different the last few days?"

She collected her thoughts. When she began, her voice was quiet. "I must admit, I failed to notice any changes in him. He certainly did not share his intentions with me. I consider myself a perceptive woman." As she spoke, she twisted and untwisted the handkerchief. "But it appears I have deceived myself. I had no idea my husband planned to end his life. Nor do I have any idea why."

Winston cleared his throat. He needed to steer her away from thinking about her husband's death as a suicide. "This is a delicate question, Mrs. Pierce, but I must ask it. How was your marriage?" Sweat broke out under his arms. He caught the scent of the soap he'd used in the bath that morning.

"Our marriage?" She let the handkerchief drop. The question was intimate and personal. "It was fine, I suppose. I have nothing to compare it with, other than what my friends share about their own domestic lives. Perhaps it is different among policemen, but married life is not something I commonly discuss." She swatted the idea away and another burst of heat swept through him. "We didn't quarrel. I left him to his business affairs, he left me to mine."

"You have business affairs?" His question came out harsher than he intended.

Mrs. Pierce let out a laugh that stirred Winston. Deep and throaty, it heightened the warmth of the room. "No, of course not. My sister and I spend an afternoon each week making sure families who are not as fortunate as our own have enough to eat."

A noble pastime. Winston's mother spent some of her time doing a similar thing in Toronto. Despite both cities being home to men who had achieved great success, there were also those who struggled. "And your husband supported you in this?"

"Yes, he made sure we had funds if we needed them. Though I preferred to encourage other women of means to donate money if they wouldn't donate time."

As she spoke, Winston relaxed. Business, whether hers or her husband's, was a safe topic to discuss. "What was your husband's business?"

She closed her eyes for a moment as if gathering her thoughts. "He had many interests. He financed businesses. Helped his associates invest in others. I do not know the details, I'm afraid."

"He was successful?"

Her eyes narrowed and she looked around the room. "We live here, don't we?" She brought the handkerchief to her eyes again.

"Have you any children, Mrs. Pierce?"

"Our son is in Ontario studying. The schools here are less established. I will send for him, but it will take days for him to arrive."

Winston nodded. "You mentioned your sister's husband. Was he familiar with Mr. Pierce's business?"

"Yes. Arthur was helping Reginald, though I got the impression neither was pleased with the results. Arthur shared no details directly with me, but he implied Reginald was not prepared to work hard. That's one thing I know about Arthur: he worked to earn his money."

Winston wrote Reginald's name and circled it in his notebook. "What will happen to your husband's business now? Who inherits it?"

Abigail Sawyer entered the room and held out her hand. "Really, Detective. Is that an appropriate question to ask at this time? Surely the chief constable will leave my sister to her grief?" She sat and placed her hands around her sister's.

Winston stood, flustered and unsure whether to defend himself or his uncle.

"Sit down, Detective." Mrs. Pierce pulled a hand from her sister's grasp and motioned to Winston. She turned to her sister. "The detective explained the reason for his questions already, Abigail. Though I appreciate your concern."

Winston cleared his throat. "I am simply gathering information. I have no wish to trouble your sister."

Still looking at her sister, Mrs. Sawyer frowned. "Is there really a need to speak to her today?"

Mrs. Pierce patted her sister's hand. "Abby, Detective Winston is simply doing his job. Let me answer his questions, and he will leave. You're making this more difficult than it need be."

A flicker of anger flashed in Abigail Sawyer's eyes before she turned her head away. Was there tension between the sisters? Was it greater than one might routinely expect between siblings? He thought about his own relationship with his brothers. Despite the difference in age between Winston and his older brother, they'd been close before Ellis had disappeared. He pressed his brother's stone against his thigh. Winston didn't remember tension, only good times. He thought of his younger brother, George. With Winston in Vancouver, they hadn't seen each other in some time. He should write to him, find out how he was faring at the railway, working with their father.

Winston leaned forward, forcing his thoughts back to the woman sitting opposite him. "Mrs. Pierce, would you like me to repeat my question?"

"No need, Detective. Our son is too young. I am not sure who will inherit the business. My husband's lawyer will have that detail. I'm sure it's set out in his will."

"With whom should I speak about the future of the business?"

"Won't it be Reginald? He's the closest relative." Abigail Sawyer focused her gaze on her sister.

Caroline Pierce shrugged. "I don't know, Abby. The decision was Arthur's. And I heard the two of them arguing." She turned to Winston. "I will ask our lawyer to get that information. Can I have it sent to the police station?"

Winston nodded. "If you don't have it at hand, yes, please send it to my attention at the station." He held his finger up. "The argument. Was it recent? Do you know what it was about?"

"It must have been about business. It is all they really spoke about. I do not recall the specific date, but it was a couple of weeks ago now. Reginald and Arthur had seen each other since and I sensed no tension between them, so whatever it was about, it had blown over. I shouldn't have even mentioned it." She slumped into her sister.

Abigail Sawyer placed a hand on her sister's arm and fixed her gaze on Winston. "As you can see, Detective, you have upset my sister. I do hope you have what you came for. Moreover, I hope we will not see you back here tomorrow."

Hearing this, Mrs. Pierce straightened. "Abigail. That is no way to speak to someone in my home." Tears welled in her eyes.

"You need rest, Caro. This ordeal has exhausted you. I will see the detective out."

Caroline Pierce nodded, and her sister followed Winston to the door. She leaned in close. "You may think I have been harsh, but I'm concerned for my sister. Losing her husband so suddenly has been a terrible shock. It doesn't help to have you asking so many questions."

Winston turned to face her. "Mrs. Sawyer, I understand your wanting to protect your sister. However, I must do my job. And today, that job is to gather information about Mr. Pierce's death. The sooner I gather information, the sooner I can leave your sister alone."

Mrs. Sawyer bit her lip. "Very well, Detective."

"If I may ask you one question before I go. . ."

She lowered her chin, and Winston took the movement as her agreeing.

"Did you notice the tension between your husband and Mr. Pierce that your sister spoke of?"

"Oh, they were great friends. Relied on each other for much. But as friends sometimes do, they had occasional differences." She waved her hand. "Quickly resolved and easily forgotten."

"They spent a lot of time together?"

"That's two questions, Detective. But yes, they did."

"Thank you, Mrs. Sawyer."

"Good day, Detective Winston."

Winston retrieved his hat and coat from the butler, who held the open door wearing the same frown he'd answered it with.

During the twenty-minute walk to the station, Winston sifted through the bits of information he'd gleaned from the morning's interview. There were trails worth following, but he'd need clearance from the chief to pursue them.

CHAPTER 7

Jack

AT THE STATION, Winston checked with the desk clerk to find out whether Doctor Evans had delivered his report. The clerk pushed a folder toward Winston. "He just dropped this off. Asked to speak to you."

"Has he left?"

The desk clerk shook his head. "He's speaking to the chief constable."

Chief Philpott had shown little interest in the doctor's work, except to ask whether Winston trusted it. Why would he speak to Doctor Evans now? He nodded to the clerk and walked to his uncle's office.

Hearty laughter filtered through the office door. A good sign. Winston was raising his hand to knock when the door opened. "Jack, I was just speaking to the chief constable about you," Doctor Evans said.

Winston tilted his head. "You were?"

"Is that Jack?" called Philpott from behind his desk. "Come in, come in. Your ears must have been burning, lad."

"I suppose they were, Chief Philpott. I have just returned from speaking with Mrs. Pierce, sir."

Concern flashed across Philpott's face. "I thought we agreed you would not bother her. She's mourning her husband."

"I know, sir. But I need to learn more about him—his relationships, his business, his habits—if I'm to investigate who is responsible for his death."

Beside him, Evans stared at his feet. Winston looked from Evans to Philpott. Both men avoided eye contact with him. Did the men share a confidence about the investigation?

"I know enough about the man to say there is no need to investigate further," Philpott said.

"You knew the man, yes, but he's dead, and I'd like to look into why."

Philpott shook his head. "No need, Jack. Nathaniel here has just confirmed Arthur died at his own hand."

Winston noted his uncle's use of the doctor's first name. He looked between the men again, trying to gauge what had passed between them. "He hanged himself?" Winston stepped back and searched the doctor's face. "At the park—the tree?" His hand involuntarily reached into his pocket to grip his stone. His breathing calmed as he rubbed its smooth surface. "He couldn't have."

Doctor Evans nodded. Something flickered in his eyes, though Winston couldn't place what it was. Embarrassment at a mistaken assessment yesterday? Discomfort with changing his mind? What had altered his earlier decision?

"You're certain?" He searched the faces of Evans and Philpott again to identify what was influencing the doctor.

Philpott rose from behind his desk and walked toward Winston and Evans. He clasped both men on their shoulders and guided them toward the door to his office. "Nice work, gentlemen. We can call this closed."

Winston shrugged from his uncle's grasp. "You're not at all concerned with why your friend killed himself? And yesterday, we saw no evidence at the park of how he'd climbed the tree himself."

Philpott placed his hand on his nephew's arm. "I'm deeply sad for Caroline. But we can never truly know someone. And what is to be gained by trying? I have asked Evans here to mark this as a death due to unknown causes to protect the family from the shame."

Anyone who had been to the Hollow Tree yesterday could not doubt Pierce's cause of death. Ruling it as unknown to protect the family was a kindness, but it was a misrepresentation of fact. Why was Philpott avoiding the truth? "Sir, with respect—" Winston protested.

"That's right, Jack." Philpott reddened. "With respect. If not for your uncle, then for your boss."

Confusion coursed through Winston. He felt the force of Philpott's rebuke as a slap. Questions churned in his mind. Had Evans been pressured to change his findings? Had Winston misjudged his character? And Philpott. Winston understood wanting to avoid scandal. Generations of choice marriages and political adjacency had bred Philpott for skillfully navigating delicate situations. But to do so at the expense of an investigation left Winston feeling uncomfortable, almost unclean.

He fought to contain his frustration. He wanted to shout. Instead, he closed his gaping mouth, straightened his waistcoat, and nodded.

"Good lad." Philpott held up a finger. "And one more thing."

Winston met Philpott's gaze.

"Leave Caroline alone to mourn."

Winston spun on his heel in a flood of heat as Philpott closed the door. He stole a glance at Doctor Evans as the men stood outside Philpott's office.

"If you'd like, I can show you what I found."

The gesture did little to soothe Winston, but he saw it for the peace offering it was. "I'd like that, Nathaniel."

Evans paused outside the examination room. "What's troubling you, Jack?"

Winston sighed. "You saw at the park. There was no way Pierce did that to himself. There's something about this, and it needs investigating, despite what the chief constable just said."

*

THE AIR INSIDE the police station's morgue was kept artificially cool thanks to large blocks of ice lining the perimeter of the room. To prepare for the cold, and to mitigate the smell, Winston had stopped at his desk for a scarf to tie around his neck. Doctor Evans, seemingly unaffected by the temperature, rolled his sleeves to his elbows as he walked to the centre of the room. Arthur Pierce's body lay on a table covered by a light sheet.

Doctor Evans signalled for Winston to approach. He focused on the sound of his footsteps on the tile floor. When he reached the body, the detective closed his eyes and took a shallow breath as Evans lowered the sheet to the dead man's waist. He was unclothed. Where had they taken his clothes? Winston made a mental note to find them and search the dead man's pockets for clues.

Arthur Pierce, in his forties, appeared not to have overindulged in drink or food. Winston could see the shape of the man's leg muscles underneath the cloth. "He was a sportsman?"

"It would seem so," Evans answered.

Pierce's knuckles were raw. Winston pointed. "What happened here?"

"He may have clawed at the rope or banged them against the tree shortly before he died. I have no way of knowing."

Winston swallowed against bile rising in his throat. "What about other injuries?"

"I found some bruising on his legs, but, like the fingers, I cannot tell whether he sustained it before he died, perhaps in a fall, or whether it occurred when we removed him from the tree. Our bodies can sustain damage after we die, Detective."

Winston recalled the moments he'd had his arms wrapped around Pierce's legs. He'd been squeezing, but not strongly enough to cause bruises, surely. "How can you say unknown causes?" Winston made an effort to keep his voice even, pushing his frustration aside. He was determined to remain calm, but equally determined to get answers. His uncle must have said something to change Evans' mind.

Evans shifted his weight. "Upon reflection, I believe Pierce could have tied the rope around the branch and been seated on a horse. When the horse walked away, the rope strangled him." He raked his hands through his hair. "I'm thinking of the family."

Winston searched Evans' eyes. He could hear his uncle's influence in the doctor's words, yet a seed of doubt formed. Was his uncle right? Had Winston made an incorrect judgment at the park? "What makes you now believe he hanged himself? You were the one who first suggested murder yesterday." Winston winced at the frustration that had crept into his voice.

Evans pulled the sheet back over the body. "I admit it seemed clearer yesterday, at the park." As if to busy his hands, he arranged and rearranged the instruments set out on a wheeled table near the body's head. "How do you plan to proceed, Jack?"

As the doctor's hands moved, Winston noticed the care he took, moving slowly and deliberately. He, too, could take care and move slowly. He clenched and unclenched a fist. "I intend to answer my questions. Do you object to my doing so, Doctor?" Winston held his breath. The man's reply would confirm whether Winston had misjudged him or whether his interest lay in finding the truth.

Evans set down an instrument and locked eyes with Winston. "I'll help you where I can."

Hearing this, Winston relaxed. His uncle could be persuasive, and Evans was new to his role. The chief constable had the power to determine whether Evans continued as the constabulary's medical examiner. "Let's start with what you can be certain about. Did the hanging kill him?"

"Definitely. He would have lost consciousness when he could no longer breathe."

"And as you pointed out at the park, there was nothing the man could have used to suspend himself. If he wasn't on a horse, he would have needed to. . ." Winston looked around the room. "Do you have his clothes? Pierce was strong. With enough determination, he could have climbed the tree. And that might explain his injuries."

Evans walked to a low cabinet and removed a pile of neatly folded clothing. He placed it at Pierce's feet and stepped away. Winston unfurled the first article, the trousers, and held them in front of him, turning them to inspect the front and back. "These would be dirty, if not damaged, had he climbed to the branch," he said, remembering the pieces of bark that had caught on his hand when he'd rubbed it.

"And it would have been dark," Evans added. Was that excitement in his voice? The doctor was intrigued. "Unless he regularly climbed that tree, it would have been nearly impossible without some light."

"Okay. We can be certain he didn't climb the tree." Winston checked the pockets, finding a few coins. He folded the trousers and set them on top of the other clothes.

"Can you tell if he'd been on a horse?" Evans' voice rose as he asked the question. He averted his gaze, but not before Winston caught the growing doubt in the doctor's eyes.

"I see nothing on the pants to suggest it, but I will ask Miller to look at them more closely and to find out whether any riderless horses have been found." Winston made a note to remind himself. "Can you show me the bruising you spoke of earlier?"

Evans removed the sheet from the right side of the body and pointed to a bloom of deep purple on Pierce's lower leg.

"How much force would be required to cause this?"

"Once you're dead, less than you'd think." Evans stepped closer to the head and lifted the sheet. "He also has bruising here." He indicated Pierce's lower arm. "It could have resulted from being squeezed." He mimed a gesture with his hands.

"What does that mean?" Winston's heart raced.

"He was alive when these injuries were inflicted."

"But they occurred..." Winston let the unfinished question hang.

"Shortly before death."

Winston stood in front of the doctor with his back facing him. "How would you restrain me, Doctor?"

Evans frowned. "I'd grab your lower arms. But I'd look for something to tie you with. And I'd want another man with me." He reached around Winston and clasped both of his wrists. Winston twisted and Evans squeezed to stop him.

"Would you say the same about Mr. Pierce?" Winston turned to face Evans.

"I'd say that about anyone larger than a small child."

At the same time, the men reached for the cover to look at Pierce's wrists. Faint marks, paler than the bruises on his legs, appeared on Pierce where Evans had moments ago been holding Winston.

"Can we agree Pierce was unlikely to have been alone when he died? And if that was the case, he was almost certainly murdered?" When Evans nodded, Winston fought an urge to slap him on the shoulder. Their original conclusion had been sound. Instead, he reached into his pocket and ran his thumb over Ellis's stone. Winston walked to the counter where the rope sat coiled and picked it up. "Does this tell any stories?"

"It's common enough. Sold at any of the gold rush outfitters around here. I didn't look closely, but I see no way to tell it from any other piece."

Winston brought the knotted end closer to his face. "You're right. One piece is like any other. Still, I will send Miller to shops along Water Street. We may be lucky." He moved back to the body in the centre of the room. "Does he have any injuries on his head? Something that would have knocked him out, allowing whomever he was with to tie the rope around him?"

Evans slid his fingers underneath Pierce's head. "There is a lump here." Evans pointed to the back of his own head before reaching across to Winston's. Evans eased his hands under the body again. "It doesn't feel like the skin was broken. Judging by the size, it could have been enough to knock him unconscious."

Winston turned the idea over in his mind. "He must have been attacked and brought to the park. Doctor, you suggested Pierce was a sportsman. Could he have been injured during a game?"

"Only if it was within hours before his death," said Evans.

Winston made another note. "How long did you say Pierce has been dead?"

Evans answered this question with ease, regaining his confidence. "Since a few hours before he was found. His body would have cooled more quickly last night than if he'd died during the summer, but rigor mortis would have been slower to set in."

"When does it usually occur?"

"Within four to six hours at room temperature. It would take much longer outside."

"I need to go back to the park. We may have missed something."

Evans stretched his hand out. "Jack, the chief constable was clear he doesn't think it was murder. What we've found suggests it was. How will you investigate further without his support?"

"It doesn't matter what the chief constable thinks. He will have to see the truth."

CHAPTER 8

Riley

Dear Riley,

I visited Arthur Pierce's widow again today. Her sister, Abigail Sawyer, was present as well. It is clear Mrs. Sawyer expects her own husband to inherit Pierce's business. She seems to wield dominance over her elder sister. I am not sure if this is a recent change in their relationship or their natural state.

I fear I have angered Mrs. Sawyer, though I'm unclear how. Perhaps she is concerned the investigation will compromise her husband's claim on the business he shared with Pierce. Mrs. Pierce has agreed to send me a copy of Arthur Pierce's will so I may confirm whether Reginald Sawyer will take over the business.

Lastly, a disturbing development occurred today: Doctor Evans temporarily reversed himself regarding the cause of Arthur Pierce's death. His report found the man died of "unknown causes," a conclusion I'm certain he was pressured into by my uncle, the chief constable. My uncle tells me that's the end of it: I am not to investigate this death further. But Doctor Evans and I have re-examined the body, and he has confided in me that his original conclusion was sound. I will have his support in continuing my investigation, but I will need to tread very carefully until I have enough evidence to restate my case to the chief constable.

Until next time,

Jack

Riley balanced the journal on her lap as she read. Poor Jack. He was really walking a tightrope this time.

A buzzing from her phone drew Riley's attention from the journal. She had just finished scanning newspaper clippings for Arthur Pierce's name and rewarded herself with a few moments in the book before she began searching death records. Nick had caught her with the journal before, but at the moment he was so engrossed in his research she was certain he wouldn't notice if she wheeled a body into the archive.

A quick look over her shoulder confirmed he was absorbed in his work. Riley slid the book back into her bag and checked her phone. A message from Jules.

Riley! I'm coming to town. A surprise for my mother.

She typed back and turned the phone on silent.

Amazing! When will you be here?

Actually, I arrived last night.

And you're only texting me now?

Jet lag

How long?

A week. When can I see you?

Tonight?

At the pub. See you at six.

XXO

She set her phone down and looked up to see Nick, a grin stretched across his face. "What?" Heat prickled the back of her neck.

"You look like a kid waiting for Santa. What's up?"

Riley frowned. Nick read her emotions with such ease. "I just heard from a close friend. He's in town and I'm going to see him tonight."

"That's cool. Is he an ex or something? You're practically bouncing."

"What? No, we grew up together. It's just been a while since I saw him. He recently moved overseas, and we have lots to catch up on."

"How's the research coming along?"

"It's slower than I thought it would be. Remember that guy I mentioned? He's a business leader from over a hundred years ago. I still haven't had any luck finding much related to him."

"Where have you looked?"

"I was just about to search for a death certificate," she said, pointing to her screen.

"Are you sure you have the right name? And he was a business leader?"

Riley's ears burned. Jack was unlikely to be wrong about the prominence of the victim in his case, but she couldn't tell Nick that. "I'm sure. But maybe I'll try just his surname rather than his full name." Riley's fingers moved over the keyboard. She exhaled while the results loaded. "Huh."

Nick moved closer to Riley, bending to look over her shoulder. "You find something?"

"A few results for his wife."

"But nothing more on the husband?"

She shook her head. "The same matches I found earlier on his name, and they all have to do with his death. Nothing much about his life."

"What about variations? I've found names inconsistently spelled in the past."

"Good idea. Thanks." She typed "Pearce" instead of "Pierce" and shook her head. "Nothing."

"What do the wife's results say?"

She clicked on the first result and skimmed it. The article, published six months after her husband died, described a garden she'd had planted, though it didn't refer to Arthur Pierce specifically. It also mentioned her charity work, and referenced a donation she'd made to the city for the upkeep of Stanley Park.

Disappointment washed over Riley. "A dead end. You must be right, and he wasn't as influential as everyone said." Stroking Nick's ego sparked his interest. He leaned in to read over her shoulder again, moving his finger along the screen and leaving fingerprints. She shoved her hands in her pockets to avoid knocking his away.

After a moment, he paused. "Are you sure you weren't looking up the wrong man? You didn't want his business partner?"

"Who?"

"Reginald Sawyer. You probably don't even think about it, but the Sawyer name is everywhere—the library, university buildings, Sawyer Hill Park. Did you confuse the two?"

Riley's cheeks flushed warm. "I don't think I confused them. This says an early business venture had failed when Sawyer's partner died. His partner must have been Pierce." Her fingertips tingled as she made the connection.

Nick walked back to his end of the work table. "Why don't you look up Sawyer and see what else you can find?"

"Thanks, Nick." Her toes curled at having missed the connection.

"We're working together on this, remember? Teamwork." He extended his fist toward her.

"Teamwork," she said and shot her fist forward, wincing when their knuckles collided. She'd never fist bumped before, and judging by Nick's chuckle, she'd done it wrong. Should she have done more of an air bump, like an air kiss? One more thing for him to teach her.

Riley returned to her screen. Sawyer and Pierce. Jack's note this morning had mentioned the widow's sister. Wasn't her surname Sawyer? She must have been married to Pierce's business partner. Maybe Sawyer was the brains behind the business. Clearly he'd gone on to achieve big things.

Questions surged through Riley's brain. Had Sawyer killed his partner to take over control? That was... ruthless. But wasn't business ruthless? She jotted a note to herself. *Partner—Sawyer—killer?* How much of this could she tell Jack? Not much, yet. She needed more information before she could figure out what to share.

Riley felt in her bag for the journal but decided against bringing it out again. She looked at the clock on her laptop. How long could she stay in the bathroom without Nick noticing? Probably not long enough to write to Jack. She'd wait until she got home.

"I'll look up Sawyer now. See what I can learn." When Nick didn't reply, Riley looked up. He had walked to the back of the archive.

"Did you say something?" he shouted.

Instead of shouting back, Riley opened a new window in her browser and entered Sawyer's name into the search bar. Nick was right: Sawyer's name was peppered throughout documents relating to the city's history, but the earliest record she found was 1900, after Pierce died. If Sawyer didn't appear before then, perhaps Pierce had been the more prominent of the two at the time he died, or Sawyer didn't receive credit for his work until after Pierce's death.

The remainder of the afternoon passed more quickly than Riley had expected. Doing research for both a new exhibit and a new case ate up the hours. Around five, Nick waved. "I'm heading out. What about you?" he asked.

"I'm meeting my friend later, so I'll keep working on this for a bit."

"Don't let your mistake frustrate you. We all make them."

Was he referring to the fist bump? Not so much a mistake, just awkwardness.

With Nick gone, Riley pulled the journal from her bag, brushing her fingers against its cool leather. The crisp pages—one of the things that had first drawn her attention to the book when she'd found it in the box of early Vancouver police records—looked nothing like the yellowing, sometimes ragged pages of other books from the same era. Something about the journal's magic—what else could it be but magic?—preserved the pages as pristine as they appeared to Jack, for whom it was a new book.

Before she started to write, Riley poked her head out the archive door to make sure Nick was truly gone. She picked up her pencil.

Dear Jack,

I sympathize with the awkward place you find yourself in, needing to look into the death of Arthur Pierce without your uncle finding out you're continuing your inquiries. I hope it doesn't hamper your investigation.

I, too, have been looking into Mr. Arthur Pierce and have been surprised at how little I have managed to find about him. It seems that though he was prominent in the business community during your time, he is all but forgotten over one hundred years later.

She paused. Nick had interrupted her when she'd been searching for Pierce's death certificate. She pulled her laptop closer and entered his name. While she waited for the results, she continued her note to Jack.

What little I found follows:

Article in the Vancouver Voice: "Local Businessman Found Dead at Hollow Tree." The brief article mentions Arthur Pierce and describes him as a prominent financier. Perhaps you've already seen this one.

Article in the Vancouver Voice: "Arthur Pierce Buried." This article contains a short description of the funeral attendees. Sounds like a who's who of the city.

Article in the Vancouver Voice: "Investors Lose Following Pierce Death." This article states that several investors in Pierce's business lost money after he died but omits mention of any specific names.

She checked her laptop screen.

Arthur Pierce's death certificate shows "death by unknown causes." Other death certificates of the same period contain few details (more than one lists "dropped dead"). Some omit information about the cause of death entirely, so I'm not sure whether to read anything into this determination. I suppose if it wasn't clear whether Pierce hanged himself or was hanged, it may be accurate to indicate "unknown causes."

That said, for someone as prominent as you suggest, I'm surprised I couldn't find more. Perhaps some information has been lost to time, but I would have expected something about his earlier life, especially if his funeral warranted such high-profile guests.

In contrast, I have found several resources detailing the work of his business partner, Mr. Reginald Sawyer. It seems his legacy has stood the test of time; Vancouver boasts several landmarks that bear his name. I wonder if it's possible Mr. Sawyer's reputation has somehow become confused with Mr. Pierce's? Another possibility is that Mr. Sawyer only started to receive credit for his work following the death of Mr. Pierce, as I haven't found any mention of Sawyer before 1900.

Until later,

Riley

Riley held her hand on the book, waiting for her heart rate to slow. No matter how many messages they exchanged, she reacted the same way every time she wrote to Jack. Each word had the potential to alter history. Since they had first connected, she had taken great care not to reveal much about the future. She reopened the journal and scanned her message. Jack would see the newspaper articles soon enough, and the information about Sawyer's place in the city's history helped the investigation but didn't reference any specific deeds. She released the breath she'd been holding. She hadn't crossed the boundary she'd set.

She checked her watch, and though she had a few minutes before she needed to leave to meet Jules, she packed up. Her footsteps echoed off the hallway walls as she walked toward the exit, punctuating the low hum of the overhead lights. While she liked being alone in the archive, she preferred it at the beginning of the day rather than the end, when the spirits became restless. She shook her head at this silliness, but it was hard not to believe in spirits when the museum was home to so many relics of past lives.

*

Outside, fine rain coated Riley's face. Of Vancouver's many forms of precipitation, this kind was the most deceptive, appearing to be light yet somehow managing to soak anyone without rain gear within minutes. She pulled her hood tighter and swerved to avoid an umbrella held by someone walking in the opposite direction. Tourists.

Warm air brought feeling back into Riley's cheeks when she opened the pub door. As she hung her jacket on a hook, she spotted an empty booth. She patted herself down, assessing her dampness. Her clothes protected by her jacket were dry, but the exposed sections of her jeans clung to her legs.

Quiet music allowed pub patrons to speak to each other without shouting. Later in the night, the pub would become uncomfortably loud, with competing conversations bouncing off the wooden floor, tables, and chairs.

Riley slid into the booth. The once-plush fabric covering the seats was now felted by the shapes of the many guests who'd occupied the booth before her. She caught the eye of a waitress and ordered a drink. While she waited for Jules, she looked up pictures of the Hollow Tree on her phone. Several city archive photos showed smiling visitors in various poses. One boasted nearly a dozen people squeezed into its opening. Riley was bringing her phone closer to get a better look at the photos when she heard her name. Jules beamed at her while water droplets fell from his hair onto his tailored coat.

They embraced for nearly a minute. "I didn't realize how much I missed you," he whispered in her ear.

"Same," she whispered back. She pulled away and examined her friend. "London looks good on you," she said. In truth, the physical distance his move had imposed had messed with the spontaneity of their friendship. More than once she'd seen something she'd thought Jules would like—something that normally she would have instantly messaged him about—but decided not to bother him about it. Navigating a 120-year time gap with Jack seemed easier than navigating an eight-hour difference with Jules. She wished he were still in Vancouver. "How much longer are you staying there?"

Jules settled into the booth across from where she'd been sitting. "At least another couple of years. Work is going well. Steve is great."

"You're enjoying it."

"I love it, Riley." He brushed his hand through his hair, releasing another wave of drops. "But I love this place too. Even when it's raining, this city is home."

Seeing her friend's smile as he spoke made her regret her selfishness of wanting him home. She smiled back. "Did you bring Steve?" Riley looked toward the entrance.

"He had to stay for work. But he says hello."

"I'll send him a text," she said as she sat down.

"How often do you text?"

She smiled at the memory of the video call Jules forced Riley and Steve to have shortly after he'd arrived in London. Through their stilted conversation, Riley realized that speaking to a stranger is considerably more difficult than writing to one. "Not too often. If I haven't heard from you in a while, I check in with him, make sure you're okay." She regretted her words once they were out of her mouth. Why was she trying to make him feel guilty about leaving?

She shifted in the booth. The damp fabric of her jeans was clammy against her legs. "You're here for your mom's party? She told me she hoped you could come, but you told her you were too busy."

Jules grinned. "Such a great surprise, right?"

"I guess, but I think she would have enjoyed looking forward to your visit. I would have too." Why couldn't she be happy about seeing him?

A brief frown creased Jules's forehead. "Next time. I wasn't even sure I'd make it until a few days ago, so it was a surprise for me, too." His smile returned. "But your mom is coming, right? Mom mentioned your mom sounded excited about something when they last spoke. Was she talking about your sister's wedding? It's coming up, right?"

"The wedding is in two weeks, and as you'd expect, Lucy is going a little overboard." An image of suspended forks flashed through Riley's mind. "My mom is catching the ferry on Thursday. Lucy has a final dress fitting, so Mom will go with her. Of course, she's coming for your mom's party too."

"Good. It wouldn't be the same without her."

Riley leaned forward. "Get this: Lucy was complaining yesterday that our mom is investing some money for her rather than giving it to her as a wedding gift. So selfish, right?"

"Investing?"

"Yeah, in some company using the investments to build schools in Africa. I haven't spoken to my mom about it, so I don't have any details."

Jules tilted his head, mild concern pinching his features. The waitress approached and took his order, and by the time she walked away, his face had relaxed.

"What do you love about London?" Riley asked when they were alone again.

"It's so vibrant, and there are so many people. Vancouver seems a sleepy village in comparison."

Riley sat back, unsure whether she was upset by Jules insulting the city she loved or upset by her reaction to him expressing love for another city. Her stomach soured. Was she jealous? At his happiness? She shook her head. "We don't have nearly as many people. But London doesn't have our mountains."

"True. I wouldn't change this city for anything. It's perfect for you. But I think London might be perfect for me."

The waitress brought Jules his drink and hurried to another group. Riley appreciated that she hadn't lingered at the table.

"Are you ever coming home?" Her stomach flipped. Why couldn't she be pleased for him?

Jules shrugged. "I don't know. Like I said, not for a little, at least."

"Just don't forget where you're from." Riley frowned at her drink.

"Riley, are you upset?"

She waved her friend away. "It's nothing." The pang in her belly grew, making it harder to ignore now. "Tell me more about life in London and being with Steve."

As Jules described the flat he and Steve shared and the neighbourhood they lived in, her stomach relaxed. Jules was, as ever, Jules. He enthused about the elderly woman living in the flat below them who relied on Jules and Steve to help with her recycling and rubbish.

"Every week she bakes us a batch of cookies or a loaf to thank us. They're inedible, but we love her for trying." Jules sipped his beer and reached to hold Riley's hand. "It's so good to see you. As much as I'm enjoying London, I do miss you."

"I miss you. Lucy moved out. Sometimes I feel alone." As she spoke, Riley's throat closed. Why had she fought this admission?

"What about this guy you met just before I left? John? And do you see our friends?"

She swallowed at the mention of Jack's great-grandson. "Johnny. We've seen each other a few times." Riley recalled their last date, a hike on a local mountain. When they'd shared a parting kiss, she had been shocked when an image of his great-grandfather had flashed through her mind. It had unnerved her, so much so she'd avoided seeing Johnny since. She had to get past this irrational feeling, almost like she was cheating on Jack when she was with Johnny, and cheating on Johnny when she wrote to Jack. There was clearly no conflict, the logical part of her brain reminded her. "I've invited him to Lucy's wedding."

Jules smiled broadly. "I'm glad. He sounded promising." He raised his eyebrows and gestured for her to continue. "And. . .? Our friends?"

Riley turned to look at the lights reflecting off the puddles outside the window. She loved the dark, wet Vancouver winter months. Others moaned about yearning for spring, but she was grateful for an excuse to stay inside and read. "The others are really your friends," she said, turning back to face Jules. "I met up with them once. It was Simon's birthday, I think."

Riley did enjoy spending time with the group of artists and musicians Jules was friendly with. Whenever she did, she felt a surge of her own creativity, as if theirs fed the people around them. She wasn't sure they got anything from her and she didn't want to be a creativity vampire, so the birthday celebration was the only invitation she had accepted.

"Riley, you've known some of them for nearly a decade. They're your friends. If you're feeling lonely, you need to do something about it. Get out."

Jules was being kind, but she bristled against his words. "I'm not lonely. Just alone." Riley drew her hand through her hair. She was unwilling to argue with Jules, but firm in her belief in the difference between loneliness and aloneness. The settled calm of her stomach confirmed she was right.

Jules blinked at her. "I like this more assertive Riley. Where did she come from?"

"Maybe she's always been here." She sat back and looked at him. They stared at each other until they both smiled. They'd moved past whatever was blocking her.

"What have you been working on?" he asked after sipping his drink.

"At the museum?"

"Yeah. Any exhibits I should see?"

"Nick, a guy I work pretty closely with, worked on an exhibit about hidden rivers that's on right now. It's worth checking out. Will you have time to see it?"

"I'm here for a week, and most people work during the day. Maybe I'll come by tomorrow."

"Sounds good. Nick and I actually just started working on another exhibit this week. It's about how the city's business leaders have shaped Canada and the world. You might be surprised at who has come from this little backwater in the last one hundred and thirty-five years."

"Who?"

"I was looking into a guy named Arthur Pierce today. He was business partners with Reginald Sawyer."

Jules furrowed his brow in confusion. "Should I know either name?"

"Probably. And you must know Sawyer's. The university's business faculty is named for him."

"Oh, right. But we pronounced it 'Say-yer?' Is the park also named for him? Sayer Hill Park? Sawyer Hill Park?" Jules chuckled. "I can't believe I never questioned the pronunciation. Which is correct? 'Sawyer' or 'Say-yer?'"

Riley bit her lip. A good question for Jack. "I'll look into it. Either way, there's something odd, since Pierce was meant to be the more successful of the two. When he died, Sawyer took over the business and must have really done well. I haven't found much at all about Pierce. Tomorrow I'll dig deeper into Sawyer."

"When did Pierce die?"

"1897."

"Maybe the records don't exist."

Riley scraped the table with her fingernail as she recalled Jack's latest message. "Some do, but I found something that talks about how Pierce was a prominent member of the business community. Only I couldn't find his name anywhere in the newspaper archives except for a brief mention, and we have everything they published. I expected to find more."

"Is your original source reliable?"

"He's reliable."

"He?"

Riley flushed. "I mean, his records." Riley grabbed at her glass and sipped. "They've been accurate about everything else."

"I guess it's not like you could ask him."

"Right?" Riley wiped her palms on her jeans.

"You okay, Riley?"

"I'm suddenly quite warm." She looked at her drink. "I guess it's the beer."

Jules nodded, concern in his eyes. "Are you sure?"

"Of course."

"So are you going to stick with this guy Pierce? Sounds like you've hit a roadblock."

Riley shrugged. "I'm not sure. I mean, there are several others I need to research for the exhibit. I can't spend too long on Pierce, but his story intrigues me. Something about it doesn't add up. Why would someone be essentially erased from history?"

"Maybe there was a scandal."

Her breath caught. "A scandal?"

"Sure. Maybe he did something his family didn't want remembered. If he was influential, like you think, they could have paid for him to be forgotten. It's not like they were using social media."

Riley nudged his foot under the table. "I bet you'd be a pretty good detective, Jules. You've just given me an idea."

At home that evening, Riley dashed off a quick note in the journal before climbing into bed.

One more thing: What is the name of Arthur Pierce's business? I'd like to look into the records associated with it.

Thanks,

R.

PS: How do you pronounce Sawyer? Saw-yer? Or Say-yer?

CHAPTER 9

Jack

THE DIN OF the station faded to a faint hum as Winston read what Riley had discovered about Arthur Pierce. His prominence will be lost to time. Winston scratched at his temple and puzzled over what this could mean. When he died, Arthur Pierce was more successful than Reginald Sawyer. Yet, according to Riley, Sawyer's accomplishments are memorialized as the city grows. Either Sawyer becomes considerably more successful than Pierce, to the degree that he overshadows his mentor completely, or Pierce's work is forgotten, wiped from public record. Which of the two scenarios was more likely? If Sawyer's star rose so high so quickly, why would that mean Pierce's accomplishments would be obliterated?

And "death by unknown causes." A muscle tightened in Winston's jaw. There it was. Just as Philpott had requested. But the cause is known. Now he had to get out and gather the evidence to prove it. He made a mental note to encourage Evans to be as precise as possible with his paperwork. Winston felt a duty to the future, to one researcher in particular.

He wrote a quick reply to Riley, thanking her for the information, confirming the pronunciation of Sawyer, and providing the name of Pierce's business. He needed to better understand Pierce's business and what role it may have played in his death and, ultimately, in Sawyer's future. But first, he needed to visit the Hollow Tree again.

"Miller, collect your things. We're going to the park."

"The park, sir?"

"Yes." Winston walked to the small window at the rear of the room. "Rain is threatening. Better bring an umbrella." As he left the room, he called over his shoulder, "And a ladder, please."

A few minutes later they were in a carriage, winding their way up the park drive. The canopy of trees blocked the greying skies. Winston recalled his father telling him how the city had been given the park by the railway as part of a land exchange negotiated in the city's earliest days. What a marvellous gift!

When they arrived, Winston asked the driver to return in two hours.

Miller hitched the ladder under his arm. "Two hours, sir?"

"Yes. I want to look around, and I'd rather not be in a rush. And I'd like to speak to anyone we see. I imagine most people visiting the park at this time of year would come regularly, no matter the weather. Perhaps we'll meet someone who recalls something significant."

"Okay. What are we looking for?" Miller fell into step beside Winston.

"The rain and falling leaves will have covered footprints. Let's not waste time searching for them. Instead, let's look at the tree itself. How did the rope get onto the tree? Could a man easily climb it? Could the rope have been swung up to the branch?" Winston carried a rope of similar weight and length to the one recovered from the scene. He spooled out a length, gathering it in one hand, and hurled it overhead toward the branch. After a few tries, he was successful. "In the dark, it may have taken longer," Winston called out to Miller.

"There would have been a lantern, sir."

"A lantern, Thomas?"

"If Pierce was alone, I mean. He wouldn't have made it up here, found a suitable branch and swung a rope around it, and hanged himself in the dark. He would have brought a lantern. And we didn't find one yesterday."

As Winston followed Miller's explanation to the conclusion he'd been hoping for, his heart rate accelerated. "So he wasn't alone. Whoever he was with took the lantern, likely to return to the city." He tugged on the rope and it coiled at his feet. "Well reasoned, Thomas."

Winston pointed to the Hollow Tree. "What do you think of this location?"

"There was intention behind its choice, sir."

Winston nodded. "I agree. In picking this place, Pierce's murderer must have wanted the body to be found."

Miller walked in a slow circle around the tree. He stood in front of where Pierce had been hanging. "He could see the tree." He nodded toward the tourist attraction.

"Meaning?"

"A message?" Miller offered.

"To whom? What kind of message?" Winston surveyed the Hollow Tree. "Something about the hollowness? Age? The once majestic height this tree must have stood?" He shook his head and turned back to Pierce's tree. Winston pointed. "Some of the rope was left behind."

Miller set up the ladder, then steadied it as Winston climbed its rungs. Winston reached for the branch and pushed against it. It was sturdier than it had appeared from the ground. For the briefest of moments, he wondered if the chief constable's theory was correct. Then he recalled the missing lantern.

Winston switched hands to relieve the cold biting at his skin. His hand came away from the branch with flecks of bark and moss clinging to it. He remembered the man's clothing at the morgue—clean, no evidence of moss or bark. Pierce's trousers and jacket were intact. Still, Winston inspected the branch for pieces of torn material. Nothing.

He noted the knot on the remnant of rope left behind when they'd cut Pierce down. He untied it and let it drop to the ground beside where Miller stood. Carefully, Winston returned to the ground, where he brushed off his clothing.

"Can you check the mining supply stores to see whether anyone recognizes and remembers selling this? And if so, who they sold it to?" Winston nudged the rope with his foot. "I don't notice anything distinctive about it, but perhaps someone who trades in ropes will."

Miller bent down to collect the rope, but rose quickly. Both men turned toward the notes of someone whistling. A man emerged from the woods, a bag slung over his shoulder.

"Hello," Winston called out.

The man adjusted his bag and approached the policemen. "Police here again?" He directed his question at Miller.

Miller nodded, tugging at the hem of his uniform jacket. "Were you here two days ago?"

"Here?" the man asked, looking up and moving in a circle. He raised his arms toward the sky to reveal dirty, frayed cuffs. "This is our park. I can spend as much time here as I like."

"Yes, you can, sir," Winston said. "Did you happen by the Hollow Tree in the last two days?"

The man scratched his unshaven chin and wiped his nose with a sleeve. Miller stepped away from him. "I come here every day."

"To this spot?"

"To the park." He shook his bag. "I make new homes for these." He opened the bag to show the policemen hundreds of acorns.

"New homes?"

The man nodded. "I give them to the forest. Some of my trees have grown a foot this year."

Winston looked around. "Your trees?"

"The ones I gave before."

"You gave the forest trees?" Winston continued to engage the man, letting him unfold his story. Miller cast him a pleading look to let the man continue on his way. Winston shook his head.

"I am giving these seeds new homes among new friends." The man rolled an acorn between his fingers.

"Did your planting bring you to this spot recently?" Winston asked gently.

"I plant the trees where they need to be. I have been drawn here for the last week or so. The park is guiding me."

Miller stepped forward. "Are you guided here during the day? Or at night?" He matched Winston's tone, and Winston gave him a slight nod to encourage him.

"This isn't a safe place in the dark." He looked directly at the tree where Arthur Pierce had been hanging.

"Did you see what happened here?"

"I don't leave my home at night." The man closed his bag and walked away.

"What's your name, sir? Where can I find you if I need to talk to you again?" Miller followed the man and guided him back to Winston.

"I'm Jessop. Otto Jessop. I don't want any trouble."

Winston extended his hand. "It's a pleasure to meet you, Mr. Jessop. We will not trouble you if we do not have to, but it is important we know what happened here. You said this is not a safe place. Why did you say that?"

"A man died here."

"Did you see him?" Miller asked.

Jessop shook his head, his eyes fixed on the tree behind Winston and Miller. "No. I heard him."

"When?"

"When he died."

"Where do you live, Mr. Jessop?" Winston asked.

"I have a room downtown."

Miller stiffened and whispered to Winston. "How did he hear when the man died?"

Jessop switched his focus to Miller. "I didn't hear him then. The next morning, when I came here, I saw him hanging. There." Jessop pointed to where Pierce's body had hung. "He cried to the trees, and they told me." He cupped his hand to his ear. "Listen."

A breeze picked up, and brown and orange leaves fluttered to the ground. Miller mimicked Jessop's gesture, then frowned. Winston held a hand to his ear for three breaths.

"I appreciate your speaking to us, Mr. Jessop." Winston offered the man a smile. "One final thing. When you heard the man crying, did you see any horses or a carriage around?"

"It was just after sunrise. A carriage passed me, but I didn't see who drove it. Driver had his head covered."

"Would you recognize the carriage if you saw it again?"

"They all look the same to me." Jessop turned and began walking away. The policemen watched as he bent down every few steps to push an acorn into the ground. Then he paused to wipe his hands on a cloth dangling from his rear pocket. He called back over a shoulder. "I didn't see any faces, but I saw a colour. It was a maple on fire." Jessop returned to his rhythm of kneeling and planting.

"He wasn't very helpful," Miller grumbled.

"He might have been more helpful than we realize, Miller. Did you hear what he said? He saw a carriage leaving the park when he arrived. What would a carriage be doing here before the sunrise?"

"What about his mutterings about the trees speaking to him? Or the maple on fire? Did he set a tree alight?"

"I will ask Evans if a hanged man makes noise. It could be that Jessop heard Pierce's final sounds."

Miller crinkled his nose.

"As for his reference to fire, look around. What colour are the maple leaves?"

Realization dawned on Miller's face. "Red. He saw something red. Still, Jessop doesn't seem very credible."

"Why do you say that, Miller?" Winston turned to watch the man in the distance stooping to his planting task. "He is unusual, I agree. But that doesn't make him unreliable. It would be a shame to dismiss this man only because he is different."

Miller frowned. "So many witnesses contradict each other. Or are unhelpful."

"True, Constable. Our job is to hear it all and figure out what it reveals."

Miller nodded. "Hear it all. I understand. This man, even if he is different, might know something."

"I know he does. He told us about the carriage."

"You think whoever was in the carriage was involved in Pierce's death because it was here before daylight."

"Precisely."

"But what good does that do us if he didn't recognize the carriage?"

Winston dismissed the comment with a wave. "That doesn't matter. I'm certain Pierce was not here alone."

"And Jessop saw his murderer?"

Winston nodded. "I think so. Mr. Jessop's information certainly supports that." He turned to survey the scene a last time. "We've learned all we can from here. Collect the ladder. It's time to look more closely at Mr. Pierce's business."

CHAPTER 10

Jack

THE CAB DRIVER dropped Winston and Miller in Vancouver's business district. Winston thanked him and instructed him to return the ladder to the station.

Arthur Pierce's business operated out of a three-storey building on Granville Street. Several other professionals had offices in the same building. Winston spoke to a man sitting at a desk near the entrance for directions to Pierce's office on the third floor.

Winston and Miller's footsteps echoed as they climbed the stairs to AP Investments. Winston knocked on the door's frosted-glass pane before turning the knob.

Inside the office, a young man with a dark, close-cropped beard sat at a small desk. He stood as Winston and Miller entered. "We are closed, gentlemen," he said, his voice cracking. His eyes widened, pleading for them to accept his pronouncement. His gaze flicked to Miller. "Unless you were looking to invest? We have an exciting—"

Winston held out his hand and motioned for the man to sit. "We are not looking to invest. I am Detective Jack Winston, and this is Constable Thomas Miller. We attended the scene of Mr. Pierce's death." Something about this man discouraged Winston from offering further explanation.

The man gestured to two chairs positioned opposite his desk. Winston and Miller removed their hats and sat. Pierce's name was stencilled on the glass of another door behind the man. A single bookshelf adorned with a handful of books occupied the wall next to the door.

Colour had drained from the man's face. "Then you will know why we are closed. I am Charles Macey, Mr. Pierce's assistant." Macey blinked rapidly as he spoke. "He was such a good man."

"Do you plan to reopen?" Winston asked.

Macey reacted with a shrug so slight, Winston wondered if it had been a shiver. "I don't know, sir. I am waiting to hear from Mr. Sawyer on what to do."

"You're just sitting and waiting for him?" Miller had spoken more sharply than Winston would have liked, but the question was a good one.

"No." Macey indicated a box beside his desk. "I am organizing our paperwork for Mr. Sawyer."

"How many boxes have you to go through?" Winston looked around the sparsely furnished room. The files must be stored elsewhere, perhaps in Pierce's office.

"Just this one." As Macey pointed toward the floor, Winston noticed a tremor in his hands. Winston leaned to peer around the desk and saw the edge of a single box. "How many clients did Mr. Pierce have?"

The man sighed. "To be honest, I'm uncertain. I looked after our smaller investors. Mr. Pierce and Mr. Sawyer handled our larger ones, but we kept the paperwork separate." He nudged the box with his foot. "That's what's in here."

Winston thought of the year he'd spent working for his father before leaving Toronto to become a police detective. How different that office—a loud, dynamic business environment—had been to this spartan space, staffed by this single, nervous man. As a police detective, he had visited several company offices. This one lacked the energy he associated with enterprises of the sort linked to Pierce's name. Very peculiar.

"How long have you worked for Arthur Pierce, Mr. Macey?"

"A year. He hired me when I moved here."

As Macey spoke, Winston fished for his notebook from his satchel. "What can you tell me about Mr. Pierce?"

"He was kind, very generous with his friends. I believe he entertained often. Always speaking about fine dinners." Macey paused, then added, "And he was very well dressed." He brushed the lapel of his own jacket. "A professional appearance was important to him."

"You mentioned investments for Mr. Pierce. That's the business, isn't it?" Winston asked. "What did the company invest in?"

"I didn't do the investing."

"But you just said you handled the smaller investors," Miller said.

Macey looked from one policeman to the other, then dropped his eyes. "I did. But I was never directly involved in the transactions."

Winston sensed he would need to be direct with Macey. "Please describe the exact nature of your involvement."

"I found some investors, received their money, and gave it to Mr. Pierce."

"The rest was handled by Pierce?" Winston tempered his voice.

"You are correct." Macey offered a curt nod.

"Is this a typical arrangement for investment firms?" Miller asked.

"I wouldn't know. Mr. Pierce's is the only one I've worked for."

Miller considered this. He looked at Winston, who dipped his head to indicate Miller could continue asking questions. "What made a man a small or big investor?"

"My investors gave smaller sums. No greater than one hundred dollars."

Miller shot Winston a glance.

Winston noted the arch of Miller's eyebrows. He agreed; one hundred dollars was a significant sum for most men. How much, he wondered, did men in the other category invest?

"Where did you find these smaller investors?" Miller asked.

"They were men who were interested in supporting miners but were unable to do any prospecting themselves."

Macey's response didn't directly answer Miller's question, but it had revealed the focus of the investments: mining. Winston marvelled at how many of the city's businesses were associated with the industry, even indirectly. Shipping, trains, supply shops—all had some connection. "How did they support miners?" he asked. "Did they fund expeditions?"

Macey shook his head. "Not exactly. One miner. He has had considerable success finding gold deposits. Pierce funded his expeditions in exchange for a percentage of the finds. People have already doubled their investments."

"And your small investors?"

"Also contributed."

Winston noted Macey didn't say how much return these smaller investors may have seen on the money they'd contributed. He decided not to press the man on it now, but jotted a reminder in his notebook. He swivelled in his seat, scanning the other walls for another door. The entry door and Pierce's office door were the only ones. "Does Mr. Sawyer not keep an office here? Doesn't he have a role in the company?"

Macey shook his head. "He is Mr. Pierce's partner. But he kept his office elsewhere. At home, I believe. He spent very little time here. Though I suppose I'll see more of him now that this is his enterprise." His face clouded.

Winston waited for the man to collect his thoughts. Silence was a powerful tool; people were often compelled to fill it.

Macey leaned forward as if to share a confidence. "I wouldn't mention it if Mr. Pierce hadn't died, but I heard him and Mr. Sawyer arguing recently. I had the impression the partnership wasn't working as well as either of them had hoped."

"What makes you say that, Mr. Macey?"

"Mr. Pierce told Mr. Sawyer he was losing patience. I assumed he thought Mr. Sawyer was not performing as well as he might. It seemed he was not as skilled as Mr. Pierce at finding clients." He looked away. "At least, that's what I overheard Mr. Pierce say. 'You'll need to do better at finding clients if you want to succeed at this.'"

Miller adjusted his position in his chair. "How did you add clients to the roster? Did they come here?"

Macey reached down and moved a single glove from the lid of the box, setting it on the desk. The sight reminded Winston of the one they'd found in the park. The flicker in Miller's eye revealed he'd also noticed it. "Are you missing a glove, Mr. Macey?" Winston asked. Miller leaned forward to hear the man's answer. Had they already found their killer?

"Yes, I seem to have mislaid one. I'm sure it will turn up somewhere," he said. "As to your other question, many of the clients I worked with came in without appointments, having been referred here by other investors. In fact, this morning I thought that's why you'd come."

Winston stood and stepped toward Macey's desk. "I would like to look at the business's records, Mr. Macey. But first, may I have a look at your glove, if you don't mind? And please tell us where you were two nights ago."

"My glove? Why?" Macey recoiled. "Two nights ago?"

"I'm interested in a pair." Winston reached for the glove. "I find the dampness makes my fingers stiff."

Macey looked at his own hand before reluctantly handing his glove to Winston. "They were a gift."

Winston turned the black glove over. It was leather with a small gap in the outer seam. He handed it to Miller, who had joined him at the edge of Macey's desk.

Miller examined it briefly, then returned it to Macey. He leaned toward Winston. "The one we found was for a left hand, sir."

Winston nodded. Macey's was also for a left hand. "And your whereabouts two nights ago?"

"The night Mr. Pierce died? I was at home. I live with my mother. She needs some assistance," he said, eyes cast toward the floor. He looked up suddenly. "Why do you need to know that?"

Winston ignored Macey's question. "Now the records, please."

Macey stood and moved in front of the box at his feet. "I don't think I can let you," he said. "The identities of our investors are confidential. You'll need to speak to Mr. Sawyer."

"We will," Winston said. "But it would save us time if you let us look at the accounts now."

Macey set his jaw and shook his head, surprising Winston with his assertiveness.

"Very well." Winston turned to his constable. "Thomas, stay here with Mr. Macey. When I return, it will be with permission from Mr. Sawyer to remove the files for our review."

"Will he grant it to you, sir?" Miller asked.

"He will. Make sure Mr. Macey doesn't destroy anything."

Winston turned on his heel, leaving Miller standing beside the office door, frowning deeply at Charles Macey.

CHAPTER 11

Jack

REGINALD SAWYER CLEARED his throat from the doorway of his sitting room, where Winston warmed himself in front of the fire.

Sawyer bore a friendly, almost inviting expression, despite the prospect of having a policeman standing in his front room. "Detective Winston. I understand you are here about Arthur."

His tone as he said the dead man's name interested Winston. The men were business partners as well as brothers by marriage. Surely Sawyer had held some affection for Pierce, yet he spoke his name as if he were referring to a butcher or gardener, betraying no hint of the depth of their relationship. "Arthur Pierce was also your business partner, wasn't he?"

Sawyer drew his hand down the length of his moustache, a gesture Winston recognized as buying Sawyer time to think. "Perhaps we should meet in my study, Detective."

Winston followed the man through the house. Family portraits lined the walls, but Winston couldn't identify much resemblance in any of them to either Reginald Sawyer or his wife. "Has your family lived in the area long, Mr. Sawyer?"

"Not long, no. We, like so many residents, are transplants from elsewhere. What about you?"

"Our stories are similar, I suspect. I moved here a year ago. My parents remain in Toronto." Winston took the opportunity to build Sawyer's trust. "When did you arrive? I am amazed by the pace at which the city is developing, even in the short time I've lived here."

Sawyer stood in the doorway of the study, gesturing for Winston to enter. "We've been here slightly longer than you, but I agree, we have seen considerable change."

Was the man evading Winston's questions? He tried another approach. "Still, I don't regret coming here."

"Nor I. Vancouver has much to offer."

The lighting in the study was subdued. Book-filled shelves lined the full length of the far wall. In the centre of the room, Sawyer cleared away a pile of paper from the top of a writing desk and gestured to Winston to sit in an overstuffed chair.

Winston waited until Sawyer settled before continuing. "Now to my earlier question. Were you and Pierce business partners?"

"Not exactly." Sawyer folded and unfolded his hands. "Arthur was giving me guidance regarding starting a business similar to his own."

"What kind of business?"

"Investing. Arthur was investing in mining exploration. But there are other opportunities as well."

"And what opportunity are you planning to pursue?"

Sawyer's face clouded as he sighed. "I haven't decided, and I was hoping Arthur would continue to serve as my guide. He had a nose for successful ventures, and what I really wanted to learn was how to develop that same instinct."

"How long did you work with him?"

Sawyer rubbed his face. "This was our first project. He was keen to have me involved, show me the ropes."

"Will you take over his business?"

Sawyer's brow furrowed as if he was considering the idea for the first time. "Will I?"

"Your wife seemed to think so when I saw her yesterday with Mrs. Pierce. And Mrs. Pierce's lawyer has sent a letter confirming it was her husband's intention you run the company in Pierce's son's name until such time he is old enough to assume the responsibility himself."

"Better me than Macey," Sawyer said, though he didn't sound convinced.

"Why?" Charles Macey had seemed competent enough, if not particularly assertive.

"I don't trust him. In the past few months, Arthur had missed a couple of appointments. He said it was scheduling confusion due to mistakes made by Macey. Why he kept the man, I have no idea."

"When I spoke with him, he suggested Pierce was also offering him some instruction."

"Macey was working with Arthur to find small investors. But to me, that seemed a waste of time. Why not seek out the bigger players? The ones who can provide real capital?" Sawyer raised his eyebrows, forming neat arches that nearly met his hairline.

Winston considered the question. In a city Vancouver's size, even though it was growing rapidly, the pool of investors with large sums of capital would still be relatively small. Pierce's strategy was clever: recruit who he could from the bigger players through his own connections, and employ someone else to deliver smaller investors. Was that why Macey had concluded Sawyer was struggling? Was Pierce impatient because the man was reluctant to go after anyone but the biggest of fish?

Sawyer leaned his elbows on the desk and clasped his hands in front of him. "Macey has always seemed... evasive."

"He refused to let me inspect Pierce's files," Winston said. "Will you grant me permission to do so?"

"Yes, of course. I'll write you a letter." Sawyer reached into a drawer for a piece of paper and scrawled a few words on the page.

Winston waited until Sawyer handed him the document, then asked, "How much did you interact with Pierce's clients?"

Sawyer relaxed into his chair. "He introduced them to me at the club. They were always eager to speak to him. He'd made some of them quite wealthy. Word spread. Others wanted the same."

"Did that make it easy for you to find your own clients?"

"I think so. My association with Arthur was known at the club. Being able to point men to others who've been satisfied with the returns they've enjoyed helps when one is attempting to convince people to part with their money." Sawyer paused. "No matter how wealthy they are."

Winston edged forward in his chair. "And when they parted with their money? What happened next?"

Sawyer leaned toward Winston as if preparing to share a confidence. "Arthur handled everything after the money came in."

"He was funding mining exploration, correct?"

Sawyer furrowed his brow. "In a manner of speaking. It was a device to make mining extraction easier, more efficient."

Winston noted the difference in how Sawyer and Macey spoke about the investment opportunity. Why would the men describe it so differently? "Not a specific expedition? A specific miner?"

Sawyer pursed his lips. "Well, sure. Arthur had a man testing it. Billy, his name was. And he'd had considerable success."

Here Sawyer's wording mimicked Macey's. "He'd found gold?" Could this miner have found enough gold to repay investors in such a short time?

"Yes, and that's what made the investors happy. Arthur's plan was to have Billy continue his search for more. And eventually to have other miners use the same device. He just needed new investors so he could purchase the equipment."

"It sounds like you'll be able to continue despite Pierce's death."

"I'm not sure I can rely on Macey's help. The man doesn't seem to be particularly ambitious. Nonetheless, he may have connections I can use. I will check on him."

"He would appreciate that. I saw him this morning and he looked rather lost." Winston surprised himself with his comment. Something about Sawyer's manner invited sharing more than one intended. "Do you know how I can find Billy, this miner?"

Sawyer rubbed his chin. "I don't. Apparently, he doesn't like the city. He would check in with Arthur occasionally, at some predetermined time. Maybe you will find more detail among Arthur's papers. Search away. Especially if it will help you understand why he killed himself."

Winston didn't correct Sawyer on his assumption. "Thank you for your time, Mr. Sawyer." Winston extended his hand.

"If you have other questions, I will try to answer them." Sawyer led Winston through the house. At the door, Sawyer's servant handed Winston his coat and hat.

"One last thing. Do you know how many clients Pierce had?"

Sawyer shook his head. "Arthur never told me."

"Thank you, Mr. Sawyer. I'm sure I'll be in touch."

CHAPTER 12

Riley

RILEY STARED AT the screen of her laptop. No results came up when she'd searched AP Investments, Pierce's company. It either hadn't been registered, or the records hadn't survived the decades since Pierce's death. She took a mouthful of her morning tea.

Jack's note had also confirmed Sawyer's name was pronounced as it was written—"Saw-yer." Why had the pronunciation changed? Was this another detail lost to time?

Riley was writing some thoughts on a pad of paper when her phone rang. "Hi, Mom."

"Hi, honey. Did Lucy tell you I am planning to come a day early, tomorrow instead of Thursday? I'm not sure if I can stay for the weekend, so she's moved the dress fitting."

"She didn't mention it. Do you want to stay here?" Riley pictured her mother biting her lip during the silence that hung on the line.

"No, thank you," her mother finally answered. "Too many memories."

Too many, or not enough? Riley's father died shortly after her parents had bought the condo. "I have a spare room if you change your mind." Silence again. "Mom?"

"I'm here," she said at last. "I'll stay in a hotel, but I appreciate your offer." Muffled sounds followed, as if her mother was covering the phone with her hand. Was she with someone? A faint rustle, then her voice returned, clear again. "I've decided on a gift for your sister and Alex that might be unconventional."

Lucy certainly thought it unconventional, but Riley couldn't tell her mother that. "Like what?" It was better to let her reveal the plan.

Her mother explained the gift was an investment in the couple's name in a company that supports building schools. "Is it a charity? A donation rather than an investment?" Riley asked.

"We invest the money. Some goes to build the schools, and some goes back to the investors."

She'd said "we." What did that mean? A flutter of unease awakened in her stomach. She'd leave it unchallenged—for now—and just get her mother to talk more about the investment. "How does it work?" Riley pulled out a fresh piece of paper. She could look up the company after the call.

"I've made ten thousand dollars back. I reinvested it, of course. But I'm quite pleased." Her mother spoke quickly.

Riley inhaled sharply. "Ten thousand dollars?" How much money had she invested to make so much? "Mom, something about this sounds risky."

"That's the beauty of it, dear. It's not risky at all. We buy these coins. Educoins, they're called. A percentage of what we buy goes to the schools. When the coins go up in value, so does the amount going to build the schools."

Riley wrote *Educoin* on the paper. Was this a cryptocurrency? She wrote *crypto?* "What happens if the coins don't go up in value?"

"It's never happened. They're extremely secure, and people are racing to get them."

She spoke with such confidence. It didn't sound like the first time she had pitched the soundness of the coins. Riley rubbed her jaw and forced her tongue to the top of her mouth to relax it. "Mom, don't take this the wrong way, but what do you know about investing? I mean, you're a teacher."

"I'm teaching part time. Educoin is bringing in a little extra. You can start by attending a training session."

"I'm not really interested. My salary covers my expenses. I don't have much left over, but I'd rather just put it in a savings account. In a bank."

"Your money isn't doing anything for you in a bank, dear." Riley bristled at her mother's condescending tone. "I'd like to give you some to invest, like I've given to your sister. I can't see you miss out. There are a few sessions this week while I'm in town. Say you'll come to one."

"I'll think about it, Mom."

"Why don't I send you some information? Look it over. Then we can talk again."

Her mom disconnected and Riley stared at her phone. Such a weird conversation. What on earth had her mom become involved in? She pulled her laptop closer and typed "Educoin" into the browser's search bar.

The first result took her to the company's website. It was sleek and minimal, its images alternating between those of smiling children standing outside a simple building in what she suspected was Africa, and of happy-looking middle-aged and older couples, all looking active and healthy. She looked for the About Us section and found a write-up similar to the description her mother had given her. An endnote explained that while not all investments are profitable, Educoin investors had been successful so far, and children receiving education had been the true beneficiaries. Educoin had already built three schools in its relatively short existence. Impressive, though there were no details about the locations of the schools.

Next, Riley searched "Educoin" and "investors". A few social media posts surfaced. People shared their pride in investments that were benefiting others. Educoin was touted as a new model for investing. One post referenced something called a "digital wallet" with a considerable sum of money in it. "My balance after two months.

$$$," the caption read. So far, it seemed, nobody had any criticisms of the venture.

Riley entered "Educoin" and "complaints." Perhaps the company was too new for someone to have had a bad experience, or maybe it really was great. But the way her mother had talked about it, Riley had the impression it had been around longer. She typed the company's domain name into a domain lookup tool to see how long the website had existed. One year. That seemed a short time to have already built schools. She checked the dates of the discussion board postings. All within the last few months. She wrote *too new?* in her notes. She checked the domain registration again. The associated physical address was in downtown Vancouver. She could visit the offices at lunch tomorrow.

*

THE NEXT MORNING, Riley stood outside a low-rise commercial building with three retail units on the ground floor: a print shop, a convenience store, and an alterations shop. She double-checked the address she had written down from the domain registration office. Unit B, the convenience store.

Posters promoting low-cost calling cards and international money transfer services obscured the view into the shop. An unlikely place for a successful investment company to be operating, and definitely not what the Educoin website conveyed. She checked the address a third time before pulling the door open. The door chimes rang as she stepped in. Rows of shelves displaying packaged foods, mostly potato chips and chocolate bars, filled the small space. A bored-looking woman stood behind the counter. Riley approached her. Should she even mention Educoin? Nothing about this seemed right.

"Excuse me," Riley said.

The woman ignored her.

"Excuse me," Riley repeated, adding force to her voice.

The woman looked up at Riley. "What are you buying?"

"I don't want anything. I mean, not from here. But maybe you could help me. . ." She pulled her phone out to show the woman the Educoin website. "Do you know about Educoin?"

The woman shook her head. "We don't make change," she said, pointing to a handwritten sign on the back of the cash register.

"No, I don't want coins," Riley said. The woman was infuriating. She measured her words to avoid losing what little was left of her patience. "I found an address for a company called Educoin. It's here." She pointed to another browser window on her phone's screen.

The woman pointed to the back of the room. "Must be a PO box. Anyone can rent them. I can check the mail weekly for an additional ten dollars a week."

"Can you confirm you collect the mail for Educoin?" Riley asked.

"Nope. Unless you're police and have a warrant?" The clerk raised her eyebrows. Bored, but not gullible. "But if they list the address, they must use our service."

"Can I take a look? At the PO boxes, I mean? I will be fast."

"Customers only."

Riley fished change from her bag. "If I buy something, will I be a customer?"

"If you rent a box, you're a customer. Prepay for the year, please." The woman held out her hand. "It will be two hundred and fifty dollars."

Riley flushed. She wasn't going to pay to check out what a block of PO boxes in a convenience store looked like. She'd have to learn more about Educoin another way.

CHAPTER 13

Jack

Constable Miller's smile suggested relief, rather than pleasure, when Winston entered Arthur Pierce's business office. Winston produced Sawyer's letter and handed it to Macey. "I've spoken with Reginald Sawyer. He has granted me permission to search wherever necessary and review business records," he said as he cast his gaze around the room. "We'll start in Mr. Pierce's office."

Macey stood, frowning. "I haven't a key for his office."

Winston closed his eyes to quiet the frustration bubbling inside him. Why was every part of this case proving to be so unnecessarily difficult? "Is there a building caretaker? Surely he'll have a key." Without having to be told, Miller escorted Macey from the room.

Winston took a deep breath and sat at Macey's desk. He pulled out his journal and jotted a quick message to Riley.

Dear Riley,

I trust you are well. The Pierce case is proving perplexing. I am currently sitting in the office of AP Investments, waiting for Pierce's secretary, Charles Macey, to return with a key to open the door to Pierce's office. The man seems to be going out of his way to hinder my investigation. First, he refused me entry to Pierce's office without written permission from Reginald Sawyer. I secured a letter of permission, redeeming the time to also ask Sawyer about his business arrangements with Pierce.

Then, on my return, letter in hand, Macey reveals he hasn't a key to Pierce's office.

Winston sighed. Writing to Riley eased his frustration. He set his pencil down and fanned the remaining blank pages in the book. There looked to be ten left. Winston dismissed, again, the question too uncomfortable to ponder: how would he continue his connection with Riley when the journal was filled? For now, he'd try to keep his entries concise, look for ways to conserve space on the page.

Sawyer and Macey each reported different versions of what Pierce offered investors. According to Macey, it was the opportunity to fund a particular miner with a record of success. Sawyer suggested that rather than a man, it was mining machinery they were raising money for. I suppose each man might focus on separate aspects when speaking to potential investors, but I wonder why they seem to understand the business so differently. They were after different investors: Pierce and Sawyer sought wealthier ones, while Macey worked with men who had less to invest. I'll get more detail from Macey.

Neither Sawyer nor Macey seemed to understand what happened after Pierce received investors' money. They just recruited investors and handed the money to Pierce. Once I get a look at Pierce's records, I should learn more.

Thank you for the information about the death certificate. I am trying to encourage my police colleagues to keep better records. I am more convinced now than ever of their value to future reviewers.

Until next time,

Jack

Winston had just returned the journal to his satchel when he heard footsteps approaching from the hallway. But rather than Macey and Miller, a tall man in workman's clothing stood in the doorway. Winston rose and motioned for the man to enter. Before he could introduce himself, the man began to speak.

"I'm looking for my money. I just heard Mr. Pierce died, and, well, I wasn't sure I wanted to give him my money in the first place. Now that he's dead, I'd like it back."

"Please have a seat." Winston gestured to a chair. "Tell me, how much did you give him?"

"I actually gave it to the other guy, Macey. He was sitting here, where you are." He nodded toward the desk. His eyes narrowed as he scrutinized Winston. "Do you work for Mr. Pierce too?"

"You gave your money to Macey?"

"Yes. Seventy-five dollars. He said he would return one-hundred-and fifty to me if I waited two months. I'd rather not wait. I'd just like my money back now."

Winston wrote the information in his notebook. When he finished, he set down his pencil and looked at the man. Seventy-five dollars was more than most men earned in a month. This man must have given Pierce his savings. "I am a detective with the constabulary. I'm investigating Mr. Pierce's death."

"A detective? Investigating? Why?" The man edged forward in his chair, his eagerness to learn something from Winston evident in his posture.

The office door opened, and Miller and Macey walked in. Macey stopped short when he saw Winston sitting behind his desk and another man sitting opposite him. He turned back to Miller. "What's going on?"

The investor swivelled to look at Macey. "I've come to get my money back. You're the one I gave it to." His voice had taken on an accusatory tone.

As if a switch had been pulled, Macey assumed an authoritative stance. "Mr. Pierce has just died, so we are presently pausing any investments or withdrawals. I can take your name and information, and I'll contact you when I have more information."

The man stood. "I suppose I'll have to accept that," he muttered, but his face betrayed his dissatisfaction.

Winston stepped away from the desk so Macey could note the man's name and details.

When he was finished, Macey extended his hand. "Thank you, Mr. Felter. I'll be in touch as soon as I can."

Winston stepped forward. "Mr. Felter, my name is Detective Winston. I neglected to introduce myself when you asked. Should you have any questions, you can find me at the constabulary."

Felter nodded. Macey promised again that he would contact him as soon as he knew more, and the man left.

"He's the third man who's been here since you left to speak to Sawyer, sir," Miller said after he'd closed the door behind Felter.

Winston turned to Macey for confirmation. "They all want their money back?"

Macey nodded. "I've told them all the same thing, as your constable will confirm. I hardly think it's appropriate for people to ask for their money so soon after Arthur's death." He narrowed his focus on Winston. "Were you searching my desk, Detective?"

Winston bristled at the question. "I was making some notes. But, as I have Sawyer's permission, I could have searched the desk had I wanted to." He took the opportunity to open the drawers, finding them neatly organized. "These other men, were they investors you have met before? Were you expecting them to ask for their money?"

"I had met them." Macey raked his hands through his hair. "And no, I was not expecting them to ask for their money. Mr. Pierce had just received payments from newer investors. It's too early for them to see any returns. It's too treacherous to head out at this time of year to search for gold."

"Why take their money now, then, if no mining is happening? Did the investors realize they'd have to wait to realize any returns?" Miller asked.

"They understood. We needed the money now to order supplies, make preparations. That kind of thing. Billy needs equipment."

"Doesn't Pierce have some money in reserve? To pay investors like these fellows?"

Macey's cheeks flushed. "There should be some money. But if every investor asks, there will not be enough. And what would we use to fund Billy's expedition?" His sentences came out in sharp bursts.

"You'll need to speak with Sawyer. The two of you will need to reassure investors. Explain how Pierce's death doesn't impact the exploration plans." The words were out of Winston's mouth before he could stop himself. He wasn't there to dispense advice, but he would have offered the same counsel following the unexpected death of a business owner. "Speak to Sawyer," he repeated.

Miller, eyes wide, stepped forward, wiggling a key between his fingers. "The building manager gave me this. Shall we conduct our search now, sir?" He waited for Winston to nod his approval, then approached the locked door.

Winston, resuming his detective role, squared his shoulders. "Please let us know if you intend to leave, Mr. Macey."

Miller closed the door behind them and looked at Winston. "What did Sawyer say?"

"He described the investment differently than Macey had," Winston said, and explained Sawyer's definition.

"Why would they represent the investment so differently?" Miller asked.

"A good question. One we need to answer. Let's see what we find in here." Winston surveyed the office.

The room appeared as Winston had expected: solid wooden desk, upholstered chairs, landscapes on the walls. He pulled open the drawers on one side of the desk to find they contained writing materials, but no files. He continued his search, which yielded nothing of relevance. "Miller, what is in the drawers on your side?"

"Nothing much, sir. An empty notebook." Miller shook the book before replacing it in the drawer. "Not much here at all that you'd expect to find in a business office."

"Agreed. There should be investment records. Money they paid in, money investors were paid. Very odd." Winston scratched an earlobe. "I will visit his home."

Miller slid the art to the side, checking to see if there were any secret storage spaces behind the pieces. Winston smiled at the man's thoroughness. It was a shame that Miller's ingenuity, along with their combined efforts to investigate, remained unrewarded.

Winston closed the door to Pierce's office as they exited. "Mr. Macey, please leave this room unlocked. We may wish to search it again." No need to tell the man where they intended to search next.

Macey nodded slowly.

"The other men who were here earlier. How much did they invest?" Macey produced a paper on which he had written the men's names. Most had sums of less than one hundred dollars beside them. "One man had invested one hundred and fifty dollars?" Winston had thought Felter's investment of seventy-five dollars a considerable sum. "Where does the money go?"

"I don't know. Mr. Pierce took it."

"You have no record of which bank holds it?"

Macey looked down at the desk. "I don't think it went to a bank. Not at first. Mr. Pierce used it to purchase supplies."

"And where are those supplies?" Miller asked. "You said before, no exploration happens during the winter."

Macey offered a shrug. "They're not here. Perhaps Mr. Pierce kept them at his home."

"He never told you what they were, where he kept them?" Winston hadn't searched the Pierce home looking for mining supplies, but shovels and axes would surely have caught his attention had he seen them.

Macey shook his head with a glum expression.

Winston sighed and pinched the bridge of his nose. He scanned his notes. Despite the business training his father insisted he complete and the brief time he'd spent working in his father's office, his head swam with the details of this case. Nothing about how these men had run this investment business made sense. "We will take any records you have here, Mr. Macey. Whatever you used to produce this." Winston waved the sheet in his hand.

Macey looked stricken at Winston's demand. "What if others come?"

"Repeat what you told the other men earlier: the company is pausing operations for now and they will be contacted. Miller will copy out the records, and we'll return them to you as quickly as we can. Thank you, Mr. Macey. That will be all for today." He signalled to Miller they were leaving.

Macey pushed forward the box that had been at the side of his desk. "Before you go, if I may ask, when you spoke with Mr. Sawyer, did he say anything about my job?"

Winston paused. "He mentioned Arthur Pierce missed appointments because you'd failed to schedule them."

Macey blanched. "I haven't arranged any appointments for him recently. If Mr. Pierce missed something, it wasn't because of me."

"Why would Sawyer blame you?"

Disappointment crinkled the corners of Macey's eyes. "I've always had the sense he didn't care for me. I'm not sure why. He spent far more time with Mr. Pierce. I don't suppose Mr. Sawyer will be interested in sharing anything that he knows about the business with me."

"You'd be best to speak to him yourself. Good day, Mr. Macey."

Winston waved Miller ahead of him into the hall. As he closed the door behind him, he caught sight of Macey at his desk, his head in his hands.

✷

ON THE STREET, Miller and Winston waited to hire a cab. Winston pointed to the box in Miller's arms. "Take this to the station, Thomas. Tomorrow, you can review the documents inside. Copy anything that contains information about Pierce's investors. I'd also like you to speak to the men who visited Pierce's office today. Find out how they heard about Pierce, where they work, what they know about investing. And, last thing, send someone to check whether any horses have been reported missing at the stables."

Miller shifted the box's position as if weighing how much time copying its contents was going to take.

"Get another man to help you transcribe if needed. I'll go to Pierce's house first thing in the morning. His office held none of his business records. He must have kept them at home."

A cab pulled up, and Winston opened the door for Miller. "Oh, and please don't discuss with anyone which case this information relates to." He caught the flash of surprise as it crossed Miller's face.

"Is this a secret?"

"Not exactly. But I'd like more evidence before I bring it to the chief constable." He leaned into the carriage wall. "I'll speak to him tomorrow afternoon."

CHAPTER 14

Riley

AT THE MUSEUM, Riley pushed herself away from the work counter. Since visiting the address of the Educoin offices, she'd struggled to focus on the exhibit. What did it mean if Educoin's listed address led to a PO box? Clearly, many people used them. The store wouldn't offer the service if it didn't make them some money.

Nick was off tracking down a CEO, leaving Riley alone in the archive. On an impulse, she dialled Johnny's number. He answered on the second ring.

"Hey, Riley. Everything okay?" She heard the concern in his voice and kicked herself for phoning instead of sending a text. They spoke on the phone rarely, usually only to confirm details for meeting places or times.

"I'm fine. Sorry to call during your workday." She rubbed a clammy hand against her pant leg. "Actually, I'm calling in a semi-professional capacity. Do you have a minute?"

"Absolutely. Just let me close my door," he said. She heard the muffled sound of footsteps. "I'm back. What is it?"

"Have you ever heard of something called Educoin?"

"Educoin?"

"It's some sort of investment fund people pay into," she said. She gave Johnny a brief explanation. "I went to the address listed on its website today, and it's a convenience store. The clerk there wouldn't confirm, but she said some businesses use its address if they rent PO boxes." She bit her lip. "Have you heard of anything like that?"

"There's no issue with a company using a PO box. But you said there wasn't another address listed on the website?"

"Nothing I could find."

She heard him typing on his keyboard. "The website looks well put together."

"I thought so too."

"Is this for the museum?"

"My mom has offered to invest some money as Lucy's wedding gift. I wanted to learn a little more about it."

"Okay, I haven't come across the name before, but I'll see if I can dig anything up. At first glance, it seems slightly unusual. Is it a cryptocurrency?"

"I wondered the same thing. Are they legal?"

"Yes, but not they're not well regulated. I'll let you know what I find."

Riley thanked him and ended the call. She smiled back at his smiling face in his contact photo. A warmth spread through her, setting her toes to tingling.

*

THAT EVENING, THE sound of rain pelting the window drew Riley from her position on the couch to check that her window was closed and latched. A bus hissed as it collected and deposited passengers at the stop below her building. People caught without umbrellas or rain jackets hunched over their bags. Who in this city goes out in November without a rain jacket?

She pulled out her phone and sent a message to Jules.

Need somewhere to dry off?

How did you know?

I expect your policy on rainwear hasn't changed. Come by any time.

Despite growing up in the middle of a temperate rainforest on Canada's West Coast, Jules refused to bring a rain jacket if it wasn't raining when he left home. He had explained to Riley once that he was never far from shelter if the skies opened. Did he keep track to see how many times his theory had failed him? Likely, given his number-crunching profession.

Riley didn't love her rain jacket, especially its crinkly fabric and unflattering cut, but everyone—except Jules—wore one. Vancouver was a sea of coloured waterproof fabrics from October through May. Riley was convinced Jules adhered to his policy out of sheer stubbornness.

After five minutes Jules buzzed, and Riley let in her wet friend.

"I'm glad you're here," she said, handing him a towel. She started the kettle.

"You are?"

"Of course. We can catch up on Lady Smallington's latest mystery."

"Sounds good." Jules passed the towel back to Riley with a nod of thanks.

"Before we do that, I have a question for you."

"What is it?"

"Two questions, actually. I thought you were going to come by the museum today?"

Jules frowned. "I did. But my mum wanted help with a last-minute detail for her party. We looked at flowers at Granville Island. We wandered around a little and caught an Aquabus back across to Yaletown."

Riley could hardly fault Jules for spending time with his mother. She looked down as she pushed a pang of jealousy away. "Sounds like it was a nice afternoon."

"It was. You had a second question?"

She returned her gaze to her friend. "Right. What can you tell me about investing?"

Jules arched his eyebrows. "Whoa, I didn't see that one coming." He shot her a teasing smirk. "Well, I'm not a financial adviser, but I can give you a basic rundown." He cut out the kidding and continued with a quick overview of registered investments. "Are you looking to get into the market? If so, you want to find an adviser who is independent. Not associated with a particular fund."

Riley understood this but appreciated Jules starting with the basics. "And how does someone choose what to invest in?"

"The adviser would have information about past performance of funds."

"What if the money isn't in a fund? What about unregistered investments?"

Jules folded his arms across his chest. "Unregistered is riskier. Are you planning to invest in something?"

"Riskier how?"

"There's some protection in investing through an adviser. They work with specific companies. You know where the money is going. They're regulated."

"But haven't there been cases of investors being defrauded?"

"That's usually when one person is pitching an idea to another. 'Give me five thousand dollars. I can turn it into fifty thousand.' That kind of thing." He narrowed his eyes. "Why are you asking?"

"Imagine a situation where one or two people promote an opportunity. They gather the funds and give them to someone else who is supposed to do the investing. But investors never hear anything about how it's going or what happens to the money."

"That is a lot of red flags. I would tell the person who is considering investing to be careful. I would want to know how the returns are funded—they should be the result of profit. They shouldn't be funded by other investors." He placed his hand on her arm. "Have you invested in something like what I've described?"

The concern in his eyes touched her. "Not me. I'm researching something. What should potential investors look out for?"

"High returns, little in the way of documentation, investments not registered with a bank or investment fund, complicated plans." Jules raised a finger with each point.

A knot formed in Riley's stomach. Educoin sounded like it matched some of the criteria Jules had just listed. Come to think of it, the same red flags existed in the case Jack was investigating: unusually high returns, minimal documentation. "How would I tell if the investments were registered?"

"The government has a website," Jules answered.

"What about in the past? Pre-internet?"

"A bank would have been able to look them up, I suppose. Or maybe confirm via letter. Everything was slower before the internet, wasn't it?"

"What if the investments had to be made in person? Imagine we didn't have phones or email."

"Like after an apocalypse?"

Riley laughed. "I guess so."

"Whose first concern is investments after an apocalypse? Have the zombie hordes been defeated?"

She waved her hands in front of her. "No apocalypse. No zombies. No phones or email, either." Riley fixed two mugs of tea and led Jules to the couch.

Jules perched himself so he could face her. After a moment, he furrowed his brow. "Okay, let me get this straight. In this hypothetical situation, you're not using technology to communicate but want to make an investment. In that case, you'd need to do the transaction in person. How else would the money move around? These circumstances would make me think something fishy was going on. Is this something to do with the man you were looking into the other day?"

"Yes. It's for my project at work."

"Your job is more interesting than I thought. Didn't you ask me about bodies last time, how victims of drowning would look? It was when you first began working there, just as I was leaving town."

Riley's cheeks pricked with heat at the memory of the first case she'd helped Jack Winston with. "I did. For a different exhibit. This one is about businesses in the city."

"Fraudulent ones?"

"I don't know yet. But I think I might have found something to dig deeper into."

Jules wrapped his hands around his mug, ribbons of steam weaving in front of his face. "Two things pop into my mind. First, we have the person responsible for the investments, the broker."

Riley nodded. "I'm following you so far."

"Let's say the broker takes money from new investors to pay off early investors. Those early investors see great returns and invest more. They talk up how great the investment is, and the broker uses that because he needs to convince more and more people to invest in order to keep the returns going."

"Using Peter to pay Paul?"

"Exactly."

"Isn't that how most investments work?"

"Not if they're legitimate. If it's an actual investment, their money goes to fund research or production, or something related to the company. What are they investing in? What asset?"

"I think it was a mine."

Jules pressed his lips together. "All investments bear some risk. You put in some money with the promise that if the investment succeeds, you'll get your money back with interest. Brokers rely on hope, but they are supposed to warn investors of the risks."

"And?"

"And if there is no identifiable asset, investors weren't handing their money to a company so it could expand or buy more materials or do research. They were handing it to someone so he could eventually run off with it."

Riley curled her legs underneath her as worry gnawed at her. She needed to speak to her mother about Educoin. "You said two things come to mind."

"The investment vehicle. People don't just hand over money without expecting they will get something for it. They do it believing they're investing in something."

"Like a mine?" Or schools in Africa.

"Right."

A hum of excitement passed through Riley. "This has been helpful. Thanks."

"Any time." He sipped his tea. "Now, should we find out what Lady Smallington is up to?"

Riley glanced at her bedroom, where she'd put the journal when she landed home. She could write to Jack later. And waiting a couple of hours to phone her mom wouldn't make a difference. "Let's do it. The investors and mystery broker can wait."

After two episodes, Jules stood. "I should go. My sweater is dry, and the rain has stopped. My mom's party is on Friday. You'll be there?"

"Of course. I was going before I knew you would be in town."

"Lucy?"

"Lucy is bringing Alex."

"What about your mom? Is she bringing anyone?"

For a moment, Riley remembered her mother's deep sadness after Riley's father had died. "I don't think she is seeing anyone, if that's what you're asking. She gets offended when I mention it." Riley crossed her arms. "I mean, I don't think I'm ready for her to run off and marry someone, but I want her to be happy, and my dad would have wanted the same for her."

Jules pulled on his sweater. "I'm glad it started pouring. It was nice to catch up like this."

"I'm glad too," Riley said. As soon as the door closed behind him, she reached for her phone. She needed to speak to her mother.

After three rings, her mother answered. Riley took a calming breath. "Mom, can you tell me a little more about Educoin?"

"Of course, dear. I'm so excited you're interested."

Riley began to correct her mother, then thought she might learn more if she played along. "I am. What more can you tell me? How do you know your money is growing?"

"When I see you tomorrow, I'll show you my investor dashboard. You can see how it's just gone up and up."

The excitement in her mother's voice was infectious, and Riley realized how easy it must be to convince people if someone like her mother was extolling Educoin. "And the schools—how many have been built?"

"That's on my investor board, too. I can't show you because I'm speaking to you right now, but I can't wait to tell you more."

Riley considered helping her mother share her screen, but she didn't want the headache that exercise would be sure to cause. "I'm looking forward to it. Mom, can you wait before you invest any more money?"

"Why, dear?"

"Educoin sounds great. It's just there are lots of scammers out there. You know, people who will take your money."

"Oh, Peter wouldn't take my money. He's not a scammer."

Riley's throat tightened. "Peter? Who's that?" She tried to keep her voice light.

"I didn't tell you about Peter? He's coming to Vancouver with me this week. You can ask him directly about Educoin, or come to a seminar we're holding. Listen, Riley, I need to go. Looking forward to seeing you. Kisses."

Riley stared at her phone after her mother had hung up. Who was Peter, and how involved was her mother? She would have to wait to answer that question, but she could send a quick message to Jack about what Jules had told her about investments.

Dear Jack,

As you look into Pierce's investment company, here are a few things to watch for. Investment fraud is common in my time, especially investments with high returns, investments made directly with individuals, overly complicated investments, and investments with little documentation.

Hope that helps,

Riley

CHAPTER 15

Jack

THE NEXT MORNING, Winston decided to walk to the Pierce house from the constabulary. The air was chilly but fresh, and he used the time to think about Riley's note. Which of the warning signs she'd mentioned were present in what little he knew about Pierce's business? There certainly was little in the way of documentation so far. And Sawyer's and Macey's differing descriptions of the investment didn't necessarily mean it was complicated but presented challenges to finding answers.

Finding answers. Winston drew the condensation from his moustache with his hand. All this runaround wasn't helping him find answers to who may have caused Arthur Pierce's death. He must uncover something soon to begin making progress on the case.

He pulled his collar around his neck. Puffs of steamy breath bloomed from the horses waiting on the street as he passed. A strong overnight wind had blown the rain and clouds away, leaving the sky clear and the air crisp. Winston savoured the break from the grey and turned his head toward the east, hoping the sun might warm his cheek.

The shout of a delivery man roused Winston from his thoughts in time to avoid a collision in front of the house. He hurried up the front walk and knocked on the door. The butler showed Winston to the sitting room, and he'd hardly stepped into the inviting, though darkened, space when Caroline Pierce appeared in the doorway.

"Mrs. Pierce, I am sorry to trouble you. It's just that I went to your husband's office yesterday, and although I had help from Mr. Macey,

I am still missing some information. I thought perhaps it might be here among Mr. Pierce's papers."

Caroline Pierce stiffened. "I rarely saw Arthur with paperwork, but I suppose he might have something in his study."

Winston stepped toward Mrs. Pierce, then retreated. It wouldn't serve to intimidate the widow. "Perhaps if I take a look, I'll find something?"

"Why didn't Macey come?" She shook her head. "It seems wasteful to send you here for these papers. Haven't you more pressing demands on your time, Detective?"

He clasped his wrist behind his back. "It's no trouble. I cannot comment on Mr. Macey's usual work ethic, but I think he is rather upset about losing his employer and likely his livelihood. The news of your husband's death has already spread, and Macey found himself spending time yesterday speaking to the company's clients, reassuring them their money is safe."

Mrs. Pierce waved her hand in front of her face and looked away. "We're all upset, Detective Winston. I apologize for my outburst. You may, of course, search as you need. I will have Mr. Clifford show you to my husband's study."

"Before you go, Mrs. Pierce, was your husband an active sportsman?"

At this, she paused. "Yes, he was. He played in some sort of game or match the day before he died. Basketball, I believe he told me. Some new sport he had taken interest in." She pinched her eyes shut as if to collect herself. "I will get Mr. Clifford now."

She left the room, dabbing her eyes with a handkerchief as she walked past Winston. Caroline Pierce wore her grief as elegantly as any woman Winston had ever seen. Her dress, though black, was cut in a striking fashion that suited her features. Instead of appearing red and puffy from crying, her eyes were almost brightened by her tears. With hot shame, Winston remembered how her deep, throaty laugh had affected him on his last visit. In his line of work, he had little cause to hear women laugh. What did Riley's laugh sound like? What made her laugh?

Winston closed his eyes and scolded himself silently. He followed Mr. Clifford, the butler, giving himself until he reached the study door to get his mind back on the case. The sooner he uncovered who murdered her husband, the sooner Mrs. Pierce would laugh again. A second wave of shame swept over Winston.

Mr. Pierce's study was built for comfort, although the furniture looked as if it hadn't seen much use. The spines of the books lining the shelves were uncracked. Winston bent closer and noted their covers were uniform in colour and height.

Clifford made a point of leaving the door open when he left. Winston jotted a note to learn how long Clifford had worked for Pierce. Long enough to develop deep loyalty to the man, judging by how closely he studied Winston before he left the room. No doubt the butler would assign himself some activity that meant he had to cross the hallway several times, thus allowing him to monitor Winston. He couldn't fault the man; Winston's mother's staff possessed the same instinct to protect their employer.

Winston focused his thoughts on his task by pulling out each of the drawers of the writing desk. They revealed little more than a few pencils and sheets of paper. He tapped the drawer bottoms to ensure they didn't hide anything.

He moved to the shelves. A desk is an obvious place, but not the only one, to store documents. He set his cheek against a shelf, looking to see which book received the most attention. As the room was dusted regularly, there were no obvious indicators signalling spots in repeated use, save a single book that bore little resemblance to the others. It was taller and had a wider spine than its shelf mates.

Winston eased the book from the shelf. Its weight surprised him, and he nearly dropped it. Inside, he found a second book nestled within a cutout in its pages. After using his fingernail to pry the second book from the first, Winston flipped the smaller one into his hands. His heart raced with the thrill of a good clue.

Rather than a work of forbidden literature, Winston held a small ledger. The notebook contained two columns of entries using letters and numbers. Footsteps sounded in the hall and Winston tucked the ledger into his satchel. He returned the outer book to the shelf. If Pierce had hidden it so carefully in his home, few other people, including his staff and his wife, would likely be aware it existed. Why keep it tucked inside another book in his personal library? Winston licked his lips, relishing the anticipation of uncovering what was inside.

At the sound of a polite cough, Winston turned around to find Clifford. Heat pricked his cheeks. He was getting ahead of himself. Did the butler's stern expression convey loyalty to his employer and a protective attitude toward Pierce's belongings, or a bald distrust of Winston? "Mrs. Pierce wishes me to ask if you would like a cup of tea."

"I appreciate the offer, Mr. Clifford. However, I must return to the station and see how my constable has got on with a task I gave him this morning. Please pass along my regrets."

"Will you need to visit this house again, Detective? I fear your presence flusters Mrs. Pierce and disrupts her mourning." Clifford opened and closed his mouth while adjusting his waistcoat, appearing to be unsure whether his comments had just overstepped the line of propriety.

"I have no intention of disturbing Mrs. Pierce, yet I must follow my responsibilities to the law and other citizens of this city. I will do my best to minimize how my investigation disrupts your household, as I'm sure you all feel your loss deeply."

Clifford allowed the corners of his lips to turn up. "I worked for him for years, Detective. I knew him before he moved to the Coast."

He looked over his shoulder and stepped closer to Winston. "He even offered me the opportunity to invest with him."

Winston leaned toward the butler, his pulse quickening. "Did you? Invest with him, I mean?"

"I did. I'm meant to receive my first return payment next month." The man's shoulders sagged. "Will that still happen, do you think?"

"How long did you invest with him?"

"He brought me in as a trusted friend. Said it was his way of thanking me for my loyalty." He squeezed his hands. "I declined the first time he asked, but two months ago I ended up giving Arthur—Mr. Pierce—my savings." Clifford coloured at his informal reference to his employer.

"I can't tell you whether your payment will happen, but I'll look into it for you."

Hearing this, Clifford relaxed. "I've been so worried. Please don't think I was being rude to you earlier. It's just this family, they have done so much for me. I don't want to compromise that."

"I understand." Winston decided to take advantage of Clifford's change in attitude. "Where did you say Pierce moved from?"

"Out east. Two years ago."

"You travelled with the Pierces when they moved?"

The man's facial expression became blank, unreadable. "I followed Mr. Pierce."

Winston noted the man's evasiveness. It reminded him of the men who worked for his father in Toronto. Their loyalty was secured simply by the kindness he showed to his staff. Winston's mother didn't always agree with her husband's approach, worrying the staff would become unruly, take advantage if they felt they could get away with underperforming their duties. But Winston's father was fair and firm. Once, when he had learned of a stableboy who had abused a horse, he relieved him of his duties. But rather than casting the boy out, Winston's father had given him a job on the railway, with the promise that any similar behaviour would result in a considerably harsher penalty. Before Winston left Toronto, his father reported that the boy—now a man—had been leading a railway crew and had expressed interest in further advancement. "Yes," Winston agreed. "I understand why you followed. It can be hard to find a good employer."

Clifford nodded, then swallowed in an exaggerated manner.

"Did you notice Mr. Pierce behaving unusually in the weeks leading to his death? Was he more distracted, more worried, or angrier?"

"Not that I noticed. I had no idea he was going to—" Clifford's face fell. "Going to do what he did."

"How often did Mr. Pierce entertain here?"

The butler composed himself. Winston had moved to more comfortable territory. "He spent most of his time at his club or at his office."

"Recently?"

Clifford's eyes looked to the side as if reviewing the past few weeks. "A few days before he died, maybe a week, he had a visitor, someone he hadn't expected, sir. I didn't see who it was, but I heard them speaking."

"And?" Winston coaxed.

"And they exchanged heated words. By the time I reached the study, Mr. Pierce had regained his composure and the visitor, whoever he was, had left."

Heated words. Surely Clifford would recognize Sawyer's voice. Or Macey's. Had Clifford heard his employer arguing with his murderer?

"You didn't see the guest?"

"No. It was evening, and I was about to close the house for the night. I had not let him into the house, and I was in the kitchen when

I heard them. The front door closed as I reached the study to check on Mr. Pierce. I assumed it was the visitor leaving."

"Can you describe anything about him?"

Clifford shook his head. "Nothing."

Why wouldn't Clifford have looked out the window? He was not a curious man, this butler. "Can you describe the man's voice? What were they discussing?"

"They spoke quietly. But I heard Mr. Pierce ask the guest whether he could wait a few weeks. I didn't hear the response." Clifford looked down. "I thought it had something to do with Mr. Pierce's business. He retired to bed shortly afterward, and I continued with my task."

"Was Mr. Pierce fond of all his staff? Were any jealous of how you were treated?"

Clifford pressed his lips together for a beat before answering. "I don't know if everyone had the opportunity to invest. He asked me to keep it to myself and I did." The butler scratched his head. "I haven't heard anyone speak ill of Mr. Pierce."

"Any staff leave suddenly?"

The butler shook his head. "Our newest staff member is Daisy, and she's been here for over a year. Nobody wants to leave the Pierces." He pulled a piece of cloth from his pocket and used it to polish a smudge on the brass door handle. Pausing, he added, "I've remembered something." He turned to face Winston. "After Mr. Pierce's guest had left, I found a glove near the door. The Sawyers had been here for dinner, so I thought it may have belonged to one of them. Mr. Pierce had just given each of us a pair in anticipation of the cooler weather." He replaced the cloth in his pocket and cleared his throat. "I should really get back to my duties."

A single glove. They had found one in Stanley Park. Had someone from Pierce's household been involved in his hanging? "Before you go, would you mind showing me the gloves you received, Mr. Clifford? And if you have it, the one you found the other night?"

The butler blanched. "I'm sure we have an extra pair. Shall I send a maid?"

"Please. I'll wait here." Clifford set off, and Winston held up a hand. "One more thing, if you don't mind. What do you know about Pierce's family? Their background, I mean?" Winston lowered his voice. "There isn't a delicate way to ask this, but did they come from money?"

Clifford pursed his lips. "The Pierces are well respected. He was a kind and generous man and he will be missed. Mrs. Pierce, I knew her as Miss Rallston before she married Mr. Pierce. She's a generous woman, like her husband." He motioned for the door, then paused. "Does it matter, sir? Whether he came from money, I mean? He's made such a difference in people's lives."

Winston considered the question for a moment. "Perhaps it doesn't matter."

Clifford waited for Winston to nod, then closed the door. A few minutes later, he returned holding a pair of gloves. "Mr. Pierce gave these to everyone."

"And the one that had been left behind?"

Clifford shook his head. "I couldn't find it, sir. I'll ask the maids. Perhaps they've put it away somewhere."

Winston examined the black leather gloves. He held them out, then brought them close and inspected the stitching. They were unremarkable save the small letters "From AP" embossed near one seam at the wrist. Winston handed them back to Clifford. "They are all the same?"

"They are." He stashed the gloves inside his jacket. "But I can't say that for certain about the one I found."

"Thank you for speaking to me so candidly. I'll show myself out."

Winston left the house without seeing Mrs. Pierce again. The churning in his stomach suggested he'd be back sooner than she expected.

CHAPTER 16

Jack

CONSTABLE MILLER WAS sitting at the largest desk in the station's common room sorting a stack of papers when Winston found him. "Thomas, have you already finished with the records from Pierce's office?"

Miller stood. Winston motioned for him to sit and settled himself into another chair. "They're here." Miller pointed to the documents. "Once I read through them, I realized there were only a few pages that needed copying right away." He pointed at a smaller pile. "A list of all the investors, with their names, addresses. I had the desk clerk do it."

A glimmer of hope. Perhaps Macey was more organized than Sawyer realized. "And the other papers?"

"There were a couple of copies of this photograph." Miller handed one to Winston. A heavily bearded man stood looking at the camera with what appeared to be a wooden box beside him. "Billy" was scrawled across the back of the image. "I think it's the man Macey said Pierce was funding."

"And the equipment Sawyer mentioned?" Winston asked, pointing to the box.

"Must be. I wonder what it does."

The constable's eyes shone as he spoke. Winston hoped he wasn't becoming enchanted by all this talk of gold and money. He'd begun to show real promise as an investigating officer. "Did you find anything else?" He redirected Miller's attention to the papers, away from the distracting photograph.

Miller regained focus, shifting to pick up a piece of paper. "I copied out the list. The other papers in here are about mining, but not the clients." Miller pushed the pages toward Winston. "I would have thought there might be... more."

"I agree, Thomas. My father's business produces pages and pages of information daily. These men seemed to manage the enterprise with surprisingly little in the way of records." Riley's note flashed in his mind as he said the words. Her last point: be wary of investments with minimal documentation. Had Pierce been running a fraudulent enterprise?

"What do you think that means, sir?"

Winston wasn't ready to answer that question yet. Instead, he motioned for Miller to continue.

"After I copied Macey's list, I went to visit the first man. He works at Hastings Mill in False Creek." Miller explained, "He learned about Pierce from a friend. The others I spoke with said the same thing."

"The same friend?"

"No, but each knew someone who knew Pierce. Or knew of him. They'd all heard good things and met with Macey."

"They're friends?" Winston asked.

"They all work at the mill. Macey promised them their investments would be safe." Miller checked his notes. "It was each man's first time investing, but after seeing their friends double their money, they didn't want to miss out." Wistfulness crept into Miller's voice. "Is it really that easy?"

Winston thought of his father, who had amassed what most would consider a fortune but had worked hard to do so. "It sounds like it was easy for Pierce. At least easy for him to find clients." Winston looked at the list. "Macey made promises to these men. They gave him their money, and he gave it to Pierce?" Another echo of Riley's message. Investments made directly with individuals.

"One man told me he invested because he wished he could travel to the north and find gold, but he has a family here and couldn't risk it. Investing in another man's quest seemed as close as he would get, and less risky."

"This is good work, Thomas."

Miller flashed a smile. "There's more. I recognized a few of the names on this list and thought they might be members of the Vancouver Gentlemen's Club. I went to the club and asked to see a roster to confirm. I spoke to a few of the members who were there." He lowered his voice. "I had to use the chief constable's name. He's a member. Do you think it will get back to him?"

Winston inhaled sharply. "Quite likely. We'll need to be careful." His uncle would not be happy to find out about the continued investigation. "Did you learn anything there?"

"It seems Pierce was a popular card player at the club."

Winston considered this. "Had he any debts?"

"None to mention, according to the club's manager. Though he stressed wagers are between the members, so he may not have been aware of them."

"How long had Pierce been a member?"

Miller checked his notes. "Just shy of two years, sir."

"Around the time Pierce arrived in the city. But that was also when the club opened." Winston waited while Miller made a note.

When Miller finished, he waved a set of folded papers. "The member roster, sir."

"Good." Winston opened his satchel and pulled out the ledger he had retrieved from Pierce's home. "And I've found something else we need to look at. I'm not sure what it means yet."

Miller looked at the growing pile of papers in front of him. "Should we set up a board?"

Winston swallowed. "Actually, I wonder if we need to be cautious about curious eyes."

"Curious eyes?" Miller whispered as he leaned in. Colour drained from his cheeks.

"From what you've just said, this investigation appears increasingly likely to involve rather high-profile individuals." Winston swallowed, weighing his next words. "And Philpott doesn't want me continuing."

Miller blinked. "You mean. . ." he stammered, his colour returning in a flush, "we're not supposed to be investigating this?"

"Philpott believes Pierce killed himself. The evidence we've seen does not support that. And now we have some serious questions about Pierce's business. His butler—Clifford—said he was asked to keep his involvement quiet. I imagine the same is true for the others."

Confusion clouded Miller's face. "What happens if the chief constable finds out we're investigating when he told us not to?"

Winston's toes gripped the inside of his boots. "Our duty as police is to uncover whether there has been a crime. There has been at least one: I am now certain Pierce was murdered. It also appears his business may not have been what it seemed. Nothing will happen to us if we are seeking the truth. And we are." He took a breath to slow his racing thoughts, willing Miller to accept his answer. When the man nodded, Winston continued. "Let's start by considering why. If Pierce was successful, why did he ask investors to remain quiet?"

"Could the investments be a motive? The men we've spoken with so far seemed to hear from friends about the opportunities, but nobody was immediately forthcoming about investing with Pierce. At least, not the men at the mill. It seemed like they wanted me to keep the information secret."

Winston pressed his hands into his knees. "If, like Clifford, they thought they were brought in on a secret deal, that might have been part of Pierce's plan. It would be rather clever on his part to exploit people's inability to keep secrets as a means to find more investors." Or to keep the true nature of the business secret.

Miller nodded, weighing the explanation. "He used their gossipy enthusiasm to recruit others."

"Exactly, Thomas."

"What about opportunity?"

"Anyone could have arranged to meet Pierce at the park under the guise of wanting to give Pierce funds to invest, especially if the investment was supposed to be secret." Winston remembered the gloves. "The glove we found at the tree, I'd like to look at it again. I saw a pair at Pierce's, and Pierce's butler, Clifford, mentioned having found a single glove left behind by someone, possibly the person he'd overheard arguing with Pierce."

"The killer? Or did someone from his own household kill him?" Miller rooted in a box at his feet and produced the glove.

Winston inspected it, finding the same distinctive "From AP" embossed on the cuff. Now he would need to ask Clifford to produce his gloves, and all the others who had received the gloves as a gift.

"If we can find who is missing a glove, it may very well be someone connected to this case." He set the glove aside. "Let's take a closer look at the member roster against this ledger." Winston pointed to the book he'd found hidden at Pierce's house. Unease tightened his stomach, and he spun his head to survey the room. They needed somewhere else to work. "Do you think we could bear setting up in the morgue? We would have privacy, and we could spread out on the table there."

Miller blanched.

"No, you're right, Miller. Let's go to my rooms."

✳

Although the rooms Winston rented from Mrs. Bradley were small, they afforded the policemen privacy. As he held the door open for Miller to enter, he realized the constable was the first guest he'd had since arriving in the city. He often found himself picturing Riley sitting near him as he wrote to her. Instinctively, his hand felt for the journal in his satchel. It was high time he spent a little more time with people in the here and now.

On Winston's instructions, Miller moved the writing desk and the table upon which Winston occasionally took his meals to the centre of the room.

Winston lit a fire to guard against the chilly November air. Mrs. Bradley would frown at his use of a log during the day; she thought little of "such luxury." Winston disagreed. He saw no sense in suffering unnecessarily for the sake of a few coins. He would offer to replace the log nonetheless.

While the room warmed, Miller reported he'd received confirmation that no horses were missing from the stables Pierce routinely used. Further evidence the man hadn't killed himself.

Winston began by examining the documents that had been copied. The thin stack of pages and the ledger from Pierce's house had yet to reveal their significance to the case. He handed Miller the ledger. "Can you start by looking at this? I didn't have a chance to inspect it when I found it. It was hidden inside another book, so I gather it's of some importance."

Miller thumbed through the book's pages. He pointed to entries in the first column. "Are these initials? Of clients?"

Winston leaned over the ledger. "I had the same thought." He drew his finger down the page. Not all entries in the first column had a corresponding entry in the second column. He flipped forward a few pages and found that some entries had a third column.

HTC20095 42595
TB52595   81596   2403BW763AR
OS5095   12595

Did that mean the columns were linked so each row was a unit? Winston returned to the first page and pointed to the first column. "And these numbers beside them, could they be dates?"

"I don't think so. If they're dates, I can't make sense of them and they're inconsistent."

Winston reached for the copied list of names. "Let's start with these, then. I will read out each one. See if you find corresponding initials in the ledger."

The policemen worked together, Miller ticking off a line as Winston read each name. When they arrived at the name of a man Miller had spoken to, he raised his hand. "He has a family, sir. Young children. He gave Macey everything he'd saved because of Pierce's reputation for doubling monies invested."

"Had he ever done any prospecting?"

"Nobody I spoke with had. What about Pierce's butler?"

"I don't think so. Though he looks like he has powerful hands. He may have had a job that required working with them at some point."

The talk of prospecting brought to mind the stores Winston had seen around the police station that offered prospectors all the goods required for a successful trip. Men came from all corners of the continent and beyond to seek their fortune. It would be easy enough for these stores to convince them—unfamiliar as they were with their pending journeys—to purchase unnecessary supplies. If Pierce had been taking money from people who had no experience with mining, just like the green prospectors had been taken advantage of by shop owners, they wouldn't know whether Pierce's "opportunity" made sense. The only evidence they could go on would have been the "double your money" reports of previous investors.

"Pierce's clients were investing in a device," Winston puzzled aloud, "but Macey said they were investing in a man."

"Do you think it was the same thing? Maybe Pierce just changed how he spoke about it, depending on who he spoke to." Miller pointed to the photograph as he spoke. "Something that made finding the gold easier. Such a device would appeal to men who had more money. While investing in a person—someone who was like them, someone who worked—that would appeal to the men at the mill. These mill workers, they invested because it was going to change their lives." Miller dropped his voice. "This man was so certain, sir. So certain he was going to give his family a better life than the one he'd had."

Winston stared into the fire. "That's what Pierce was really offering," he said. "Hope." He returned his gaze to the sheets on the table and resumed reading the names, pausing after each one so Miller could nod or shake his head as he searched the ledger.

"They're all in here, sir, toward the end." Miller flipped to the beginning of the ledger. "But there are more entries." He fanned his thumb against the pages. "The men from the club?"

Winston nodded. "Likely. Let's check them." They continued through the member roster the Vancouver Gentlemen's Club provided to Miller. When they had finished, Winston ran his finger down the list of checked names, pausing at a few he recognized, including the chief constable's. He had said nothing about being Pierce's client. "We don't know for certain these men invested, but it seems likely this is a list of men Pierce had spoken with. I'm still not sure what the numbers mean, though."

"Do you think the numbers relate to amounts?" Miller asked.

"Of money invested?" Winston motioned for Miller to hand him the ledger. "No. These amounts are too high. Look at these first pages. I can't imagine many men in this city—even members of the Vancouver Gentlemen's Club—had the sums listed here available to them. And the number sequences for some of them are considerably longer than for others."

"Bank account numbers?"

"That's a terrific idea, Miller. We will visit the banks tomorrow." Winston's stomach rumbled. "Let's finish today by finding somewhere to eat."

CHAPTER 17

Riley

Dear Riley,

Constable Miller and I have now met some of Pierce's investors. I have spoken directly with two of them—a member of the Pierce household staff and a mill worker—who'd each trusted Pierce to invest their hard-earned money. Many of the men Miller spoke with are labourers, working at the mill or on the docks. When they appeared in Mr. Macey's office yesterday seeking to withdraw their money from Pierce's investments, he had to put them off, tell them investments had been paused in the light of Mr. Pierce's death and he'd contact them later.

I saw in these men's eyes more than a desire for financial success. These men were hungry for it and, until recent events, were certain of it. Such expectations can be hard to bear; I have seen other men crumble under their weight. Perhaps this led Pierce to make bad decisions. Because it is becoming clear; he was not as honest as he claimed to be.

That so many of the men who invested with him, particularly those who invested recently, were from humble circumstances and were unlikely to have had much money to invest suggests he was taking advantage of them. There are many suspicious aspects to AP Investments. Macey was his secretary but hadn't even met many of the men investing with Pierce. And the sparse and cryptic record-keeping is unusual too. I'm at a loss as to how I will learn more.

As always, I appreciate your thoughts on the matter.

Jack

The murmur of conversation and whir of coffee machines fell away as Riley read Winston's note while waiting for Lucy in a Gastown café. She was reminded of a recent financial scandal where an investment adviser was found to have been paying initial investors with the funds of subsequent investors. Jules's description of these shady practices had led her to do a little research. A quick search the night before had revealed pages of headlines about these Ponzi schemes, named after the fraudster who'd made them famous in the 1920s. How did people continue to fall for them?

Had her mother fallen for one?

Riley resisted the temptation to dial Jules again. Lucy would be by any minute to share lunch and to discuss their mother. Riley slipped the journal into her bag and rested her fingers on the book's spine, taking comfort in its sturdiness.

Ten minutes after they had agreed to meet, Lucy slipped into the seat across from Riley with a salad on her tray. "I will have to eat quickly. I have a designer coming in this afternoon and I really can't be late," she said. "Then we need to be at the bridal salon for our appointment before dinner with Mom."

Ice cubes clinked as Riley set her water down. "Appointment?"

"For my final dress fitting. Did you forget?" Lucy wiggled a finger at Riley. "Mom is supposed to be joining us, and then Alex will meet us at the restaurant."

Riley bit down on a sharp reply. Okay, she had forgotten about the dress, but that was because she'd been so focused on researching her mother's investment. Was this the first time she was the less responsible of the sisters? "I'll do my best to be there. But we need to do something about Mom."

Lucy stabbed at her food. "What do you mean?"

"I don't think this investment she's gotten herself involved in is good," Riley said.

"I told you. I'd much rather just have the money."

Riley shook her head. She didn't want to get into how it wasn't really the recipient's place to dictate the format of the gift. "I mean, I don't think the investment is safe. I think it's a scam. I think we need to confront Mom about it, but gently." Riley explained what she'd learned about fraudulent schemes and how what she'd learned so far about Educoin rang all the same alarm bells.

Worry creased Lucy's forehead. "I don't need this drama just before my wedding. When can we talk to her?"

Riley tapped the corner of her coaster, peeling the first paper layer with her fingernail. "At dinner? Tonight? Or at the dress fitting?" Riley paused mid-peel. "Maybe that would be better, so she doesn't feel like we're attacking her. Or we could meet her before. Do you know where she's staying?"

"She's booked a hotel. Said it was with Edumoney." Lucy rolled her eyes.

"Educoin," Riley corrected her sister. "She was going to show me her investor dashboard. If we go to her hotel room, that might be best."

"Yes, do it in private. It will be awkward if you upset her while we're eating." Lucy waved her fork in the air. "I don't have time to deal with this, Riley. I have to go meet this designer. Let me know after you talk to Mom."

The way Lucy was demanding, rather than asking, grated on Riley. Why did it fall to her, the younger sister, to confront their mother? "She said she's coming over with a friend. Peter. Did she say anything to you about him?"

"That's nice. Tell her to bring him to the restaurant later."

Riley wasn't sure she was on board with that idea. She was curious about Peter, but not quite ready to meet him yet. Lucy's absent, non-committal responses signalled that Riley had already lost her to this meeting she had to flit off to. "Okay," she said, "I'll speak to Mom." Courage, fuelled by frustration, prompted Riley's next pronouncement: "I'm bringing Johnny to dinner too."

"Okay. Can you change the reservation, then? Since you're bringing the unplanned guest?"

Riley bit her tongue. Her sister had just suggested their mother should bring a guest. She reminded herself that Lucy was pretty scattered right now, and that Riley had promised she would be supportive in these last weeks before the wedding. But Lucy was making it difficult for her to deliver on her promise.

*

AFTER HER LUNCH, Riley found a bench along the paving stone sidewalk and texted Johnny.

> *Can you come for dinner tonight? Sorry for the short notice. My mom is in town. Lucy and Alex will be there too.*

As she waited for his response, her thoughts bounced between Jack's case and her mom's involvement with Educoin. She pulled a notebook from her backpack. She needed to organize her thoughts.

Educoin

- *Invest in the cryptocurrency. A portion of money goes to support building schools in Africa.*
- *As Educoin grows, so does amount for schools.*
- *Mom invested $, made $$. How much to kids?*
- *Educoin address is a PO box. Who's behind it?*
- *Where does money go?*

AP Investments

- *No business records (now). Exist for Jack?*
- *Invest in miner and/or mining device. Why two different incentives?*
- *Where does money go?*

What was she missing? As a researcher, her job was to look for connections. She scanned her list and recalled her recent conversations. She added a final line to her column about AP Investments.

- *Sawyer name pronunciation.*

It might just be one of those things that evolves, but what if it wasn't? What if the change had been deliberate?

Her phone buzzed beside her. Johnny's name flashed on the screen.

"Riley, I'd love to join you for dinner." His words came out in a rush, causing a butterfly sensation to move through her belly.

"I'm glad you can come, Johnny. You've met Lucy and Alex before, but I thought it might be nice for you to meet my mom before Lucy's wedding." She thought of when she'd invited him a few weeks ago. Lucy had been encouraging her to bring a date, and she'd held off asking Johnny until Lucy threatened to ask him herself. "You don't have to dress up or anything. It's just a pizza place on Commercial."

Johnny chuckled, reminding her of how he had laughed when Riley explained Lucy's clear dress expectations for the wedding. "She's very specific, isn't she?" he had asked.

"She is, and if you want to be included in any photos, you'll follow her instructions. Lucy isn't serious about much, but getting a perfect wedding photo is important to her," Riley had explained. "You can say no, but it would be nice to have a friendly face there."

"Won't you know most of the guests?"

"Sure, but only because they know my sister. They're not really my friends."

Johnny had taken Riley's hand. "I would be happy to attend with you." His thumb tracing a circle on the back of her hand had sent a shiver up her spine.

"Riley?" His question brought her back to the conversation.

"Sorry. What did you ask?"

"I asked whether you want me to pick you up," he repeated.

"Actually, can we meet there? I'm supposed to go to the bridal shop with my mom and Lucy for her final dress fitting." Riley rolled her eyes as she spoke. Why did she need to see her sister put the dress on again? She was only going to be wearing the thing for one day.

"Okay," Johnny said. The butterfly's wings slowed when she heard his disappointment.

"Listen, my mom's friend is coming tonight. He's involved in Educoin."

"I haven't found anything other than the website. I asked a crypto guy I know, and he didn't know much about it either." Johnny had taken on a more professional tone, his Crown prosecutor's voice coming through. "Have you learned anything more?"

The butterfly fluttered again at the sound of his warm concern.

"Not much. Which is why I'm glad she's bringing this guy. We can ask him about it."

"Sounds good. I'm looking forward to it. Not questioning your mom. Seeing you, I mean."

"Thank you. Me too." Riley's cheeks warmed as she allowed herself to admit how much she wanted to see him. "You'll be getting quite the introduction to my mom."

She gave him the details of the restaurant and ended the call. This wasn't how she'd imagined Johnny meeting her mom. She placed a hand on her stomach to quell the fluttering.

CHAPTER 18

Riley

Now that Riley had a plan about how to speak to her mother, she could focus on Jack's case. She took another minute on the bench to text Nick at the museum.

> *I'm checking out the stock exchange to see if they have an archive. Might have some details about early business leaders.*

> *Great idea. See you later.*

The building that housed the former Vancouver Stock Exchange was on Granville Street, squarely in the middle of the business district. Though trades were now performed electronically as part of a new exchange, the old trading room floor had been preserved to show how trading had changed with Vancouver's growth. Riley was pleasantly surprised when the receptionist nodded when she asked if a historian or archivist was available to answer her questions. While she waited, she read a small display about the market's history. She was partway through a description of how traders learned the signals they used when she heard her name.

Riley spun around to find an older man in a three-piece suit standing with his arms behind his back.

"It's quite remarkable, isn't it?" He nodded toward the display of photographs behind her.

"It is. And it hits the right balance of detail and information."

"Thank you. I felt it important to make this space accessible to anyone interested. Which is why, I understand, you are here. I'm Henry Pepper. One of my responsibilities is being the Exchange's historian." He handed Riley a card.

She couldn't remember the last business card she'd received, but she thanked him and tucked it into a pocket of her backpack. "I work at the museum and we're preparing an exhibit on some of the city's influencers, the individuals who shaped what this city is now. I'm specifically looking into two men from the late nineteenth century: Mr. Arthur Pierce and his business partner, Mr. Reginald Sawyer. Do you know if you have any information about either of them?" She used the modern pronunciation of "Saw-yer" to avoid confusing Henry.

Henry tilted his head. "Reginald Sawyer was influential in financing this city's earlier years, so we have information about him." He scratched his head. "Did you know he helped establish the university's business school?"

"I knew he was involved with the university somehow." But was it relevant? She made a mental note to check with her former classmate who worked at the university, just to be sure. "When?"

"Early twentieth century. He provided some of the money to construct some of the campus. He specifically wanted an emphasis on business ethics to be taught at the university," Henry said. "Now, the other name, Arthur Pierce? It doesn't seem familiar, but I will see what I can find."

"Several men invested with Pierce in the late nineteenth century." What more could she share about Winston's case? "He died suddenly, leaving many without their expected returns. Sawyer was his partner, or perhaps more accurately, his protégé."

"It seems you already know a great deal about them. I'm not sure I will have any additional information."

"You'll still look?" She was counting on Henry being as curious as she was and being unable to help himself from looking.

His smile widened, confirming Riley's assessment of his passion for history. "We have many records I haven't yet committed to memory. Do you know what Pierce's investors were supporting?"

"Something to do with mining."

Henry's eyes brightened. "We have a rich history of mining companies in this city." He paused and lowered his voice. "You know we were home to some impressive fraudulent schemes related to the industry, too? It's not a proud part of our history, but it's one I feel we should acknowledge. Unfortunately, some parts of that history are more recent than others."

Riley had found references to multiple scandals, often involving some variation of a Vancouver-based company, fraud, and international mining. "This was a local mining operation, I believe."

"Any time there is money to be made, there is a risk someone will take advantage of you. How much do you understand about investing?"

"I'm saving a little for retirement, and the bank invests that for me."

"When Sawyer and this man Pierce were operating, investment wasn't as regulated as it is now. They could have told their clients virtually anything. Investing then was risky, and many in the industry didn't have any concerns about leaving their investors with little more than a promise."

"Some of Pierce's investors saw returns. But I don't know if the men who were out of pocket after Pierce's death were ever compensated. What kinds of practices left people open to the risk you mentioned?"

Henry guided her to a small round table and chairs nestled between two displays. She had never thought to put seating within an exhibit. Maybe something to suggest to Claire. She smiled at him to continue.

"Fraud was illegal, of course, but there would have been little regulation, so it would have been easy enough to convince others to invest in something that didn't exist. Or maybe the early investments were sound, but something happened so subsequent investments weren't as successful. Instead of admitting to the failure, the company may have continued to try to raise funds to fix the problem. Or the money from later investors was used to pay returns to earlier investors. Ponzi wasn't the first, but he will forever be associated with that illegal practice."

Still a common practice, if her suspicions were right about her mother's Educoin investment. Her stomach lurched at the thought of her mother being a victim of fraud. "If Arthur Pierce was committing fraud, why has it been so difficult for me to find information about him? I know there was a police investigation into his death, but I can't find much about it."

Henry considered this. "I suppose it's possible he could have been scrubbed from memory, so to speak."

"How would that happen?"

"Well, if he was conning his investors, they likely felt some shame and wouldn't have wanted to have their lack of judgment exposed. It isn't hard to imagine an unspoken agreement not to mark their losses so they could move on."

Pierce's investors had been influential. It might have been easy for them to scrub his record, as Henry suggested. "So you're saying everyone may have known, but nobody said anything. Then when he died, it was easier to act as though nothing had happened."

"Exactly. Assuming this is what happened in this situation," Henry said.

"You'll still look to see if you can find anything about him?"

"I will. It might take me a day or so."

Riley gave him her contact information, and he agreed to update her as soon as he found anything. She thanked him and walked back to the museum.

When she arrived, she saw that Nick had left her a note to say he would be back in ten minutes. Just enough time to share what she'd learned with Jack.

Dear Jack,

I spent some time today at the Vancouver Stock Exchange, where I spoke to their historian. He had much to say about Sawyer and is looking into information about Pierce, whose name he didn't remember having seen before.

I think your instinct is correct, and I wonder if Pierce wasn't somehow defrauding his investors. A common financial crime here is where someone uses one investor's money to pay the returns on another's investment. What they think they're investing in doesn't exist. As long as a continuous stream of new investors can be recruited, the returns keep materializing. Could that be why Arthur Pierce had been targeting poorer investors? To provide him with a necessary stream of funds? What if someone found out about the fraud and killed him for it?

I have had a hard time finding information about Pierce, yet you say he was quite prominent. I wonder if his record was unofficially cleaned up after he died, once influential people realized what he had been up to. Another thing, and I doubt this is related at all, but I figure I should share it: Sawyer's name is pronounced differently in my time than in yours.

I'll let you know if I learn anything more.

R.

CHAPTER 19

Jack

WINSTON AND MILLER learned nothing at the first two banks they visited the next morning. The managers failed to identify the numbers in the ledger. They didn't match the account numbers used at their banks, and the managers couldn't suggest what they might represent. At their third stop, Western Bank, they were shown to the office of manager Owen Scott.

Winston gave the room in a quick appraisal. "While we wait, Thomas, tell me, what do you think this office says about the man who occupies it?"

Miller turned slowly about the inviting space. He rested his hand on an overstuffed wing chair in front of the heavy desk situated at the far end, facing a window with a view of the mountains to the north.

"Mr. Scott is educated," Miller said, pointing to a framed certificate. "In Toronto, so I imagine he is from there." He bent at the waist to inspect the bookshelf, careful not to disturb any of the books. "These are well used. By him, I assume. The furniture is pristine, as is the rest of the room, but the books are not just for display."

Winston nodded. Miller's observations matched his own. "What else would you say of the man?"

Miller looked again at the certificate, then tilted his head as if performing a calculation. "Judging by the year this was awarded, he must be at least forty-five, if not closer to fifty."

"Well considered, Miller. We will see when he arrives."

Minutes later, a tall man Winston placed at fifty years of age appeared. From the corner of his eye, he caught Miller nod with satisfaction. The man's hair was longer than was fashionable, but the style suited him. Winston introduced himself and Miller.

"Owen Scott." He extended his hand. "How can I help you, Detective?"

Scott carried an easy confidence that seemed to reflect the friendly respect he expected from everyone he met. He offered Miller the same smile and handshake he had offered Winston, undeterred by the constable's uniform. Scott gestured for the men to take a seat. As he lowered himself into the chair behind his desk, he took pains to smooth his waistcoat.

Winston placed the ledger atop Scott's desk and rested his fingers on its edge. "This contains numbers we're trying to identify. Would you look at it and tell us whether it contains account numbers from your institution?"

"I will look, but I can promise nothing." Scott reached across his desk and took the ledger from Winston. "Where did you find this?" he asked as he opened it.

"It was discovered as part of an investigation. I'm afraid I can't tell you more."

The man smiled and puffed out his chest. He turned several pages, examining each closely. He frowned. Flipping ahead in the ledger to the pages where additional notations appeared in a third column, he frowned. He returned to the ledger's opening pages and raised his eyes to meet Winston's. "These do not match with how we assign account numbers. Perhaps it would help me if you told me where you found this?"

Winston shook his head. "I cannot share that information."

Scott looked at the ledger again. As he stared, he tugged at his sleeves, alternating between the two. After a minute, he sat back. When he began speaking, his voice was muted. "If I guess correctly, will you tell me whether I'm right?"

"I will be impressed if you're correct, Mr. Scott."

Scott pulled his hand across his face, pinching his lips between his thumb and forefinger. When he took his hand away, it was to release a slow breath through pursed lips. "Did this belong to Mr. Arthur Pierce?" He spoke barely above a whisper.

Miller leaned forward. He widened his eyes in stark surprise at Scott's question. "How did you know?"

Scott swallowed and pointed to a line of numbers on the page. "These initials, *OS*. I think they're mine. I gave him fifty dollars. It was in '95, shortly after Pierce arrived in the city, I believe."

Winston circled the desk to lean over Scott's shoulder.

OS5095

"Are you saying these numbers reflect the amounts and the year people gave him money?" Miller asked.

"My initials are certainly not unique, but I know how much I gave him and when. Beyond that, I can assure you they are not account numbers at our bank."

Winston pulled the ledger closer to where he was standing. He turned to a page with three columns of entries. "And these?"

Scott shook his head. "These are not account numbers either. At least not at our bank. Ours do not contain letters."

"Thank you, Mr. Scott. This is helpful information. I ask you to keep this information to yourself as we try to unravel this."

"What do you know about the device Pierce was investing in?" Scott asked. He had recovered himself, regaining some of his confidence.

"Something related to mining." Winston waited to see if Scott would ask anything further, possibly reveal something more.

Scott leaned forward. "Pierce told me the device facilitated the extraction of resources from the ground." He licked his lips. "You know, it would be a shame not to continue supporting it. Pierce provided me with occasional updates, usually when I saw him at the

Gentlemen's Club. I was impressed with what he shared. I would be happy to continue his work. I've heard others have also done well with him."

Winston didn't answer immediately. He observed Scott alter his posture, straightening in his chair to resume his businesslike manner. "He had a business partner, Reginald Sawyer. Do you know him?"

"We've met." The sides of Scott's mouth curled down. "But I conducted my business with Pierce."

"Did you make money on your investment?" Miller asked.

"I did. Pierce paid me promptly. Some time has passed, and he recently asked me to consider reinvesting. I was going to give him more money this time but did not have the chance. I had asked him earlier, and he declined. A pity." He moistened his lips again. "If you learn the details about the opportunity, the machinery, I might take it upon myself to handle it." He eyed the ledger and the rows of initials listed in it.

Winston ran his finger across the line with Scott's entry.

12596

Scott's return of one hundred and twenty-five dollars was an incredible return in a single year. Unusually high. Another of Riley's signs to watch for. Her latest description of the shady practices of investment fraud had fed Winston's growing conviction that Pierce's scheme was dubious at best. And why would Pierce have refused Scott's request to invest further? "Did Pierce say why he didn't want you investing again?"

"He didn't. But he had done similar with some other men. They were all hungry to get back in, and most did, as far as I know. Each for more than his original investment."

Winston imagined the men exchanging information about how they were going to spend their money. Had Pierce been creating a false scarcity to lure his investors back? Limiting their reinvestment opportunity to foster artificial demand? "Mr. Scott, I must ask you to please keep what we have shared with you to yourself."

"I will." He gestured to the ledger. "You have several pages of entries there. How will you identify the others?"

"Leave that with us, Mr. Scott. But, please be prepared for us to call on you at a future point if needed. You've been very helpful." Winston stole a glance at Miller, who nodded. They had enough information now to compare the ledger against the list of investors and track how Pierce's company had grown.

"Of course, Detective. It will be my pleasure." Scott cleared his throat. "If it is not too much for me to ask, would it be troublesome for you to share what you learn about Pierce's investment? I would hate to miss this opportunity."

Scott had pressed his point. He was still interested, and no doubt other investors were as well. "I cannot promise anything, Mr. Scott. My involvement in the matter is to learn how Pierce's investments relate to his death."

Panic flickered across Scott's face. Was it the mention of the investigation into Pierce's death, or was he afraid someone else would get in line ahead of him, taking advantage of the opportunity to capitalize on the venture? How many other men had invested with Pierce and had similar returns to those of Scott? They'd likely be as eager to reinvest as Scott.

There were many more questions for Winston and Miller to explore, but first he needed to speak to Chief Constable Philpott.

CHAPTER 20

Jack

IN THE PRE-DAWN darkness, the police station had yet to reach its daytime vibrancy. Winston took advantage of the quiet to review once more what Riley had written in their journal. Her description of investment fraud explained the stacks of paper spread on Winston's desk: Pierce recruited new, unsophisticated investors like Felter and Clifford to fund the returns paid to his initial investors, like the mayor or Owen Scott. Any of these men had a motive if they'd learned the investment funded Pierce directly rather than Billy the miner, if he even existed.

Winston wrote the names in his notebook. He stared at the list, recalling the interactions he'd had over the past few days. He hesitated, swallowing against the dryness in his throat, as he added the initials of a final name: *LP*. Was his own sense of guilt the reason Chief Constable Lawrence Philpott had insisted the death was suicide? Winston had avoided asking himself this question. He thought back to the relationship he'd enjoyed with his trusted uncle over his lifetime. Uncle Lawrence was a part of many of his fondest memories. No. His uncle couldn't be the murderer. But Winston needed to speak to him.

He returned his attention to the other names. Of them, Clifford had the most access to Pierce. He would need to speak to him again after he met with Philpott. Winston pulled out his pocket watch and was surprised to see how much time had passed while he'd been lost in thought. With a sigh, he pushed away from his desk, steeling himself for the conversation with Philpott.

A voice filtered into the room. Doctor Evans had said he would stop by the station to discuss his examiner's report about the body of Arthur Pierce. Winston leaped at the distraction, and all but ran to the front of the station to greet the doctor.

"Jack," Evans said. "I've got a few minutes and wanted to speak to you about Arthur Pierce."

Inside the morgue, Winston wished he had a mug of tea. The idea of drinking it beside a body caused his stomach to turn over, but having something warm in his hands would ward off the chill of the room. And the steam would help with the smell. Instead, he shoved his hands in his pockets and did his best to breathe through his mouth.

Evans brought Arthur Pierce's body from the cold storage cabinet. He pulled back the sheet to reveal the man's face. "Detective, when we spoke last, I mentioned Pierce had an injury to his head. I am confident now he suffered it before he died."

"Why?"

The doctor re-covered Pierce's head and lifted the sheet to show the knuckles, purple with bruises, and nails, broken. Winston stepped closer. "He was in a fight?"

"He was involved in something violent. I can't tell whether he hit someone or something." Evans replaced the covering. "Where we originally discussed the possibility of his climbing the tree or perhaps having played in a sporting match, the bruises have come out even deeper now, as they often do when the injury happens close to death. If he had been playing a sport, it was very rough."

Winston recalled the conversation with Mrs. Pierce. "He played basketball the day before he was found dead. But I'm given to understand it is not a violent sport."

Evans nodded. "A more likely scenario would be if his captors struck him and he lost consciousness. Hanging an unconscious man would have been considerably easier than dealing with a conscious man."

"Do you think he lashed out before they hit him?"

"That would account for the bruising."

Winston imagined the scenario. "Doctor, does this mean you agree now? This is a murder?" He held his breath, anticipating Evans' response.

"I am certain. I apologize for contradicting you earlier."

Hearing this, the tension in Winston's body eased. His instincts had been correct. Pierce had been murdered, and from what he'd discovered recently, the perpetrator could well have been one of his investors. Almost as quickly, Winston's tension returned as he considered the possibility. "Thank you, Doctor. I need to speak to the chief constable." Winston stammered the words. "Will you come with me?"

"Of course."

The men left the morgue and walked in silence to the door of Philpott's office. Winston took a deep breath to calm himself and knocked.

His uncle called from behind the door and Winston followed the doctor into the office. As he entered, Winston wiped his palms on his trousers before pulling Ellis's rock from his pocket, gripping it tightly in his palm.

Philpott stood to greet them. "It's early, gentlemen. And you look rather serious. Has something happened?"

Winston gestured toward Evans. He deeply wished he could avoid this conversation. "Doctor Evans has found something that strongly suggests Arthur Pierce was murdered." He clenched his fingers around the stone. "And Miller and I have found a motive."

A frown crossed Philpott's face. "Are you certain?" A sheen of sweat glistened at Philpott's hairline. He retrieved a handkerchief from his pocket and blew his nose. Winston recognized the actions as stalling, but waited for Philpott to speak. His response would determine Winston's next steps. Philpott turned his attention to Evans.

"If you're certain it's murder, Jack will need to investigate." He wiped his brow with his hand.

Evans stepped forward without breaking eye contact with Philpott. "I am, Chief Constable."

"What evidence do you have?" The words came out strained.

Evans explained his conclusions, describing the injuries and how they must have occurred shortly before Pierce died.

"He was a sportsman. He could have fallen from his bicycle, or. . ."

Evans shook his head. "The injuries appear to have been inflicted shortly before he died. We did not find a bicycle at the scene."

Philpott gestured toward the chairs opposite his desk with a resigned wave. Winston slid into one, planting his feet firmly and leaning forward. He locked eyes with his uncle. "I know you knew the man, but it appears he was involved in defrauding his investors, sir. I have not yet determined how much of his business was legitimate. The man kept little in the way of records." As he spoke, he thought of how sparse his uncle's own record-keeping was.

Philpott swallowed. "Fraud?"

"I'm still looking into it, but it looks like he took money from new investors to pay original investors."

"Original investors. Do you have names?" Philpott's voice wavered.

"I found a ledger that contains initials and amounts invested. Miller is reviewing it today. We have lists of potential investors we're comparing it with."

"Do you think the fraud is connected to Pierce's death?"

"It's likely. We have found nothing else to suggest another motive."

The chief constable rearranged himself. As he did, colour drained from his face. "Jack, I know I discouraged you from pursuing this earlier. And I know you continued to investigate anyway. We can talk later about your record regarding following instructions. But in this, you've made the right decision. Do you know what Pierce invested in?"

Winston understood the unspoken meaning of the chief's words. He was reluctant to discuss his involvement in front of Evans. "Not specifically. As I said, I have found little paperwork, but I have pieced together that the business had something to do with mining. He was promising some sort of tool to make prospecting easier."

Philpott winced, opened his mouth to say something, and closed it again.

Winston waited. He hadn't expected to use his silence technique with the chief constable. Though if Philpott spoke frankly in front of Evans, Winston was ready to listen.

After another deep breath, Philpott began quietly. He focused his gaze on Winston. "I heard him speak about a mechanism. To find gold." He rubbed his palm across his face. "Faster than a man. Faster than five, apparently. He said he knew a miner who'd had some success."

Winston considered the worry creasing his uncle's face. "And you invested with him." He wanted his uncle to acknowledge his involvement.

Philpott lowered his gaze. "Clarissa doesn't know."

"How much?" The question was barely more than a whisper.

"One thousand dollars."

Evans drew in a breath sharply.

Philpott looked at Evans as if suddenly remembering he was in the room. "Initially, it was two hundred. He doubled it so quickly, I reinvested it. And I gave him more last month."

Winston leaned across the desk to grasp his uncle's arm, then drew it back. The gesture would be unwelcome. As would words. He admired his uncle for pressing on.

"See what you uncover, Jack. But please keep me out of it if you can." Philpott stood. "I appreciate your sharing this, lad. Inform me as soon as you learn more. Especially if you find more about the investors." He gripped Evans on the arm. "Doctor, I trust you will keep what you've heard today in confidence."

Winston recalled Riley's words. This, she suspected, was why she was having a hard time finding any information about Pierce's business: everyone who'd been involved wanted to avoid being associated with the fraud when they learned of it. If they could pretend it never happened, they could all move on.

"Of course, Chief Philpott," Evans said as he and Winston moved toward the door.

Winston turned to face his uncle. "Do you want to see the body, sir? It's just that Evans will need to release it to the family for burial."

Philpott shook his head. "No need. I trust you."

Outside the chief's office, Winston shook Evans' hand. "Thank you for being so thorough, Nathaniel. I am sure Mrs. Pierce will also appreciate your diligence, though I don't know if it's better to have a husband who was murdered rather than one who killed himself. I must visit her today to inform her of what you've discovered."

"I will release the body today. She can have the funeral home collect him later this afternoon."

Winston followed Evans outside the station. As the man rode off in his carriage, Winston leaned against the station wall. The validation he felt at being right about Pierce's murder competed with a growing unease about his uncle's relationship with Pierce. Did he know more than he had shared? His uncle had encouraged him to see what else he could uncover, but would he really let Winston investigate without further interference? Winston closed his eyes to calm the mix of emotions swirling inside him. It was time to update Miller.

※

After they'd left the bank, Winston had given Miller a note authorizing him to collect the case file from Winston's rooms. Now he found Constable Miller in the station's main room. He explained to the constable how he had briefed Philpott about their investigation. He lowered his voice. "Philpott invested with Pierce."

Miller's eyes widened as he realized what Winston was saying. "Is he a suspect, sir?"

"We need to eliminate him. I think that's why he didn't want us investigating."

"Was he upset, sir? About our investigation?" Miller asked.

"I didn't tell him you'd been helping me. You're not in trouble."

Miller swallowed and let his shoulders relax. "After I fetched the papers, I looked at the ledger again." As he spoke, he straightened. "It looks like Pierce had cycles of investors."

"What can you tell me about them, Thomas?"

"In the first round, the amounts invested were smaller. Most men gave him between two hundred and five hundred dollars. The second round of investment was larger. Many parted with a thousand dollars, and some considerably more."

Winston whistled. Pierce had amassed a small fortune. "Go on."

"Many of the third-cycle investors were labourers, though there were a few from the original round."

Miller pulled his finger down a page in the ledger. "Look at this. Seems like the chief was among those who reinvested."

Consistent with what Winston had just learned. "How many investors?"

"He had more with each round. The new men in the third cycle invested less than those from the earlier ones. I assume the workingmen did not have as much to invest, which is why Pierce needed more. I've matched most of them, sir." Miller's shoulders squared with pride. "But a few share initials, so some are still unidentified."

Winston recalled what Riley had shared. Pierce would have paid some money back to investors after the first round to demonstrate the soundness of the scheme. He could rely on those men to boast that they had been successful and encourage other investors to reinvest their gains. But he didn't have enough to repay them if all his investors—especially the labourers—continued to expect double their money in return. "Well done, Thomas. Now we need to figure out where to start."

Convincing his uncle to allow him to investigate Pierce's death as a murder had been less of a struggle than Winston had feared. Maybe in the back of his mind, Philpott already had his suspicions Pierce wasn't as honest as he made himself out to be. What about Pierce's associates? Did they know about the fraud? Sawyer? Macey? Caroline Pierce? Winston would have to question them with care. The widow was a good place to begin.

"You've done some good work here, Thomas. I'd like you to come with me to the Pierces' house. I will value your observations about Mrs. Pierce's reaction once she learns her husband was murdered."

CHAPTER 21

Jack

THE PIERCE RESIDENCE was a hive of activity when Miller and Winston arrived. A man raked leaves from the front garden while a maid swept the steps, the two chatting brightly while performing their tasks. The policemen exchanged glances. This hardly seemed a house deep in mourning. Clifford smiled when he greeted Winston. "Oh hello, Detective. Who have you brought with you today?" He spoke as if receiving a regular, welcome guest at the home.

Winston peered over the man's shoulder, trying to see the frenzy behind him. The butler followed Winston's gaze. "Mrs. Pierce instructed everyone to clean today. 'A fresh start,' she said. We mustn't let our grief get in the way of our duties, and I hope I'm not speaking out of turn, but everyone genuinely appears to feel better for it." Clifford stiffened after a moment, as if reconsidering how his statements might be interpreted by two investigators. "We've all been at such a loss without Mr. Pierce, but with his death the way it was, none of us knew quite. . ." Although he failed to finish the sentence, the butler spoke with tenderness.

Winston matched Clifford's tone. "Is she home? I realize the time may not be convenient, but I have some pressing news for her."

"Of course, Detective. She instructed me to let you in no matter the time. I will have some toast and jam brought to you and your colleague. Before I forget, I asked about the glove I mentioned yesterday. It turns out it was Mr. Sawyer's. Mrs. Sawyer recognized it and took it with her."

"Thank you, Mr. Clifford. Would you mind showing Constable Miller the pair you received? And those of all the household staff."

"I'll have to gather them," Clifford said. "I'll show you after I've collected them from the others," he said to Miller. "First, if you'll both follow me."

Winston noted the colour climbing up the back of the man's neck as they walked toward the sitting room. Nothing about the scene was typical. Where he would normally see draped dark fabrics, the curtains on the wide windows were pulled back, allowing the meagre morning sun to filter into the space. Large bouquets of colourful flowers adorned the tables in the room.

After Clifford left, Miller turned to Winston. "Sir, I'm not familiar with how things are done among the wealthy, but this does not feel like a household that recently lost a member, let alone one they believe took his own life."

The younger man's assessment matched Winston's, though he was reluctant to criticize Mrs. Pierce. "Who is to say how a household should react, Thomas? While many follow a prescribed set of mourning rituals, Mrs. Pierce may not subscribe to their importance." He lowered his voice. "And as a leader of Vancouver society, she has a level of flexibility not afforded to other women. It seems she has taken advantage of that liberty."

A maid appeared, bearing tea, toast, and jam. Winston thanked her and retreated into his thoughts. Regardless of the freedom her status afforded her, Caroline Pierce must know the directions she had given her household were unconventional. He was about to voice this thought when she entered.

She smiled warmly at Winston. Instead of a deep black mourning dress, Caroline Pierce wore medium grey, giving the impression of a woman nearly out of mourning rather than one so recently bereaved. She noticed Winston's appraising glance and plucked at her skirt.

"Black doesn't suit me, Detective. And tears will not bring my husband back, nor will they change what he did to himself."

While Winston couldn't help but admire her plucky attitude, he expected that what he had come to say would alter her odd behaviour. She wouldn't be able to sustain this cheerful determination once she learned her husband had been murdered. He drew a deep breath and began. "Mrs. Pierce, we have some news." He pointed to a chair and waited for her to sit, and signalled to Miller they should do the same.

Caroline Pierce arranged herself, clasping her hands in her lap. Winston leaned forward and softened his voice. "Mrs. Pierce, I must inform you our medical examiner has confirmed your husband was murdered."

A dazed expression of shock overtook the woman's face. A hand flew to her chest. "Murdered?" she repeated in a halting voice. She locked her gaze on Winston, eyes searching his. "You're certain?"

He offered her the slightest of nods. "We are. I can only imagine how this news adds to the pain you're already feeling."

"Who?"

The word escaped her mouth in such a quiet puff, Winston wasn't sure she had said it. When Winston didn't respond, Miller turned to look at him. Winston raised his hand slightly, hoping Miller understood enough to remain quiet.

"Do you know who killed him?" she asked. "Why?" With each word, her voice grew stronger.

During their journey to the Pierce house, Winston had considered how he would answer this question, yet he remained silent. On the heels of telling this woman her husband was the victim of murder, he couldn't add to her burden with the news that her husband had been misleading his clients. He settled on an evasive response. "We are exploring different theories, Mrs. Pierce."

Winston inched forward in his chair. "Actually, I was hoping you might have some thoughts, Mrs. Pierce. And I apologize, but I need to ask this. Where were you the night he died?"

The woman frowned. "I was here, of course. My maid can confirm I retired to my room shortly before midnight. I thought Arthur had done the same."

"You slept in separate bedrooms?" The intimacy of the question sent heat coursing through Winston.

"Yes. He was a light sleeper. I did not hear him leave in the night."

"Thank you, madam," Winston said, unable to look at her directly. "Are you aware of anyone who might have wished to hurt your husband?"

Now in safer territory, Winston watched her reaction. She wiped a wandering tear from her eye, clutching a handkerchief she had pulled from the sleeve of her dress. "No. My husband was well loved. By everyone." She swept her hand around. "He earned this by helping others make money. People wanted to invest with him. He couldn't keep them away."

Winston sat up. "When we spoke last, you said you didn't know much about your husband's business."

"And I still don't. But I know he was successful, and that is why he brought in my sister's husband to partner with him. He had more than enough work to go around." She clenched and unclenched her hand around the handkerchief as she spoke. "When he first started, he used to tell me more about the business, but recently, he had said little about it. I assumed he discussed business matters with Reginald after bringing him on."

Winston retrieved his small notebook from his pocket. "I understood the partnership was not as successful as Mr. Sawyer had hoped?"

Caroline Pierce sniffed. "My sister can be overdramatic, Detective. Arthur and Reginald's partnership was evolving. But you're correct.

Both my sister and her husband felt it should have gone better." She tucked her handkerchief back into the cuff of her gown's sleeve. "Arthur can hardly be held accountable for Reginald's laziness."

"Did your husband tell you Reginald Sawyer was upset? You spoke of an argument between them before."

"I overheard them. One evening a couple of weeks ago. Reginald and Abigail had dined with us, but she'd returned home with a headache." She rubbed her temples briefly. "As I climbed the stairs to my bedroom, Arthur and Reginald spoke in raised voices."

Winston and Miller locked eyes. "Did you hear what they were speaking about?" Winston's heart sped up as he waited for her to answer.

"I assumed it was about the business. And Reginald sounded angry." She clasped her hands in her lap. "The next day, I asked Abigail if Reginald had said anything to her about it, and she said it was between the men, but she thought it was not serious."

Winston made a note in his book. "Who else might know about your husband's business? We spoke with his clerk, Charles Macey. He was the only person we found working at the company's office. Does that sound right to you?"

She shrugged. "I believe it is—was—just the three of them."

"When I last spoke with Mr. Macey, he wasn't certain he'd retain his position much longer."

"Nor should he, especially if he knows nothing about the business." She dismissed the notion with a wave of her hand. "I'll have Reginald let him go if he's of no use to you."

Winston frowned. "His utility to our investigation remains whether or not he continues to be associated with your husband's company. Please don't fire him on our account."

"As you wish."

This woman was confounding Winston. Did she know more about the business than she claimed? Or did she have influence over

Reginald Sawyer? "Mrs. Pierce, I must be clear. What happens is not because I wish it, but because it is the right thing for this investigation." He softened his voice. He would get further with his questions if he didn't offend her. "Can you think of anyone else who'd argued with your husband? Did he mention any troubling relationships in any other part of his life?"

She cocked her head. "There was a man working outside." She pointed at the ceiling. "A builder repairing the roof, I think. Arthur sent him away. He said he wasn't happy with his work. But the man had hardly been here half a day, so I'm not sure how Arthur judged what he'd done."

"When was this?"

The corners of her mouth turned down as she considered the time. "Last week."

"Do you remember his name?" Winston asked. Could this man have returned the same evening to confront Pierce?

Caroline Pierce pushed herself from the chair. "Abigail will know. She is the one who sent him here."

Winston made a notation in his notebook. "Thank you, Mrs. Pierce. Is there anything else you can think of?"

She frowned, then let out a sudden laugh that filled the room. Winston felt his cheeks prick with heat at the sound. She looked at Winston's expression and said, "If I can't laugh when I learn my husband has been murdered, when can I laugh?" She wiped tears away, and Winston wondered at her reaction. They'd clearly delivered enough information to cause her great dismay. He stood and motioned to Miller to do the same.

"I imagine I will be back again with further questions, but I'll leave you now to make arrangements," Winston said.

"Does this mean we can have a proper funeral for him? I had planned to have a small remembrance, just family. The shame of taking one's own life is great, Detective." She fixed Winston with a stare. "I've been forcing myself to pretend I didn't care that he's dead." She lowered her head. "When will you release his body?"

"We can release it shortly, madam. Doctor Evans will contact the funeral home for you. Which would you prefer?"

"McLure's. I'm told he is the best."

"He is certainly reputable. I'll advise the doctor."

Caroline Pierce rose, followed by the two policemen.

"One more thing, Mrs. Pierce," Winston said. "I understand your husband gave a gift of gloves to several people. Might you know who received them?"

The widow pursed her lips. "Arthur was a generous man, Detective. He gave them to Reginald, Charles Macey, the staff here." She wrinkled her nose. "They were too masculine for my taste, but as I recall, they were well made and might have fit a larger woman's hand." She held up a hand and wiggled her slender fingers. "He talked about ordering a dozen pairs." She cocked her head. "Are you interested in a pair for yourself?"

Winston shook his head. "Not at all, madam." He looked toward Miller. "We found a glove in the course of our investigation."

"Could it be his own? He was always leaving something somewhere," she said.

"Possibly," Winston answered.

Caroline Pierce thanked him and left the room.

As Winston prepared to leave, Mr. Clifford appeared with a stack of boxes. "I've checked with everyone. They all have their gloves. Most have not been removed from the boxes they came in. They are too nice to use." He offered the stack to Miller, who opened each box to confirm it contained a pair.

"Thank you, Mr. Clifford. I appreciate your assistance," Winston said. He held up a finger. "A final question for today. Where were you the night Mr. Pierce died?"

Clifford raised his eyebrows. "I locked the house after Mr. Pierce retired. That would have been midnight or so. I then went upstairs to my room."

"Did you see anyone?"

"Who can verify whether I killed Mr. Pierce?" Clifford must have been listening at the sitting room door. "I've told you I haven't, but no, there isn't anyone who can say I remained asleep." They exchanged curt goodbyes, and the butler closed the door behind the policemen.

*

OUTSIDE THE HOUSE, confusion clouded Miller's face. "Do you think Mrs. Pierce knows more, sir?"

"I do."

"Why are we leaving now? Should we not press her for answers?"

The weight of Ellis's rock bounced against Winston's leg, keeping time with their pace as they walked from the house. "It's better she doesn't know what we think. And I'm not sure she has fully come to terms with her husband's death. Her behaviour was certainly out of the ordinary for a grieving widow, even for someone who may have been unconventional in her approach to life. We will let her prepare for her husband's funeral while we continue to speak to others who might have had a stake in Pierce's death."

Winston paused his stride and turned to Miller. "Thomas, visit Sharp's Fine Goods and Tailoring to see if he provided Pierce with the gloves. His record-keeping is no doubt better than Pierce's, and he'll know exactly how many pairs were ordered."

"And the butler, sir?"

"He doesn't have an alibi, but my impression is he genuinely cared for Pierce. Still, we will have to consider him a suspect until we know otherwise." Winston began walking again. "Let's go first to Reginald Sawyer."

Miller held up his hand and stopped. "Sir, I'm still confounded. What do you take from the widow's behaviour?"

Winston paused. "You're right to return to this. She may very well be trying to hide something. We will need something more to figure out what."

CHAPTER 22

Jack

Winston cupped his hands against his mouth and blew to warm his fingers against the wind. The soft drizzle had turned into rain. Though the temperature was warmer than November in Toronto, this West Coast cold seeped into his marrow. Constable Miller, walking beside him, appeared unaffected by the chill. "Thomas, how do you manage this weather?"

"Don't know, sir. My family moved here when I was small, so maybe I'm used to it. I also have a layer of wool beneath my uniform. That really helps. So will gloves, if you can find a pair." He laughed at his last statement, and Winston had to appreciate Miller's wit.

"I hadn't thought of an underlayer. Back home, we only wore them when skating on the lake. I shall have to pick some up. Thank you for the suggestion."

Miller's face glowed with pride.

As they stood in front of Reginald Sawyer's house, Winston's pulse quickened with anticipation. "Thomas, we want to find out what Sawyer argued with Arthur Pierce about. And what he knows about Billy the miner and the machinery Pierce was raising funds for."

"Do we also want to see how Sawyer reacts to the news that Pierce was murdered?"

"Yes, that will be telling. Observe carefully." Winston tapped Miller on the shoulder.

From the street, they could see smoke puffing from the chimney. Winston looked forward to warming himself inside. His hopes were dashed when a maid answered their knock and showed them to a small receiving room without a fireplace. At least it was dry. Moments after the policemen entered, Reginald and Abigail Sawyer appeared in the doorway.

"Have you any news, Detective Winston?" Mrs. Sawyer asked before any pleasantries could be exchanged. The woman had a directness unusual for most women Winston knew. As she crossed the room, her skirts swished about her, commanding attention. Sawyer followed behind her and shook each officer's hand. His smile was broad, despite having two policemen attend his house unannounced. The Sawyers settled into a low sofa, and Mrs. Sawyer gestured for Winston and Miller to sit in a pair of chairs opposite them.

Winston decided against easing into conversation. The moment he was seated, he interjected, "We've confirmed Arthur Pierce was murdered." Both Sawyers stiffened visibly but said nothing. "Mr. Sawyer, I need to speak to you today to learn more about Arthur Pierce and who might have benefited from his death." Winston waited for the news and its implications to hit the couple.

Mrs. Sawyer was the first to react. She brought a hand to her mouth, which had fallen open in a wide O. "Reginald gets Arthur's business..." she blurted. Horror pinched the woman's features. "Are we suspects?"

"Abigail." Sawyer's voice had a pleading tone. He took her hand.

"Everyone is a suspect until they are not, madam." Winston pulled his small notebook from his satchel. Miller pulled one from his pocket. "When did you see Mr. Pierce last?"

Mrs. Sawyer sniffed. "We dined with Caro and Arthur two nights before he died. At their home." A hint of a smile crossed her face. Was she remembering a moment from that dinner? Or another pleasant memory of time spent with Pierce?

Her answer, rather than Winston's question, was enough to elicit a reaction from Sawyer, who sat straighter. "I saw him the next day."

She turned to her husband. "You did? You didn't say."

"I wanted to discuss something with him. There were other guests at the dinner, and it wasn't the right time."

"Did you discuss anything unusual during this dinner?" Winston asked. "How did Mr. Pierce seem? Relaxed? Worried? Distracted?" As he spoke, he knew he needed to slow down to allow the Sawyers to react to each question. He pressed his hand into his leg where Ellis's rock rested inside a pocket.

"He was himself," Sawyer said. "Which is why I was so surprised when you said he'd killed himself. He certainly gave me no impression at dinner that such a thing was on his mind." Sawyer's shoulders relaxed.

"Thank you," Winston said. "What did you discuss?"

Sawyer looked to the ceiling as if trying to recall the evening. "We didn't speak directly about business."

Winston reached for the opening Sawyer had provided. "But the subject came up? Were the guests investors?"

"One couple was very close to investing. The dinner was our formal introduction.

"Their names?" Winston pressed.

"Mr. and Mrs. Brooks and Mr. and Mrs. Herringsgate. Herringsgate was rather interested and signed an agreement." Sawyer made to get up. "I should have it—"

Mrs. Sawyer's arm shot across her husband's chest. "I'm sure Detective Winston can wait."

Winston nodded, then he dropped a question to test Sawyer's reaction. "Herringsgate invested in Billy, the miner?"

"Billy? No. He's. . ." Sawyer shifted. "Herringsgate was interested in the machinery."

"Which does what, exactly?" asked Miller, pencil poised.

"I won't go into the technical details, but it makes it easier for miners to find the gold deposits they seek."

"Through what means, Mr. Sawyer?"

Sawyer squirmed again, reminding Winston of a man with a rock in his shoe. "It's more technical than I can relate, but it somehow detects when a precious metal is nearby."

"What mechanism makes such detection possible?"

Sheepishness crossed Sawyer's face. "Arthur tried to explain it. I'm afraid the concept was lost on me, other than to say it somehow sensed the metals and sounded a bell when they were present."

Winston and Miller exchanged glances. Such a machine, if it truly existed, might be worth killing for. "Who else knew of this machine? How it worked?"

"Other than Pierce? I suppose the man who used it and the man who made it."

"Billy?"

Sawyer leaned an elbow on his knee. He looked deflated. "Billy doesn't exist. We invented him. Rather, Arthur invented him. Said it helped sell the story."

Heat rose in Winston. "Why didn't you tell me this the other day? Misleading information hinders our investigation."

Sawyer looked away.

"But everything else, the information you've provided, it's truthful? Complete?"

"Of course it is, Detective." Abigail Sawyer's tone was defensive, like she'd taken Winston's question as an insult. "Arthur Pierce was respected. And my husband's integrity is beyond reproach."

Beside his wife, Reginald Sawyer nodded.

"And yet you and Pierce fabricated this man and his story." Winston had allowed an air of judgment into his voice. Neither of the Sawyers responded.

He chose a new line of questioning. "I understand you argued with Mr. Pierce shortly before his death. Can you tell me what about? And I'll need your complete honesty."

Colour spread across Sawyer's neck. "We didn't always agree, Detective. That doesn't mean I murdered him."

Mrs. Sawyer placed her hand on her husband's arm. "You must tell them everything, dear. If it will help."

Sawyer shook his wife's hand away. "Arthur didn't like how I handled a potential client. He felt I should have encouraged the client to invest more. When I saw him the day after our dinner, I confirmed that the client had agreed to increase his investment."

Miller edged forward. "How much guidance had Mr. Pierce been providing you, Mr. Sawyer? When we spoke before, you didn't seem familiar at all with his business."

Redness spread across Sawyer's face. "He was instructing me."

"In what way?"

"Arthur provided introductions. A portion of what my investors gave me went to him, in exchange for those introductions."

"And if you failed to sign a client?" Miller asked. "Or the client's investment didn't result in his making money?"

"Business is business." Sawyer swallowed. "Some deals work out, others don't. But I don't know anyone who would kill for a failed business arrangement. At least not the sort of people Arthur and I work with. And all our clients made money."

Winston pictured Felter from the mill. "All of them?"

A bead of sweat glistened on Sawyer's brow and he wiped at it with a shaky hand. "All the ones I worked with."

"Was the same true for Arthur Pierce?"

"I believe so."

"Why are you asking these questions, Detective?" Mrs. Sawyer's tone had become clipped.

Her husband patted her hand. "He said everyone is a suspect." Sawyer's chuckle sounded forced. "I didn't realize he meant literally everyone."

"So we can rule you out, where were you the night your brother-in-law died?"

"I was here, with Abigail."

She straightened her posture. "Reginald would hardly want to kill Arthur."

"Didn't you go out again, dear?" Sawyer asked his wife. "On one of your starlit rides?"

She put her hand on his. "No, that was the night before, dear." She looked at Winston. "I occasionally have trouble sleeping. I find a ride around the city helps."

Winston tapped his pencil on his chin. "Tell me more about Billy, the miner. What sort of story did Pierce fabricate?"

Sawyer shook his head. "Arthur created Billy. He described the old prospector as temperamental. Preferred the company of rocks to men." He rubbed his chin. "Investors, they loved hearing that kind of thing."

"And what will they say when they learn he is an invention, that he doesn't exist?"

Sawyer's shoulders sagged. "I don't know. Pierce's clients... They'll..."

Winston leaned forward. "I'm a little confused by your business relationship as partners. The other day, you suggested Arthur hadn't been as forthcoming with his advice and guidance as you would have liked."

Sawyer held his hands in defence against Winston's question. "It's more that the process was slower than I would have liked. That is not enough for me to kill him. We were family, for goodness' sake."

Mrs. Sawyer stood, and the men followed. "I fear you are wasting your time questioning my husband when he couldn't have killed Arthur, even if he'd wanted to. He was with me."

"That may be the case, but your husband didn't need to be there. He could have arranged for someone else to do the deed, Mrs. Sawyer."

She thought this over and sat down. "He wouldn't even know whom to contact. It's not as if we socialize with murderers."

The men resumed their seats. Reginald Sawyer frowned at his wife. Miller masked his laugh with a cough.

"Mr. Sawyer," Winston said, "how is it you know so little about how Pierce managed the investments for his clients?"

Sawyer tugged on his moustache as he considered the question. "Arthur didn't invite me into that side of things. He found his clients. They invested their money. He gave them returns. It's not a complicated thing."

"What guidance did you need from Mr. Pierce? If investing is so simple." Heads swivelled to Miller as he spoke. He had a knack for timing his questions well. Winston made a mental note to acknowledge Miller's instincts once they'd finished with the Sawyers.

"The investing is easy. Building relationships is the challenge." Sawyer crossed his legs. "And that is what Arthur excelled at."

"You will," said Mrs. Sawyer, placing her hand on her husband's arm.

Winston leaned toward him. "Where did he typically find his investors? Were they friends?"

"Not initially, no. He might have become friendly with them. He certainly found investors at the Vancouver Gentlemen's Club. But I do not think Arthur offered his opportunities to our friends. I'm not sure why not, although I had the impression he thought it best not to mix business and friendship."

Beside him, Mrs. Sawyer patted his arm. "Sounds like good advice to follow." She brought her focus to Winston. "My husband is modest. He is a good businessman." Her voice rose with pride as she spoke.

"Did you invest any money with him, Mr. Sawyer?"

"Me? No."

Winston eased back in his chair.

Sawyer continued. "I know I'm meant to take over Arthur's business, but to be honest, I'm not even sure I want it, at least not to use his name. I'll benefit more in the long run from trading on my name."

Winston's neck prickled. Riley's findings indicated Sawyer would do well without Pierce. "I suppose only time will tell, Mr. Sawyer." He shifted his gaze to Mrs. Sawyer. "I have an additional question for you. I understand you sent Mr. Pierce a builder. But the man left with the work unfinished. Do you have his name?"

"I'm sure I have it somewhere. I'll send it to you at the station. The man finished a job for us rather quickly, and I suggested he check whether there was anything he could do for my sister. I hadn't heard they'd been unhappy with his work." She rose.

The men did the same. "Thank you," Winston said. "We'll trouble you no more today." As they walked toward the doorway, Winston turned. "One more thing. Mr. Sawyer, may we look at the gloves given to you by Mr. Pierce? You recently left one at his house."

Sawyer turned to his wife. "Did I?"

"Oh, I meant to tell you I'd picked it up from Caroline." She left to retrieve them. A few minutes later, she returned with a single glove. "I'm afraid I've misplaced the other." She handed the glove to Winston.

"Thank you. We'll return this shortly." He gave the glove to Miller, exchanging a meaningful glance with his constable.

Winston turned back to Mrs. Sawyer. "Your sister will likely appreciate hearing from you, madam. I provided her with the most troubling news before coming here."

Abigail Sawyer nodded, her mouth a thin line. "I must attend to Caroline, then. She has a funeral to plan, and you have a murderer to catch." She left the room without looking at any of the men.

Reginald Sawyer stood with Winston and Miller as they shrugged into their damp coats. "I'm afraid they haven't dried completely." He produced two umbrellas from a stand against the wall. "I noticed neither of you brought an umbrella. Take these. Return them when I see you next, which I have no doubt will be soon."

The kindness surprised Winston. "Mr. Sawyer, just one more question, if you don't mind. Mr. Pierce's investments. We have been unable to find many details about them. Have you any idea where he might have kept that information?"

Surprise crossed Sawyer's face. "Not in his office, nor in his home? It must be in one of those places. Shall I look?"

"I appreciate the offer, but it's best you leave it to us." Winston buttoned his jacket and took an umbrella from Sawyer, offering the other to Miller.

CHAPTER 23

Jack

AT THE STATION, Constable Miller cleared his throat. "Sir, do you think Mrs. Pierce or the Sawyers are involved in Arthur Pierce's death?" He brought Sawyer's glove close to his face. "This looks like a match for the one we found at the park, sir."

Winston brushed his hand across his moustache. "Let's compare them side by side. Thomas, would you fetch the one we found from the evidence cupboard?"

Miller returned with the glove and laid it on the desk. "This one's for a left hand." He held his left hand over the glove to show how the thumb matched up.

Winston laid Sawyer's glove beside it. "This is for a right hand. The perfect mate to the one we found," he said. Save for some evidence of soiling on the glove from the park, the two were mirror images of each other. "How do you think it got to the park, Thomas?"

"He must have dropped it. Mrs. Sawyer said she couldn't find its mate."

Winston pointed to the glove. "This might very well be the most important evidence we've found so far. It certainly puts Sawyer at the top of the suspect list."

Both men went quiet for a moment, then Winston prompted Miller. "Tell me, what did you make of the conversations we've had today? Mrs. Pierce?"

"As I've said, sir, it was her behaviour, unconventional for a widow, I mean, that gave me pause."

"Agreed. But I'm not convinced her demeanour today is enough to make her a suspect. She has access, yes. She shared a house with the victim." He tugged at a thread on his jacket. "But what was her motive?"

Miller considered this. "How much will she inherit?"

"A good point, Thomas. I'm not sure if she was even familiar with the terms of his will. She seems somewhat ill-informed on most practical matters. Pierce's lawyer sent a letter about the will to the station. She is due to inherit the house and its contents and to receive a small annual allowance, enough to cover modest living expenses for her and her son." An image of the woman in her fine dress flashed through Winston's mind. The allowance would be smaller than she might have expected. "I assume had his business continued to be successful, she would have benefited more. As it is, she will need to adjust her tastes."

Winston waited while Miller wrote in his small notebook. "What did you think about our conversation with the Sawyers?" He was about to repeat the question when Miller turned to face him.

"They seemed genuinely surprised when you informed them Pierce was murdered. If they were involved, would they have been able to imitate such a reaction?"

Winston shook his head. "I don't know. But Reginald gains the most from Pierce's death, so he has motive. And we have what we assume to be his glove at the scene. Since our investigation is no longer something we need to hide, let's write out all we know and lay it out so we can see it."

Miller set about finding paper while Winston heated water for their tea. Warmth returned to the detective's fingers as he brought the steaming mugs to the station's main room.

"Who are our suspects, Miller?" Winston asked, setting his mug on his desk. Miller had pushed another desk against Winston's. "Let's list them all."

"Caroline Pierce. As you've observed, she'd likely have fared better with him alive than dead, but we have to include her because she's his wife, right?" Winston nodded, and Miller wrote her name and relationship to Arthur Pierce on a piece of paper. "Reginald Sawyer, as his business partner. You said he benefits most."

"He does, especially if he inherits Pierce's clients." Winston scratched his nose. "But if Pierce was not as honest with his clients about their investments, which seems ever more likely to be the case, Sawyer might not want to take over the business. He alluded to having such a thought just before we left him, albeit he claimed it was for another reason."

"What about Abigail Sawyer?"

Winston inhaled. "I find her difficult to read. How would she benefit from her brother-in-law's death?"

"She benefits if her husband inherits everything."

"And she gains position over her sister. She certainly seems to be the more dominant of the two. And very concerned with appearances and status." In this, Abigail Sawyer was like Winston's mother. He'd seen her go to uncommon lengths to preserve her status. "While we're speaking of Mrs. Sawyer, please make a note that she's meant to send us the name of the builder Arthur Pierce had argued with."

Miller jotted it in his notebook. Then he raised his head and asked, "Would any of Pierce's clients benefit?"

"From the man's death? They are more likely to lose money. If, for example, he was swindling them and paying one group with another's investments, all of them stood to lose their money, if they haven't already."

Winston thought of Felter, Clifford, Philpott, and Scott. "Motive aside, none of them had access, not in the way Pierce's wife or Sawyer had." He paused. Clifford did, and Philpott's position meant anyone would open the door to him. "Actually, his butler would have had access." Winston wasn't quite ready to point a finger at his uncle yet.

"Any man who'd learned he'd lost money would feel that loss, no matter how much he'd started with, although his most recent clients would have grieved the loss more acutely. But all reports pointed to good returns. People invested with Pierce because he had a history of success."

Winston's thoughts returned to Philpott, and his stomach sank. "Prominent figures vouched for him, which no doubt led to others investing." How did his uncle feel to learn he had been promoting a liar? No doubt he felt shame, embarrassment, anger. Enough to cause him to take another man's life? But he'd only learned of the fraud today, or so he'd convinced them earlier in his office.

Winston tugged at the notion. Shame. Is that the key to this investigation? "Thomas, what causes a man to feel shame?"

The constable stared at his feet so long Winston wondered if he'd actually spoken the question aloud or just thought it. Miller raised his eyes. "Losing, sir. Losing money. Losing a wife to another man."

"Humiliation, failure, anger." Winston swallowed. "Macey, Sawyer, Felter, Scott, Clifford. . ." He sighed heavily. "Even Chief Constable Philpott. Each man was associated with Pierce and would have cause to feel any and all of these."

"Enough to kill him?" Miller searched the room. "And, more to the point, who knew the truth?"

"That's our question. Who discovered that Pierce had swindled his clients? Winston followed the stream of thought. "If there were more than one who'd uncovered the truth, who in that number would have felt the most shame? And had access and opportunity?" Winston began to answer his own question. "Pierce died at night. Someone would have had to convince him to join them at the park."

"Or in his carriage after a night at the Gentlemen's Club?" asked Miller. He paced the room. "Could someone have forced him into a carriage?"

"Or he entered it voluntarily. Accepting a ride to continue a conversation in private. Didn't he prefer more intimate conversations?" Winston flipped the pages in his notebook briefly, then set it down. "Either way, the killer likely had his own carriage, which rules out Felter. A cab driver is unlikely to accept a fare with an unconscious or struggling man."

"And Scott didn't seem aware of the fraud either. Nor would he have had access."

"You're right, Thomas." Winston raked his hair with his fingers. "What about the others? How do we narrow our focus?" He stared at the list, then tapped his finger on the sheet. "Let's go back to see Owen Scott."

"You just said... What about the others?" Miller asked, the confusion clear on his face.

"Yes, Miller, we'll get to them." Unease grew in the pit of his stomach. "There's a missing piece. We can start with Mr. Scott and see if he can shed more light on the scheme."

"Today?"

Winston pulled his watch from his pocket. "Let's wait until tomorrow, after Pierce's funeral in the morning. I will attend and see what I can learn by observing the other guests. They may reveal more than they intend." He slid into his coat. "Tonight, think about all this." Winston waved a hand in a circle, taking in the papers scattered across the two desks. "Something may sift through. I value your thoughts, Thomas."

✶

AT HOME, WINSTON wrote to Riley.

Dear Riley,

Today, Constable Miller and I made some progress on our case, yet it feels like we have so much left to answer. We met another man—Owen Scott, a bank manager—who had reinvested his money and was expecting a second quick return. This man unlocked a coded ledger I found hidden at Pierce's house. It seems Pierce had many clients, though there is no record of how he managed their investments. Apart from this coded ledger, he kept no records we've been able to discover.

Doctor Evans confirmed Arthur Pierce had been attacked before he was murdered. My uncle, in the light of this new finding, gave his approval to properly investigate the case. Neither Mrs. Pierce nor Reginald Sawyer offered any suggestions as to his killer. However, I've come to believe shame is key to this case. Someone Pierce defrauded was humiliated, lashed out in anger, and killed the man. Tomorrow I will attend Pierce's funeral. I'll observe the mourners. I will seek out more of Pierce's clients. He had many, so it may take time to uncover the man whose shame turned into revenge.

Jack

PS: My uncle, the chief constable, has admitted to investing with Pierce. I am certain he is innocent of this crime. He has, however, asked us to keep his name out of the investigation. His strong reaction supports your theory that records of Pierce's business enterprise will be altered.

J.

CHAPTER 24

Riley

JACK'S UPDATE STIRRED Riley's thoughts. Henry Pepper had also pointed to shame being a strong motivator. It made people do strange things, including, as Henry had speculated, expunging public records of their own involvement in an embarrassing scheme. If Jack's uncle was involved, that might explain why she'd been unable to find much information about Pierce. Philpott could have easily manipulated the police records and even the death certificate, since Doctor Evans worked for the police. But would he have had enough influence to ensure the newspaper didn't report on the scheme?

Riley stole a glance at the time. Her chest tightened. She was due to meet her sister at the bridal salon in an hour. And after the salon was dinner, when her mom was going to meet Johnny.

*

RILEY ENTERED THE bridal salon and was immediately embraced by her mother. "I'm so glad to see you, dear," she said. She pushed Riley away after a moment to inspect her. "You look good." She narrowed her eyes. "Are you eating enough?"

"Yes, Mom." She returned her mother's appraising look. She looked vibrant. Her skin glowed, and not just because of the soft, flattering lighting of the bridal boutique. "You coloured your hair?" Riley asked.

The door chimed and Lucy walked in. She joined them just as their mother answered Riley's question. "I used a wash-in. To cover up the greys a little." She patted the top of her head. "Not too much, as I don't want to hide them completely, but just to take the edge off."

"Pink, to take the edge off?" Lucy quipped. "It looks good on you. But it will wash out before the wedding, right? I'm just thinking about the photos."

Riley rolled her eyes inwardly at her sister. "Luce, your pictures will be great." As Lucy pulled away from her embrace with their mother, Riley caught her eye. Their mother had never coloured her hair, despite having streaks of grey for as long as Riley could remember. Keeping her greys was something Riley loved about her mother, especially since she had spotted a cluster in her own hair.

A clerk took coats and instructed the women to remove their boots, handing each a pair of slippers. She directed Lucy to the centre of the fitting area and offered her a flute of sparkling wine. At one end of the room was a wall of mirrors, some angled to provide views from all sides. An elegant bench sat at one end of the space with a low table in front of it. The latest issues of bridal magazines were fanned across the table.

Lucy's dress hung from a high hanger outside a fitting room, still encased in its protective cover. The clerk unzipped it with a dramatic flourish and Riley made the appropriate sounds of appreciation. Unlike the ones she'd practised before leaving her apartment, these were genuine. Even on the hanger, the dress was stunning, and her sister was bound to look breathtaking in it. No wonder Lucy wanted to try it on again and show her mother and sister. The Finch women looked at each other, tears brimming. Riley thought of her father and how proud he would have been of Lucy. Their nods and gentle squeezes suggested they shared the same thoughts.

Lucy and the clerk entered the fitting room, and Riley and her mother moved back to the plush bench. The clerk had set two flutes of sparkling wine on the low table. Riley leaned back into the pillows and sipped from her glass, the bubbly, the soft light, low music, and emotion combining to create a floating sensation. The feeling lasted for about thirty seconds until her mom cleared her throat. "Riley, I'm glad we have a moment alone. Did you have a chance to think about Educoin?"

Riley listened as her mother explained the strong connection she felt to the company and the good work they enabled. Hearing her describe it, she saw how her mother had found the idea so attractive. "But how do your investments make money, Mom?"

"Look, I'll show you." She pulled out her phone and tapped on an app, showing the screen to her daughter. "This is my balance as we speak," she said.

Riley's mouth went dry when she saw the sum under the Educoin logo. "I thought you said you'd invested ten thousand dollars."

"I did. And I'm investing ten for your sister and another ten for you. Either I can open an account for you, or we could have a family account. That twenty thousand for you girls should grow to one hundred thousand within a few months, if not less. Would you like to add any of your own money?"

Making five times what she invested sounded like a great opportunity, but that was the trick, wasn't it? Riley plucked at the faux fur draped over the bench. "I want to look into this a little more, Mom." Lucy and the clerk emerged from the fitting room. "I'm worried, that's all," Riley whispered. She gripped her mother's arm when she saw her sister, and a sideways glance confirmed they shared the same dropped-jaw reaction. Lucy looked incredible.

They leaped to their feet and crossed to meet Lucy, her mother leading with her arms outstretched. Riley walked beside her, breathless. "Lucy, you look... absolutely... amazing. Stunning." The Finch women embraced each other and shed another round of tears and laughter as they tried to avoid crushing Lucy's dress. Riley's heart was full. Educoin could wait.

CHAPTER 25

Riley

AT THE APPOINTED hour, Riley found Johnny outside the restaurant and greeted him with a hug. Head still swimming from the emotion of the bridal salon, she lingered in his arms longer than usual. "You don't have to do this, you know," she said, admiring the pink collar of his shirt peeking out from underneath his jacket. "Aren't you cold?" she asked, pulling her scarf tighter around her neck.

"Not at all. I hopped in a cab and haven't been out here long." As he spoke, small puffs of breath formed clouds in front of his face. "But before we go in. . ." He laced his fingers around hers and locked eyes with her. "Riley, if your mom is in trouble and I can somehow help her, I will."

"Thank you," she said, squeezing his hand. His return squeeze sent a shiver through her, erasing thoughts of her mother, sister, and Educoin. For the briefest of moments, she imagined what marrying him would be like, until his voice broke into her thoughts.

"Riley?"

She focused on his eyes, so warm. So much like his great-grandfather's. "Thank you, Johnny." She turned to walk toward the restaurant and lost her footing. He reacted quickly, supporting her at the elbow and waist. She leaned into him and breathed in his soapy scent.

"You okay?" Johnny asked, concern deepening into a crease between his eyes.

Riley nodded and smiled up at him. "Should we go in?" Warmth flowed from his hand to hers as he led her into the restaurant.

Lucy and Alex were already seated. Johnny shook Alex's hand and slid in next to him in the booth. Riley sat next to Lucy, and they exchanged a brief hug.

"Johnny looks delish tonight. Guess he wants to make a good impression on Mom," Lucy whispered, not quietly enough for Riley's liking. But she'd noticed the care Johnny had taken too, and liked that he wanted to impress her mother.

Five minutes later, their mother arrived. "My girls, it's so lovely to see you twice in one day." She leaned in to peck their cheeks. "And Alex, of course." She blew him a kiss. "Riley, who's this? Or are you Alex's friend?" She looked from Riley to Alex.

"Mom, this is Johnny Winston. I told you about him before, remember?" Riley kept her voice quiet, not wanting to embarrass him. "Johnny, this is my mom, Nancy Finch."

Riley's mother leaned into the booth toward Johnny and said, "You're a handsome one, aren't you?"

Riley struggled to keep her expression neutral while Johnny shook her mother's hand and politely accepted the compliment. Her mother was awkward about boundaries, like the line between being confident and being creepy. She'd have to talk to her about that. . . again.

"I wasn't sure how serious this is, but he looks like a lovely man. I'm happy for you." Her mom's voice was quiet now, thank goodness. She squeezed Riley's forearm.

Behind her mom, a man Riley had initially thought was the waiter stood patiently. It was only when her mom sat and he moved to sit across from her, wearing a broad smile, that Riley realized he wasn't there to take their drink order. Was this Peter? Why hadn't her mother mentioned he was only a few years older than Lucy? Riley clenched her jaw, then forced herself to relax. If she wanted to understand what was going on, she would need to be polite, not unapproachable.

He extended his hand. "I'm Peter Lucas. You're Riley? Your mom has told me so much about you."

Riley shook his hand reflexively, scanning his face as she did. She stole a glance at Johnny, who was deep in a conversation with Alex, and her sister, who was chatting with their mother. "Nice to meet you, Peter." Heat coursed through Riley as her mom turned to mouth something at him.

He introduced himself to the others at the table. Lucy leaned closer and whispered, "Peter is not what I was expecting. Is Mom trying to set you up with him? You should have told her about Johnny."

"I don't think she brought him for me." The sisters looked across the table and caught him winking at their mother.

"Ooh." Lucy's voice was a breathy squeal in Riley's ear. "He's a bit young for her, don't you think?"

"I don't know. If they're happy, does it matter?" Riley asked. Did the age difference matter?

The conversation moved to the weather and local politics. Riley sensed Lucy stealing glances at Peter with increasing frequency until, finally, she pointed a bread stick at him. "How do you know our mother?"

"We met at a yoga class." It was their mom who answered. "He asked me for pointers." When she spoke, she stared directly at Peter.

"She was really helpful, and we got to talking," Peter explained with a slight shrug.

A waiter appeared and took drink orders from the group. Lucy pinched Riley when Peter ordered for their mother. "What do you do, Peter?" she asked.

"Oh, he's very clever, Lucy. He has several businesses." What was up with their mom speaking for Peter? Could the man not answer for himself? Riley tensed when her mom patted his hand across the table.

Peter slipped a finger around hers. Riley checked to see if Lucy had seen. Lucy scrunched her nose.

"Look, I can see the worry on your faces," Peter said. "You're thinking, 'What is this young guy doing with our mom?' I get it. The class we were in was Yoga after Loss. Your mom has been a great support to me."

"At least I had thirty years with my Leo." Their mom turned to look at her daughters. "Peter only had three years with his wife. We started as friends, but we quickly realized how deep our connection is." Her hand still rested on his.

Connection. Her mother's words reminded Riley of their conversation at the bridal salon. She'd spoken of having a strong connection to Educoin. How deeply was Peter involved? Riley forced a smile. "Peter, I'm glad you and my mom have met, if that means you're making each other happy." She elbowed Lucy.

"Yes," was all Lucy could manage before she reached for her water.

The conversation picked up after everyone had taken a few sips of their drinks. Her mom asked Johnny a few questions about himself. Johnny answered with his usual ease and quiet confidence. Her mom moved on to give the men a glowing description of how beautiful Lucy had looked at the salon. Riley relaxed into the booth, comforted by her mother on one side and her sister on the other.

"Mom, I forgot to mention. Jules is in town to surprise his mother for her party." Riley popped a hand to her mouth. "Oh, I probably shouldn't have said anything. Then you wouldn't have to keep a secret."

"It's okay, dear," her mom said. "I'll be arriving a little late. Surely Jules will have made his grand entrance by then. But what a lovely surprise for her."

Riley stiffened. "But she's your best friend, Mom. Why are you showing up late?"

Across the table, Peter sat up. "I'm afraid it's my fault. I asked your mother to help me with a meeting."

"A meeting? On a Friday night?" Lucy sounded genuinely upset. Riley elbowed her, but she continued. "She'll be disappointed, Mom."

"I'm still going. But Peter asked, and I agreed before I knew about the party."

Lucy narrowed her eyes. "What is this meeting?"

"It's for one of my businesses," Peter said.

"My mom is a teacher," Lucy said, tilting her wineglass toward her mother, then to Peter. "No offence, Mom. But Peter, if you need her help, you're probably in a lot of trouble."

"Lucy." Mom used her that-was-not-appropriate voice.

Lucy coloured in response and looked away. "Sorry."

"When I learned about the party, I told Nancy to go, but she's a committed friend. I won't keep her any longer than I need to."

"What sort of business is it, Peter?" Johnny asked. Riley offered him a quick smile to thank him for trying to defuse the situation.

"I'm an entrepreneur. Right now, I've got a couple of things on the go." He fished business cards from his breast pocket and handed one to each of them.

Riley looked at the card, then at her mother. "Do you work for Educoin, Peter? Mom was telling me about investing with them."

Peter leaned forward. "I don't want to take up time answering your questions now. This is a family event. Why don't you come to a presentation?"

"Is that the meeting our mom is helping with on Friday?" Riley nudged her sister. "One of your presentations?"

Peter nodded. "I've also got one tomorrow afternoon. Will you come?"

"I'm busy," Lucy said.

Riley could attend alone. She needed to find out more about the scheme. "I'll try to come."

Their mom clapped her hands. "That's wonderful, Riley. You'll love it." To her other daughter she said, "Are you sure you can't attend, dear? It relates to your wedding gift."

"We don't want it, Mom. Can you just give us the cash?" Alex started to object, but Lucy held up a hand to stop him. "Alex, it's much better if we have the cash."

"If you leave it in Educoin, it will grow at a faster rate than any stock," Peter offered. "And your investment helps to build schools."

"And what happens if it doesn't?" Lucy asked. Then her expression changed, like a light bulb had come on in her brain. "Wait," she said. "How quickly does it grow? We're thinking of putting an offer on a house."

Riley turned to look at her sister. She hadn't mentioned anything about buying a house. Lucy shrugged, looking a little sheepish. But it was clear that Lucy was considering their mom's offer in a new light. And who wouldn't? Extra money toward a down payment? In Vancouver's overpriced housing market? Lucy would be foolish not to jump at such an opportunity. Which was, Riley reminded herself, exactly the point.

"Even just a few weeks will make a difference for your down payment, Lucy," their mother said. "Think about it." She gathered her belongings. "Peter and I need to leave. Riley, I hope to see you tomorrow at the Educoin presentation. And Lucy, please think about my offer."

Riley and Lucy scooted out of the booth to exchange hugs with their mother and shake Peter's hand. As she watched them make their way to the door, Riley promised herself she'd get the straight goods on Educoin, especially now it seemed she'd need to warn Lucy about it, too.

CHAPTER 26

Riley

Outside the restaurant, Lucy and Alex said their goodbyes and left. Riley could tell from her sister's stiff body language that she was uninterested in discussing anything that had happened over dinner. She turned to Johnny. "So that was—"

"Interesting." He wrapped his arm around her waist.

"I'm surprised my mom didn't ask you twenty questions. I think she was too focused on Peter." She inhaled deeply, picking up his clean scent again. "What did you think about him? Did he tell you anything about Educoin?"

"He didn't say much, other than attending a presentation would answer all my questions." He brushed his hand through his hair. "Honestly, I couldn't get a good read on him. I was nervous to meet your mom, and I imagine he was nervous to meet you and Lucy."

The knot in Riley's stomach started to loosen. "I think Lucy felt something was off about him. She got close to being hostile with him a couple of times. I think she actually wanted to confront Mom, but because they argued so much when she was growing up, they don't really know how to speak to each other." She looked up into Johnny's eyes. Did Jack's twinkle the same way?

"Do you want me to go to the presentation with you?" he asked.

"Thank you. I'd like that. Maybe we can get some answers." She squeezed his hand.

"How are you getting home?"

Riley almost invited Johnny to her place for tea, but she needed some alone time to think. "I'll take the bus. It stops right outside my place. Finding a cab would be a challenge."

Johnny put his hand on Riley's back and guided her toward the bus stop. "You're getting cold. Go home, get some rest. We can figure this out."

Wind danced an empty coffee cup in front of Riley's feet. She picked it up and placed it in a garbage can. "Thanks, Johnny. I appreciate it." She gave him a quick kiss when the bus pulled up.

"Good night, Riley. It will be okay."

At home, Riley changed into her pyjamas and pulled out the journal.

Dear Jack,

I think I understand your uncle's request to keep his name out of the investigation. When I realize I've made a mistake, I don't really want everyone else to know.

Riley rested her hand on the journal, noting again how close they were to the end of the book.

What will happen when these pages run out, Jack? How will we continue to communicate?

R.

She snapped the journal closed to avoid scratching out that final sentence.

CHAPTER 27

Jack

Mourners gathered in small groups outside the church. As he approached, he saw the McClure's proprietor and was reminded of his visit to the funeral parlour in relation to a case of missing men who ultimately turned up dead, the first case Riley Finch had assisted him with. And now she was helping him with another. He pulled his wool coat tighter against the damp air.

He nodded as he passed the groups, one or two men frowning when they recognized him. He paused when he saw Melodia Spectre, a woman with whom he'd consulted on his first murder case in the city. She claimed to have psychic powers. Something about her intrigued Winston, though he couldn't identify what. Even seeing her here today, she seemed more familiar to him than having met her just the once before.

When she saw him, a warm smile brightened her face, a contrast with the faces of other mourners. Her eyes took him in from head to toe. "Detective. You have been keeping well. And keeping secrets."

Clamminess dampened his shirt despite the cool November day. "Melodia, it is a pleasure to see you, though I must admit I am surprised to find you here. Did you know Mr. Pierce?"

"I'm familiar with the family," she said, searching the crowd. "You'll forgive me. I was expecting to see your uncle with you."

Had he spoken to her about his relationship with Philpott? Had Philpott himself revealed the connection? They hadn't formally discussed it, but Winston had been under the impression Philpott did not widely share their familial relationship with others, just as he himself avoided divulging that information. "Chief Constable Philpott is meeting me here." Winston pulled his watch from his waistcoat pocket. "I am expecting him shortly." After he snapped the face shut, he slid his hand into his pocket and felt for Ellis's rock.

A look of concern crossed Melodia's face. "Your parents meant no harm when they made their decision about your brother." She placed a hand on his arm.

Winston tilted his head and tried to read her face for meaning. What was she talking about? Before he could ask, she continued with her questions.

"And your golden bird, Detective Winston. Is she keeping well?" A wave of heat prickled Winston's neck. Golden bird. Riley Finch? How could she possibly know about her?

Melodia squeezed Winston's arm. "I have no intention of sharing your secret. Though it is a fascinating one. I am so glad the book has brought you something you value. You can always get another from me when you need it."

He stiffened at her words. Get another? What did this woman know about it? He cast his mind back to when he'd purchased the journal on his arrival in Vancouver. His recollection was more a jumble of sensations than actual memories: a jostling crowd exiting the station, the shouts of cab drivers offering rides to the city's newest inhabitants, the breathless excitement at having arrived mixed with a bone-deep fatigue after the journey. With a few minutes until his uncle was due to collect him, something had drawn him into an alley that housed a small shop. He'd bought the journal on a whim to document his new start, but remembered nothing of the clerk who'd sold it to him.

Had Melodia Spectre been the shop clerk? As if he had voiced his question, she nodded. Her lips turned up in a slight smile. Winston took a deep breath, quickly regaining his composure. He couldn't quite fathom her relationship to the journal, but perhaps she represented the answer to how he and Riley would continue their correspondence. As for her statement about his brother, he would have to puzzle that out another time. The guests were moving indoors.

Winston wanted to secure a spot that would allow him to observe the mourners. He offered Melodia his arm. "Shall we go inside?"

The glow from electric lights reflected off the polished wood panelling, and though the temperature of the room was cool, judging by the crowd outside, the room would soon be stiflingly warm. Winston and Melodia found seats toward the rear of the room, leaving a chair empty for Philpott, who had just appeared in the doorway. Philpott greeted Melodia with a curt nod and slid into his seat as the service began.

"He's one of Pierce's early investors," Philpott whispered when the mayor stood to welcome the crowd.

"Much sadness in that house," Melodia said when Timothy Collins, owner of a shipping company, rose from his seat to speak of his friend. Collins' son had drowned, and his wife had died shortly after that loss.

Winston studied faces as the service wore on. Nearly everyone in the room had some influence in the city, he realized. How had Pierce established relationships with so many of them in the two short years he'd lived in the city? Some he may have known from Ontario, but most must have been new acquaintances. The man's commitment to meeting people must have been unparalleled, decided Winston. None of Pierce's more recent investors—the ones handled by Macey—appeared to be in attendance.

After the ceremony, Winston and Melodia joined Philpott in his carriage. They followed others who made their way to the city's cemetery, a line of carriages snaking through the city. The three sat in silence as they rode. Winston was unwilling to discuss the case in

Melodia's presence, though he wasn't sure whether it was to spare her the details or to preserve Pierce's privacy.

When they alighted, Melodia thanked Philpott for the ride. "It's been as pleasurable as passing time with someone at a funeral can be. Until we meet again," she said to Winston with a wink as she slipped something into the palm of his hand. His pulse quickened at her comment, and he glanced briefly at the card before tucking it into a pocket. Sitting with her had been pleasant. He watched her slip into the crowd, mourners parting, almost instinctively, to make space for her as she approached.

He wondered again what she'd meant when she said his parents had meant no harm. She'd said it just as he'd reached for Ellis's stone. Winston's heart sped up again at the thought: did she know something about Ellis? After all the searching he'd done, did a woman on the west coast of the country who claimed to have second sight possibly hold the key to solving the mystery of his brother's disappearance in Ontario?

Remembering his purpose, Winston caught up to his uncle at the edge of the group of mourners. They were far enough away not to be overheard, yet close enough to be respectful. "Sir," Winston whispered. "Do you think every man here invested with Pierce?"

Philpott raised an eyebrow. "Every man? No. You didn't, did you?"

Winston forced his features to remain passive.

"Of course not," Philpott answered his own question. "But many men here did. And they made money from Pierce. You won't find your murderer here, Jack." His uncle straightened his tie and scanned the crowd.

Winston's gaze fixed on a circle of mourners surrounding a woman. One mourner moved to reveal that the woman was Caroline Pierce. She wore a dark dress more fitting for a widow than the one she'd been wearing when Winston told her Arthur had been murdered. Although a veil obscured her face, he thought he could make out the hint of a smile. Was she amused or simply responding politely to condolences?

Philpott tapped Winston's elbow. His face bore a frown, as if he had swallowed something distasteful. "Best leave the family, Jack. At least for today. They cannot provide you any answers, and I assure you Caroline is not involved. She loved Arthur far too greatly to kill him."

Winston made no comment. Philpott continued to survey the crowd. Winston watched as he spotted the mayor speaking to two men. "Do you see those men, Jack? They're Theodore Bloomington and Charles Steele, the owners of the *Vancouver Voice* and *Western Daily News*. I'm going to say hello." Philpott strode off in their direction.

Winston knew his uncle was right: Caroline Pierce was unlikely to have been involved in her husband's death. Although if she had discovered her husband had defrauded his investors, she would have felt the same emotions as the other suspects—shame at being associated, by name, with a scandal, and anger at being lied to. And as his wife, she had access to him. She could have found someone to carry out her wishes. Clifford, for instance. Did his greater loyalty lie with Mr. or Mrs. Pierce? Winston mentally added the butler to his list of people to look at more closely. He watched Caroline Pierce for another minute. The chief had vouched for her character and devotion with great confidence. Winston was inclined to believe his assessment was valid.

Not far from where Winston stood, Reginald and Abigail Sawyer spoke to another couple, accepting condolences. She held her head high and when she noticed her husband stood half a pace behind her, she reached behind to pull him next to her. Their dynamic was interesting. Winston edged closer to them, but was still too far away to hear. As he watched Mrs. Sawyer, he was reminded of his own mother, who also exuded confidence and grace. Yet he had never seen his mother so openly direct his father the way Mrs. Sawyer did with her husband. Could she have directed him to kill Pierce? Did Reginald have the stomach for such an act?

Winston had agreed not to speak to the family, but that left many others he could approach. He saw Charles Macey and Timothy Collins with their heads together and moved closer to hear their conversation. Was Collins an investor? Winston didn't recall seeing his name among those they'd linked to the ledger. Macey seemed to plead with Collins. Winston sidestepped closer.

"We've had excellent success. You'll consider it?"

"Pierce was due to repay me next week," said Collins. He tried to speak in hushed tones, though the din of the crowd forced him to raise his voice so that Winston could hear.

Macey took no care in the volume of his response. "And I'm sure that will happen, only... Would you consider—?" The man's eyes widened when he saw that Winston was listening.

"Consider what, Mr. Macey?" Winston spoke quietly, forcing the man to lean close to him to hear. "Is there something you have remembered to tell me in relation to Pierce's business? Or his death?"

"Of course not." Macey's cheeks reddened as he sputtered the words. "I was speaking to Mr. Collins about a private matter."

Recognition crossed Collins' face, and he extended his arm. "Detective Winston. Haunting dead men's families again?" Though the words were sharp, the tone was not.

"Simply paying my respects, Mr. Collins."

Collins turned to Macey. "Detective Winston dragged up old history as part of an investigation a few months ago." His mouth formed a pained smile. "Perhaps that is the job of a detective, to dwell on the past? When those left after a death simply want to move on."

Winston's hand searched for the stone his brother had given him. His fingers gripped it and his breathing calmed.

Macey searched Winston's face. "The business with the missing men? You were part of that?" Macey's sudden assertiveness surprised Winston. Was he practising the confidence he'd need to assume a greater role in the business?

"I was. And through it, I had the occasion to meet Mr. Collins." Winston nodded at the businessman.

Collins clapped Winston on his back a little more forcefully than necessary. "I suspect you have one of those unfortunate professions in which no matter how well you are liked, nobody cares to have you around."

Winston ignored the dismissal and forced himself to remain calm. "Even so, I would appreciate hearing what business you had with Mr. Pierce." He focused his gaze on Collins.

"I'm not sure why that is particularly relevant, Detective." Collins' expression was unreadable.

"Arthur Pierce was murdered. I need to figure out by whom. If you refuse to answer my question, I will have to consider you a suspect."

Hearing this, Collins' colour deepened. "I had invested a small sum of money with Arthur. I rarely do business with friends, but Arthur was persuasive."

"I would like to speak to you tomorrow morning, if you're available at ten o'clock."

"You know where to find me, Detective."

Winston turned back to Macey. "And you, Mr. Macey. I have a few more questions for you. Would two o'clock tomorrow afternoon be suitable for you to come to the station?"

Macey hesitated before nodding his agreement. Winston watched as Macey and Collins slipped into the crowd. What more did these men know?

*

WINSTON AND MILLER met outside the bank after the funeral. "I've just been to Sharp's, sir," said Miller.

"Did he make the gloves?"

"Yes. Ten pairs for Arthur Pierce." He counted names on his fingers. "Sawyer, Macey, Clifford, their five other household staff. That leaves two pairs, but Mrs. Pierce said he'd had extra made because of his tendency to misplace his belongings."

Winston nodded. At least they had narrowed the field to two pairs unaccounted for.

"What are we going to ask Mr. Scott, sir?" Constable Miller asked. He stood with his neck arched back, taking in the bank's name chiselled in grand lettering above the entry doors.

"Good question, Thomas. When we spoke with him last, Scott was very interested in reinvesting with Pierce, or whoever takes over the venture. He may know more about the scheme than he originally let on. I'd also like his help in identifying some names on the list. Timothy Collins said at the funeral that he'd invested, but I don't recall his name being on the list."

They were shown to the open door of Owen Scott's office. The man stood when he saw Winston and Miller. "Detective Winston, a pleasure to see you again."

"And you. I am afraid this is not a social call, Mr. Scott." Winston pointed to Miller. "You remember Constable Thomas Miller, an investigator with the constabulary?"

"Yes, of course. How can I help you gentlemen today?"

"We'd like to ask a little more about your knowledge of Arthur Pierce. And his ledger. Your insight was valuable before."

Hearing this, Scott sat back in his chair. "I gave him money. He promised healthy returns. And he delivered on them. I was about to reinvest. I can't tell you more about investing, I'm afraid."

"How did you come to invest with him?"

"Arthur approached me one evening. We had been enjoying a drink at the club, and he leaned toward me. 'Scott,' he'd said, 'you've a mind for business. What would you say to an opportunity?'" Scott looked at the ceiling as he continued. "He said he would double my money. I was skeptical at first. That kind of return is unheard of."

"Yet you invested. And he did as you said."

Scott brought his gaze back to Winston. "I did. And he did. He understood my reluctance and offered to take only a small amount, to prove his claims."

"Did you ever see the mechanism he said you invested in?"

"Only a picture."

From his satchel, Winston pulled the photograph of the miner holding the box. "This one?"

"That's the one. Frank the prospector."

Winston and Miller exchanged glances. "Frank?" Winston asked.

"That's what Pierce called him. The same name as my father, you know." Scott's eyes shone with a memory. "He'd died just before Pierce approached me. Anyway, his investment was sound. And I would like to meet with Frank if I could. He's doing good work."

Winston wrote a note in his notebook, deciphering what Scott had just said. "Mr. Scott, did you encourage anyone else to invest with Pierce?"

Scott stiffened. "I did. How could I not? Though I spoke only to a few men, as Arthur wanted to keep his business small enough so that he could work with each of his clients individually."

"And being one of a few in the know made his investment opportunity special?" Miller asked.

"Exactly." Scott nodded and clasped his hands in front of him on the desk.

Winston searched for the ledger in his satchel. "May I trouble you to review this list again? I have a couple of men I suspect are investors, yet we haven't seen reference to them."

Scott accepted the ledger as Winston slid it toward him. "What are their names?"

Winston gave Scott the names of Timothy Collins and Clifford. Scott looked up when he heard Collins' name. "Timothy introduced me to Pierce. Said they'd met at some event." He thumbed through the ledger. "Here." He pointed to a line. "This is it."

Winston took the ledger and brought it closer so he could read the initials *HTC*. "Is his first name Harold?" Winston was reminded of the man's late son.

"Must be. Looks like he has invested a healthy sum," Scott said. He stood. Winston understood the gesture. They would get no more from this man. The policemen bade Scott goodbye and left the office.

Once they'd crossed the street from the bank, Winston turned to his constable. "Thomas, I think other than his identifying Billy by another name, his answers were unsurprising."

"You do, sir?"

"Yes. In fact, I predict every conversation we have with Pierce's original investors—anyone we speak to from the Gentlemen's Club—will yield much the same: no concerns, minimal details. Tomorrow I meet with Collins, and I have asked Macey to meet us in the afternoon at the station. It is time for him to divulge what he really knows."

CHAPTER 28

Riley

THE EDUCOIN PRESENTATION was scheduled for four o'clock in the afternoon at a hotel just outside the downtown core. Shortly before four, Riley was standing in the hotel lobby waiting for Johnny when her phone pinged.

> *So sorry. Something has come up and I can't meet you. Learn what you can.*

Disappointment rolled through her, but she understood. Johnny's work as a Crown prosecutor could be unpredictable. As she approached the meeting room, a friendly woman wearing a bright blue T-shirt with "Ask me about Educoin" emblazoned on the front greeted her. "Are you here about Educoin?" she asked and handed Riley a notepad bearing the Educoin logo.

"I am. I'll just sit near the back, though, if that's okay."

"It's no problem, but we're asking everyone to leave their bags out here. The room is small, and with bags and coats it gets crowded."

Riley slipped her hand inside to retrieve her phone and her fingers glanced the journal. "I have some important documents."

"I'll be out here keeping an eye on everything."

Riley nodded and eased her phone from her bag.

"No phones, either. They're too distracting."

Something didn't feel quite right about having to leave everything outside the room, but the presentation was about to start, and Riley didn't want to miss anything. She made a show of returning her phone and walked toward the coat rack. She placed her coat on a hanger and tucked her bag into a cubby. As she did, she slid her phone into her front jeans pocket. She snuck a glance at the greeter, but she was engaged with a small group of attendees.

Inside the room, most of the one hundred seats were occupied by people who looked to be in their forties or fifties, Riley guessed. She nodded to the woman seated at the end of the second-to-last row and squeezed past her. She slid her phone under her leg with the recording app running. The woman beside her noticed. "I thought no phones," she whispered, looking at Riley's leg. "Are you a journalist or something?" The woman raised her arm to signal to an organizer.

Heat flooded Riley. "I'm not a journalist. I'm just expecting a call. The woman at the door said it was okay." She waved in the direction of the door. Her mother, who hadn't been there when Riley entered, now stood near the door wearing her "Ask me about Educoin" T-shirt. She waved back, giving her daughter a thumbs-up. The woman beside Riley shrugged and lowered her hand. Riley convinced herself she hadn't lied; she was expecting a call from Johnny after the seminar. What a silly rule to have, anyway.

The lights lowered, and the crowd calmed. When the room was silent, a picture of a smiling woman wearing a cap and gown flashed onto the screen at the front. A voice rang through the speakers. "Education. The key to success." Pictures of other happy graduates flickered on the screen before it faded to black. A picture of a young child dressed in dusty clothes appeared. The setting and doe-eyed child staring into the camera suggested a developing country. "But not everyone has access to that key," the voice-over continued. "At Educoin, we want to give all children that key. First in Kenya, with plans to expand across the globe. Your Educoins make a difference. And they make a difference to you." Now the Educoin currency symbol appeared on the screen. "Turn $1,000 into Educoin and watch your balance grow." The number beside the currency symbol jumped from 00 to 100, then 1,000, then 10,000. Beside it, icons of schools flashed, the number increasing in step with the value of the Educoin. The screen faded to black.

When the lights in the room turned on, Peter stood in front of the screen. "Welcome, all of you. I'm so glad you're joining the Educoin family." He launched into his talk, essentially repeating what had just been shown onscreen. His style was warm and engaging, and the people around Riley nodded and clapped. At well-timed intervals, he stretched his arms out, making a T shape as if seeking to embrace the room, leading to a cheer from the crowd. When he asked how many people had already invested, most hands flew up. When he asked how many people were ready to invest more, Riley raised her hand, caught up in the room's energy. The woman beside her grinned at her.

By the time the presentation ended, Riley was conflicted. It hadn't answered any of her questions, but nobody in the room seemed bothered by the lack of detail. Where was the evidence that these schools really existed? Was Educoin a sham or the real deal? Anyone could make a polished video. It seemed the answers didn't really matter, as long as attendees were making money.

After the session, Riley lingered while her mother patiently answered questions from a group of attendees, her enthusiasm never waning. When the crowd thinned, her mom looked up and smiled at Riley. "What did you think, dear?"

Riley considered her answer. Watching her mother, she saw a confident woman who was at ease and proud of the work she was doing. It reminded her of the day she'd stopped by her mother's school in time to watch her in the final few minutes of class. The students adored her, and her mom's passion for her students was genuine. She'd transferred that same passion into the work—whatever it was—that she was involved with for Educoin.

"I can see you're enjoying yourself, Mom."

Her mom beamed. "Peter has asked me to join him full time. He says I'm a natural."

Riley's mouth went dry. "And quit teaching? But you love your students."

"I do, but this work is just as rewarding." She leaned toward Riley. "Actually, strictly speaking, it's more rewarding."

"What have you told him?" Was it too late to convince her mother to keep her job?

"Nothing, yet. I'm still thinking about it." She checked her watch. "I need to go."

Riley's heart started racing. "Can we speak tomorrow? Before the party?"

A frown crossed her mother's face. "We're holding another seminar, remember? But I'll see if I can work in a visit with you first." She embraced Riley briefly, then turned on her heel. Riley watched her mom stride across the room and wondered what she'd just witnessed.

*

AT HOME, RILEY sat in front of the journal and reread Jack's short note. He'd found where to get more books so that they could continue their correspondence. He didn't yet know for certain that whatever enabled them to communicate would continue in the others, but he said they'd be from the same source, so he was hopeful. A frisson of excitement ran up her spine. An answer at last? She had to trust him. What other option did she have?

Dear Jack,

I'm so pleased that you've found a source for more books. It's a great relief. I'll wait to hear more once you've worked it out.

Today I sat in a seminar where a man promoted what I am almost certain is a fraudulent scheme. I could feel the excitement of the other attendees. I have serious doubts about the validity of this scheme, yet I still found myself almost believing that what he was promoting was possible. He's slick, persuasive. And it's so easy to convince yourself that this time it will work. We all need that kind of hope. Which is what makes what this man is doing so terrible: he is preying on people's hope. He is preying on my mother's hope. So much so, she is considering leaving her job with the school to work on promoting this scheme full time.

She set down her pen, only to pick it back up moments later.

What hope was Arthur Pierce preying on?

Best,

R.

*

THE NEXT MORNING, an email from Henry Pepper, the historian with the Vancouver Stock Exchange, popped up when Riley logged on to her computer at the museum. He'd uncovered some details about the financial laws back in Jack's time. She marvelled at how little detail the few pages contained. The equivalent of a novel's worth of pages of clarification governed such documents in the twenty-first century. Riley thanked Henry for taking the time to send her this information.

Her former classmate who now worked at the university had also replied to her message about Sawyer. The university had none of his records from before it was established in the early twentieth century. Riley replied before returning to her list of points about both Educoin and Jack's case. She sighed as she circled *Where does money go?* on the page.

"What's up?" Nick Blume asked from the doorway. "Research not going as planned?"

Riley flipped the notebook over. "I've run into a snag. You know I've been looking into Reginald Sawyer, the one the parks are named after."

"Yes."

"I'm still sifting through details about him and his business partner. Something occurred to me, though. I know Claire wanted us to focus on past leaders in Vancouver's business history, but what if we also included some frauds? There have been some big ones. Would adding some scandal make the exhibit more interesting?"

Nick tucked a lock of his surfer-blond hair behind his ear. "Yeah, crime is definitely sexy. Do you want to spend some time on the fraud angle? I'll keep working on the successes."

Nick didn't want to lose his opportunity to talk to today's business leaders, though he'd probably end up speaking to their public relations teams rather than the CEOs themselves. "We should make sure Claire agrees, but I think it's stronger with both, especially the modern-day successes. People will connect with those, don't you think?"

"Sounds good," Nick said. "Take today to see where your idea goes." He checked something on his screen. "But if you don't find anything to support it today, we'll need to go back to the original plan. Claire is expecting an update tomorrow. The city has another one hundred and twenty years of history. I'm sure we can find other people who influenced how it became what it is today."

"Thanks, Nick. I'll have something for you before your meeting with Claire. How is your side of the research going?"

Nick pointed at his computer. "Just waiting to hear from a couple of companies."

"What about someone related to Greenpeace? Didn't it start in a pub in Kitsilano? It's not a business, but it certainly has left a mark on the world."

Nick nodded. "That's a great idea, but I think it's outside what Claire is looking for. Let's consider it for a future show." He paused, tilting his head to one side. "You are good at finding stories from the city's early days. You seem to have a real feel for that period. I think it could be an area of focus for you. What do you think?"

Riley swallowed against the sudden dryness in her throat. Nick was suggesting an opportunity to build a reputation as an expert on the city's early history. That would make it easier to help Jack. "Actually, if nothing comes of Sawyer and Pierce, I can think of a few others to look into. Like you said, I'm really getting a feel for the city's early days." The low hum of the overhead lights seemed to grow louder in the silence that followed Riley's burst of assertiveness.

Nick nodded his head slowly. "I get it. Wanting to find your niche. Let's see if we can make this yours, okay?"

Riley smiled inwardly. She'd take it.

CHAPTER 29

Riley

AFTER MAKING NOTES about investment fraud and compiling a short proposal for Claire, Riley had spent the rest of the day thinking about how to convince her mother that she was in trouble. Even if she came up with a strong argument, would her mother listen? Or was she too wrapped up in Educoin? Given that she was considering leaving her teaching job, it seemed she might turn a deaf ear to Riley's warnings.

She put on the kettle and laid different outfits on her bed for the party that evening. Her mom would arrive shortly. Moments like these made her miss having Lucy around more; her sister's chaotic energy hustled things along when she was getting ready to go out. At five past five, the buzzer sounded. Riley opened the door to her mother and Peter.

"Oh. . . Peter. I didn't know you'd be joining us." Riley tried to mask the disappointment in her voice. Confronting her mother would be more difficult with him there.

"I'm just dropping Nancy off. I figured you'd want some mother-daughter time."

Peter's thoughtfulness surprised Riley. Or was it really an attempt to manipulate her disguised as thoughtfulness? She wasn't letting her guard down, no matter how he may turn on the charm.

When her mom squeezed Peter's arm, her hand lingered longer than necessary. "Such a gentleman, this one. I told him I could take the elevator on my own, but he's very protective."

"You're sure I can't offer you some tea, Peter? I just put the kettle on." Riley could play at the manipulation game, as long as she didn't have to lie. Nothing she had just said was untrue.

"Thanks, but I need to get a few things before tonight. I'll be back in an hour. I'm sure that's not long enough, but we have to get to our session." Peter pecked her mom on the cheek, and she leaned in so slightly that Riley wasn't sure she'd really seen it.

"He's right, Mom. An hour isn't long. But maybe we'll have more time tomorrow." Riley closed the door behind her mother and led her to the small living room. In the kitchen, the kettle clicked off, but she ignored it. Her window of time to broach the subject of Educoin was already tight.

They settled into the couch. Riley turned to face her mother, bringing her knees to her chest. Her throat tightened, anticipating the difficult conversation that was coming. "Remind me why you think Peter's event is more important than the party."

"It's another seminar, like the one last night. Peter set up the session a while ago, and it's just unfortunate that it conflicts with the party. We're not missing the whole party. We'll come as soon as we can. I didn't want to cancel because I'd already committed to helping Peter."

"Are you seeing Karen tomorrow before her party?"

"I'm not sure, honey. Peter needs to get back to Victoria. We haven't decided yet which ferry we'll be on."

Riley's heart sank. Her mom was using a lot more "we" than Riley was expecting. And her mom's willingness to miss an important event for one of her oldest friends was out of character. "I thought Peter was just a friend."

Her mom flushed, the colour reaching her ears. "He is a friend. But he could be a very good one. If you know what I mean." She leaned toward her daughter and giggled.

Riley's cheeks burned, and she stared at her mother. They'd never had the type of relationship where they gossiped about Riley's love interests, largely because they'd been few. At least, she hadn't introduced many of them to her parents. She knew her mom had loved her dad deeply. And she didn't mind her mother dating. In fact, she'd encouraged it. Still, she had never imagined her mother being with someone so young.

"I guess, Mom. It's just... He's not what I expected."

"I was surprised too, dear. But who says I can't have a little fun?" She crossed her legs. "Now, let me tell you what's even more fun. Checking my bank balance and seeing so much money." She pulled out her phone and angled it toward Riley. The number on the screen was larger than it had been the day before. Did that money even exist? Surely it wasn't difficult to create a program that appeared to show a growing balance?

"You mentioned yesterday that Peter had asked you to join him full time. Would you really give up teaching?"

Her mom looked away. "I've been thinking about it. I'm investing what I earn now. Peter and I haven't discussed the salary. I'd want to make sure I could continue to add to my Educoin account. I've got several of the other teachers set up as well. They're thrilled."

Riley imagined her mother in the teachers' room gushing about Educoin as she had yesterday to that crowd after Peter's session. It would be hard not to get swept up in her enthusiasm. She shook her head. She needed to get to the point. "Mom, are you sure you know what you're doing?"

Her mother narrowed her eyes. "What I'm doing?" Her voice rose just enough that Riley could tell her mom was trying to remain calm. This was not going well.

"I mean, what do you know about Peter? Has he been working with Educoin long? How many schools have been built? Where is the company actually located? Does Educoin build the schools directly, or do they work with an NGO? I tried to go to their offices, but it's a PO box in a convenience store. I'm sorry, but that doesn't scream 'legitimate operation' to me."

Her mother held up her hands. "The schools are in Africa, Riley. I don't know who builds them, but Peter has shown me pictures. They really are quite sweet looking."

Riley ignored the condescension in her mother's voice as her mother continued.

"Educoin has a network of people like Peter who meet with potential investors." She waved Riley's concern away. "I told you last night. Peter's wife died suddenly. I know you miss your father, but you can't know what it's like to lose your partner. Peter does. He understands." She looked out the window for a breath and brought her gaze back to her daughter. "It is a wonderful opportunity, Riley. I'd hate for you and Lucy to miss out."

"Where did you get the money to invest?"

"I took a reverse mortgage on this place. I haven't signed it over to you and your sister yet."

Riley's stomach dropped. Her mother was gambling with her apartment. "Mom," she pleaded. "You have to get your money back. I think this is a scam. If it is, it's illegal. And you can't tell anyone else to invest. Not your teacher friends, not whoever will be at this event you and Peter are hosting tonight." Riley fought the urge to shake her mother. What was she thinking?

"You were at Peter's seminar. You saw how people were excited."

"That's the thing, Mom. I've been looking into frauds, and this hits all the right notes. Getting a bunch of people excited doesn't make it a legitimate thing. The high returns, the lack of detail. . . I mean, any cryptocurrency is shady by default, isn't it?" She reached for her mother's hand. "Please. Tell Peter you want your money back. Before it's too late."

Her mother jerked her hand back. "Too late for what? It will be too late for you to get in on this if you wait." She stood, scanning Riley's face. "I need to go. Peter will be waiting downstairs."

Judging by how quietly she'd spoken the last sentence, something Riley had said had reached her mother. Was it enough to change her mind?

Riley stood and met her mother's eyes. How could she get through to her? "Mom, I'm serious. This is illegal. You need to get out."

"I don't think I can, dear. Peter says it's best to leave your money in, especially when it's doing well, and. . ." Her mom's eyes scanned the room. "Why would he lie to me?" Her voice wavered.

"Because he needs your money. Please. Just ask for it back. Will you?"

"I'll think about it." She slid into her coat and left without hugging her daughter. Just how much would she think about it?

*

"Really, Riley, it wouldn't take much effort." Lucy's words stung as she scolded Riley in the restaurant's bathroom. Riley looked at her reflection. A low ponytail was no different from how she wore her hair most days. She tugged the ends through her thumb and forefinger. "You weren't around. . ." Riley couldn't help responding.

"I don't live with you any longer, Riley. You'll have to figure out how to do your own hair." She pointed to Riley's satchel at her feet. "And accessorize. Is that your work bag?" Lucy locked eyes with Riley in the bathroom mirror. "What's this really about?"

"It's Mom. I'm worried. And I'm worried about you. Please say you haven't invested in Educoin."

Lucy shook her head. "Alex and I talked about it and decided not to, though it is tempting. He didn't want to have our money tied up in something in case we need it for a down payment." She worked a bobby pin into Riley's hair a little more aggressively than necessary. "But why are you worried?"

Riley explained the red flags Jules had mentioned. "It's not legitimate. It can't be. Plus, his colleague said he'd never heard of Educoin, and he works extensively with cryptocurrencies."

"Maybe that's a good thing? Because there isn't any bad publicity about it?"

"There isn't any publicity about it, period, Lucy. If it's so great, why doesn't anyone know anything about it?"

Lucy bit her lip. "Okay. We're not investing in it, anyway. But what about Mom?"

"I asked her to see if she could get her money out. She didn't seem convinced. Actually, she's thinking about quitting teaching so she can work with Peter."

"What? Wow, she really seems to like him." Lucy shoved another pin into Riley's hair. Riley wasn't entirely certain that Lucy didn't intend to scrape Riley's scalp.

Riley pulled her head away. "Don't you think it's a little convenient that his wife had the same name as Mom?"

"It is definitely a coincidence." She paused. "You looked him up?"

Riley felt her cheeks flush.

"You did! What did you learn?"

"Not much. Like Educoin, there isn't much to Peter's online presence."

"What about his wife? Did you look her up?"

Riley waved her sister's question away. "My hair looks great, Lucy. And you've given me an idea." She hugged her sister and grabbed her bag, ignoring Lucy's frown.

Riley stepped out of the restaurant draped in her coat. She had tried to fit the journal inside her bag, but the pair of flats and the just-in-case sweater she'd brought had taken up too much space. She'd settle for drafting a message to Jack on her phone. Riley pulled it from her bag and shivered under the restaurant's awning.

Jules shouldered the door open and offered her a glass of sparkling wine. "What are you doing out here, Riley? They're serving delicious hors d'oeuvres inside. Should I bring you something?"

Riley shoved the phone inside her bag and accepted the glass. "I just needed a moment, Jules."

Her friend stepped closer. "Everything okay?"

"Yes. I'm fine." She pushed a stray strand of hair back into her new updo.

"I saw you pop out here and wanted to let you know I heard again from my contact who works with cryptocurrency. He has a contact in the NGO sector in Kenya. His contact said they had never heard about Educoin or any schools it funded, but he mentioned that there have been some shady charities that reuse school buildings for photo ops. One week, a set of donors poses in front of a building, and the next week a different set of donors poses in front of the same building. Each set of donors thinks they paid to build it, but it was really some unrelated group that funded it."

Riley sucked air through her teeth. "What happens to the money?"

Jules shrugged. "My colleague said it's unlikely much of it goes to the intended communities. It's a classic scam."

It would be easy enough to convince investors from the other side of the world they were doing good when all they were doing was padding someone else's pocket. "Thanks, Jules. This is helpful." Riley finished her drink, and he held out his hand for the glass.

"Don't be long, Riley. See you in there." He gave her a quick hug and returned inside.

She reached for her phone and typed in the Educoin web address. With a few clicks, she downloaded an image of one of its schools, then went to another site and uploaded it. The reverse-image search confirmed her suspicion: it was a stock image. Why pay for stock images if they were building their own schools?

*

HALF AN HOUR and another glass of sparkling later, Riley watched her mother engaged in a conversation with Jules's mom, Karen Knight. Peter stood at her side. Riley needed to begin before her infusion of bravery wore off. She moved alongside Peter, linked arms with him, and pulled him toward the door, ignoring the protests of the people they jostled.

Once outside, Riley spoke. "I know what you're up to. Let my mother withdraw what she's invested. Don't give her any of the fraudulent gains you've made. Just let her take out what she's put in."

"What?"

"Over here," Riley said, "away from the door." She led him to the opening of an alley near the restaurant, near enough to a street lamp that its puddle of light revealed the confusion on Peter's face. Riley wished she'd thought to bring her coat, but the heat rising within her was keeping her warm enough for now.

Peter held his hands up to defend himself against Riley's words. "What's all this, Riley? Your mom said you were at the seminar yesterday. What did you think?"

"I think you're a fraud. I think you're taking people's money and pretending that they're earning returns."

Peter deflected, like she hadn't just directly accused him. "Do you have questions? I'm happy to answer them."

His smooth salesperson voice only angered her further. She thought about the questions she'd been unable to answer. "How do people convert their money from Educoin back into cash? Who is buying Educoin to drive its value up so quickly? Where are Educoin's offices? Who are its founders?"

"We haven't had anyone want to convert their money back into cash. Why would they want to lose out?"

"If they did, how would they do it?" she pressed, stepping closer to him. They stared at each other and she tapped her foot. "Can you do it?"

"I... I can do it. If they really want."

"Do it for my mother, then. Now."

"It needs to be done at the Educoin offices."

"Where are those, then? I went to the address used to register the company."

His expression turned to stone. "Your mother said you were an excellent researcher."

"I am. And I haven't been able to find any answers to my very reasonable questions." She puffed out her cheeks. "Give my mother's money back to her."

"We can do it tomorrow."

Riley shook her head. "I don't believe you. I think you can do it on your phone. You have a slick app. I'll wait."

They stared at each other for another minute. Riley stepped toward him again, close enough to feel his breath now. "And you're playing with my mother's heart. You'll need to stop doing that, too."

"You don't know what you're talking about."

"I do. I just don't have proof. But I don't need any because the police can get that."

Peter's eyes widened. "If I give your mother her money back, will you still involve the police?"

Riley considered this. "Do it now and I won't tell the police."

Peter pulled out his phone. He tapped a few keys, then showed her the screen. "There. Everything your mother invested has been returned." The account showed a balance, the "gains" her mother's investment had earned. "Do you want her returns deposited as well?"

"No. Just what she invested. And don't let her invest any more."

"I won't. But you'll keep your promise?"

"I won't tell the police," Riley repeated.

"But I will," Johnny said, stepping out from the shadows.

CHAPTER 30

Jack

Timothy Collins greeted Winston with the same smile he'd offered at the funeral. "How nice to see you again so soon, Detective." This time, his delivery was more genuine. He showed Winston and Miller into his office in the building that housed his shipping company. Much of the space was taken up by an overly large desk that occupied the centre of the room.

"I don't expect we will take long to ask our questions, Mr. Collins. This is a murder investigation, and we are duty bound to gather information no matter where it leads us. How long had you invested with Pierce?"

Collins paled at Winston's explanation. "Murder? You mentioned this at the funeral, but I didn't think it proper to ask you more about it in that setting. You're certain?"

Winston nodded. "The medical examiner has confirmed it, yes. You're surprised?"

"Caroline revealed nothing. In fact, I found her mood to be a trifle more jovial than I would expect from a widow. But who are we to say how a person grieves?"

Winston exchanged a quick glance with Miller. Not for the first time, he reconsidered Mrs. Pierce: did her odd behaviour express guilt rather than grief? Winston brought his attention immediately back to the man seated in front of him. Collins had experience with grief, as Melodia had alluded to at the funeral. First his son's drowning and then his wife's death shortly afterward. He'd been deeply affected by both losses.

"As you say, grief affects us all differently, Mr. Collins." Winston allowed a moment of silence before continuing. He softened his tone. "Can you tell me a little about your business with Arthur Pierce?"

"I invested with him a couple of years ago."

"Did you approach him?" Winston asked, ready to record Collins' response in his notebook.

"He approached me. In fact, it took some convincing on his part. My son had just died, and I was still mourning him."

"Was Pierce insensitive? Asking you to get involved when you were grieving?" Miller asked.

Collins closed his eyes as he considered Miller's question. "Quite the opposite. He was respectful. Told me I could wait until I was ready."

"But he approached you repeatedly?" Miller pressed.

"He didn't want me to lose out on the opportunity. He had found a miner who had a remarkable sense of the land."

"Do you remember his name? The miner?" Winston asked.

Collins pressed his lips together. "Harry. I thought it remarkable at the time that the miner had such a similar name to my son's."

Winston noted the name as he found the photograph of Billy. "Is this the man you invested in?"

"I don't know. I have never seen that photograph before. I had the impression Harry was younger, but I didn't think to ask."

"What was the result of the investment?" Winston asked.

Wood scraped against wood as Collins pushed his chair back and crossed one leg over the other. "It did well. Very well. I made my money back, and then some, within a few months. Faster than I'd been expecting."

Winston recalled the conversation he'd overheard between Macey and Collins. "Yet you didn't reinvest?"

"My wife died." Collins leaned forward again, resting his hands on the desk with his fingers interlaced. He lowered his head, and his next words were muffled. "It was too much."

The admission hung in the air. Winston sensed Miller stiffen, likely unsure how to react or what to say. Collins still wore a wedding band, Winston noticed. He evidently loved her deeply, and such a loss so soon after his son's death would surely have caused him considerable pain. "I'm sorry to cause you to think of that time, Mr. Collins."

Collins looked up, his eyes glistening. "I think of it daily. When they died, I focused only on this business. I withdrew from everything, from everyone else."

"Did you encourage others to invest with Pierce?" Miller asked.

Winston nodded encouragement at Miller. Again, his question was what he would have asked and would steer Collins from reliving such a difficult time.

Collins looked at the policemen. His expression was one of relief, and he sat back in his chair again. "If Pierce's investments came up in conversation, I spoke of my experience, as anyone would. I saw no reason not to."

"Do you remember with whom you spoke?" Winston asked.

"I must have told Owen Scott at the bank, as he handles my finances. As I said, I had no concerns mentioning how Pierce had made good on his promise to me. Can I help you with anything else?"

Winston recognized the question as the interview's conclusion. "That's it for now, Mr. Collins." He gestured to Miller with a raised finger. They would get nothing more from Collins, and it was nearing the time when they were expecting to meet Macey at the station.

*

Thirty minutes after Charles Macey had agreed to arrive at the station, Winston squeezed his eyes shut. Macey was either incredibly rude or had no intention of showing up. Winston's face pricked with heat as he thought of his first murder investigation. Had he let another suspect evade him? The prospect of failure loomed like a darkening cloud. He slammed his hand into the desk. Miller opened his mouth and Winston shook his head. His stare was enough to silence whatever Miller had been about to say. With a gruff flick of his hand, Winston motioned for Miller to follow him. He was not going to let anyone else get away.

*

Macey kept his face emotionless when he opened the door to AP Investments and found Winston and Miller.

"I'm sure you can guess why we're here," Winston said as they entered the office. He had used the journey there to calm down, though the back of his neck was still warm.

Macey nodded and waited for them to settle. "I think you were expecting to see me earlier, Detective." He avoided looking directly at Winston as he spoke. "I mixed up the time," he stammered. "And I thought it better that I be here to go through the files again. And in case any other investors come to the office."

Winston pushed away the frustration he'd felt at the station. He was speaking to Macey now, albeit a few minutes later than he'd expected to do so.

"I'd like you to clear up some questions for me, particularly about this man." Winston produced the image of the miner from within his notebook. "I've heard him referred to variously as Billy, Frank, and Harry. How is it this man has so many names?" He pushed the photograph toward Macey.

Macey stared at the picture on the desk, his ears reddening. He stole a glance at Winston and squirmed. "He doesn't exist." Sawyer had been truthful about that.

Winston and Miller leaned forward to hear Macey speak.

"Mr. Pierce asked me to find out information about our potential investors. The ones like Mr. Collins and Mr. Scott. I learned the names of people important to them and gave that information to Mr. Pierce."

"Why?" asked Miller.

"Mr. Pierce said that investors needed to relate to the investment. If they were investing in someone who had the same name as their father, for instance, that would strike a sentimental note for them, encourage them to feel good about the investment."

"Did you not think it manipulative to use information about these men to convince them to invest with Pierce?"

Macey looked away, his cheeks reddening.

"Is that legal, sir?" Miller wasn't trying to hide the wonder in his voice.

Macey held up his hands. "We were just helping them reach a decision they wanted to reach. That's what Mr. Pierce told me."

"Does Mr. Sawyer know that these methods were used?" asked Winston. "And what about the smaller investors? The ones from the mill?"

Macey shook his head. "Mr. Sawyer was not involved in this. Once Mr. Pierce got more investors, there were too many for me to track down this kind of information about each of them. But they weren't as reluctant to invest, which is why Mr. Pierce gave them to me to handle." He looked between Winston and Miller. "It was just those first investors. I didn't think it was wrong. Was it?" His voice reached a higher pitch.

Winston leaned forward. "Wrong, as in illegal? Perhaps not. Ethical? Certainly not. You used a fabrication to trick men into investing their money."

"But they made more money," Macey whined. "Mr. Pierce didn't want them to miss out."

Winston tapped his notebook with his pencil. "Did one man find out he'd been manipulated, Mr. Macey? Did one come here? Angry because of the information you used?"

"Not that I know of. None of them said anything to me, at least," Macey replied, staring at his desk again.

"But if one did, what would he have done?" Miller asked. "Can you tell us who else you found information about?"

Macey lifted his head, the colour now drained from his cheeks. "Do you think one of them killed Mr. Pierce?"

"Their names, please." Winston said. He positioned his pencil to note them. His heart dropped when Macey recited his list and confirmed what he and Miller already suspected.

CHAPTER 31

Jack

Winston and Miller sat across from each other at the station. The photograph of the miner rested on top of the ledger. "I wonder if this man knew how Pierce was going to use him?"

"You think we need to find him, sir?" Miller asked.

"I don't think so. I wouldn't know where to start. We almost certainly do not have his name. We have other leads that will be more fruitful."

Miller set down his tea. "If Pierce was just using the photograph to find investors, who was doing the prospecting? Who was finding the gold?"

Winston sipped from his mug. "Was there any gold, Thomas? I mean, Pierce may have done nothing more than take men's money." He flipped his notebook to the page where he'd written the names Macey had given him. "If one of these men realized he'd been manipulated into investing, and that by talking about his experience he was helping Pierce manipulate others. . ." He held his thumb over a name as if that removed it from the list, though he knew he couldn't avoid speaking to his uncle much longer. "Would that have driven him to murder?" They considered the question in the silence that followed.

"What about the ledger? Can we decipher anything more?" Winston held the book by its corner.

"Can I look at it again?" Miller reached across the table.

Winston placed the book in his outstretched hand. Within a minute, Miller tapped his finger on a page toward the end of the book.

Winston leaned forward. "What is it?"

"Remember these notations that Owen Scott couldn't identify?"

"The ones he said aren't account numbers?" Miller had the ledger open to the later pages with three columns of entries.

"Right." Miller pushed his index finger onto the page to cover one set of letters. "What if this is the account number?"

"And the letters?" Winston's pulse quickened. "The account holder?"

"Sir, can you read them out to me?" Miller asked as he turned to a fresh page in his notebook.

Winston read the entries aloud. Unlike the first pages of the ledger, the format of these entries was inconsistent. Some had five digits, while others had only three or four. One letter pair—*BW*—appeared repeatedly, sandwiched between strings of numbers and followed by another letter pair at the end.

1702BW501AS
2403BW763AR
2803BW629CP
1404BW501AS
0805BW763AR
1205BW629CP

As he read the numbers, a piece of the puzzle fell into place. "Let's look at this as different information." Winston pointed to an entry in the first column on the page. "We have the investor entries. They each appear with two letters and the amount they invested. The entries in the second column show the return the original investors realized—or were told they had realized—and when. We can read them now, thanks to Owen Scott's help."

Miller nodded. "And these," he said, pointing to the third column, "the ones with letters and numbers all have *BW*. And the same number sequences." His voice rose in pitch. A flutter in Winston's stomach matched Miller's mounting excitement.

"So what could that represent?"

"The bank?"

Winston shook his head. "No banks have those initials."

"They do. Western Bank."

Winston sucked air through his teeth. Where Owen Scott worked. "He reversed the letters. But why only for the bank?"

Miller slid his finger back and forth, moving a sheet of paper across the desk as he did. The scratching echoed in Winston's ears until he dropped a finger onto the page to stop its motion.

"Sorry," Miller muttered. "There are only a few banks to choose from. Maybe he just wanted to make it harder for anyone who might find the ledger. Like us."

The idea was sound. Pierce had hidden the ledger and used initials rather than names in his records. Why wouldn't he have used another method to obscure this piece of information? "Why didn't Scott recognize the account number?"

"It's surrounded by this other information. See? The first numbers could be dates, the next, the account numbers at the bank..." Miller sighed. "And these other letters..."

1702BW501AS

"I see it now. The seventeenth of February. Western Bank, account 501." Winston ran his finger down the page. The pattern was consistent. He could see there were three accounts: BW501AS, BW763AR, BW629CP. What about the final letters?

"Another set of initials?" Miller offered.

"Could they be reversed, as he'd done elsewhere?"

Miller spun the ledger to face Winston. "I suppose. But his sister-in-law has these initials, *AS*. And he didn't obscure the initials of his investors. Could this be the account holder?" He drew the words out slowly, as if testing the idea. "But women can't hold bank accounts."

"They can, but they need their husband's signature." Winston noted the other initials. *CP*. Caroline Pierce. *AR*. Abigail Sawyer again? He thumbed through his notebook. Someone had mentioned the sisters' family name. He found the name Rallston among notes from an interview with Clifford. Winston stood and paced the room. "If Pierce was hiding money, he could have posed as Mrs. Sawyer's husband. People have described him as charming. Pierce may have convinced her to help without her realizing anything was amiss." He crossed to the board where they'd posted names of the people connected to the case. He felt an expansion in his chest, a rush of energy. "And if Sawyer found out, would he lash out at Pierce?"

"Can we interview them separately?" Miller asked.

"We should visit the bank first, see if we can look at their account information before we bring them in." He pulled his watch from his pocket. "We have time to get there before it closes. Let's end this day with success."

*

As they arrived at the bank, Miller leaned close to Winston. "Do you suppose we'll see Mr. Scott here, sir?"

"Yes, it's possible."

"What will you tell him if he asks why you've returned?"

"He will assume it is for this case. It will be better if we can deal with someone else." Winston handed some coins to the cab driver. In his haste to leave the station, Winston had forgotten his coat. Never was he more thankful that his occupation did not require that he sit exposed to the elements all day, like this poor fellow.

The man sitting at the reception desk raised his eyebrows upon seeing Winston and Miller so late in the day. "We wish to speak to someone about some of your account holders. It's related to a police investigation, so we would appreciate your prompt response," said Winston.

The man checked his watch and frowned. "I can't guarantee anyone who could assist you will be here still. The bank will be closed shortly."

"I understand, but this is for a police investigation." Winston leaned closer to the man. "I wouldn't want to close operations while we search for the information ourselves."

The man frowned again. "I'll find you someone presently."

He scurried down the hall. When he returned, he was followed by a tall man who seemed to be worn by his suit rather than the other way around. He extended his hand as he approached. "I'm Andrew Setter, president of Western Bank. You are with the police?"

Winston produced his warrant card. "I'm Detective Winston and this is Constable Miller. We are investigating a crime, and your bank may have some information we need."

"I understand." With a sweeping gesture, he invited Miller and Winston to proceed ahead of him. "We can speak in my office," he said, indicating the door at the end of the same hall where Owen Scott's office was located. Scott's door was closed.

Setter's space contained a large wooden desk, its surface free of papers or writing implements. Two overstuffed chairs sat atop a rug, facing the desk and the window behind it. A pair of maps hung on the walls on either side of the desk, above low bookshelves. Toward the back of the office sat six wooden chairs around a small round table. "Perhaps we should sit there," said Setter, pointing at the table. When everyone had settled, Setter asked, "How can I help you?"

"Mr. Setter, as part of an investigation, we need to look at the accounts of one or two of your customers," said Winston.

"You're certain they are customers here?"

"Not entirely, but your bank has a reputation of handling the funds of the city's more prominent residents." Winston made a show of looking around the office. "I assume this reputation is well earned?"

Setter's chest expanded as he nodded. "Your assumption is correct, Detective. I will help as much as I can, but I must warn you that our clients expect our discretion."

"That may be, Mr. Setter, but the law does not."

"About whom do you seek information?" Setter drew out the words.

"Reginald Sawyer and Arthur Pierce."

Setter drew in his breath sharply and leaned back. "Is this related to Mr. Pierce's death?"

Winston remained silent.

"Very well." Setter stood. "I will have to see if a clerk is available to retrieve the files. Please wait here."

Winston motioned for Miller to stand. "I'd prefer if you brought Constable Miller along. This is not a comment on your own work. It is simply standard procedure. I've learned to take every precaution to ensure that information doesn't go astray."

Setter furrowed his brow, but nodded.

As Miller rose, he leaned toward Winston. "Sir, what about accounts in the women's names?"

"Mr. Setter, can you also check to see whether there are any accounts in the name Caroline Rallston or Caroline Pierce?" asked Winston.

"Perhaps it would be better if we went together to the customer files if you're going to ask about more than one or two."

Winston stood. "An excellent idea, Mr. Setter. Please show us the way." He exchanged a glance with Miller and winked. They fell behind Setter as he led the way to the customer file room.

CHAPTER 32

Jack

WESTERN BANK KEPT customer files in locked cabinets inside a basement room, each labelled with the first letters of the files within. The clerk's shoulders fell when he saw Andrew Setter followed by Detective Winston, and fear flashed across his face when he saw Constable Miller in his uniform.

Sensing the man's concern, Winston extended his hand. "You're not in any trouble."

The man looked at Setter before slowly extending his arm.

After Winston explained their purpose, the man slid a paper toward Mr. Setter, who pushed it toward Winston. "Please write the names of the files you wish to see. Mr. Jin will look them up."

"How many files do you need?" Mr. Jin asked. By his soft accent, Winston guessed he had arrived in the country even before his countrymen had arrived to work on the railroad.

"I don't know, Mr. Jin." Winston looked at the clerk. "We will try to be as quick as we can, though taking longer and being more thorough today will save you time tomorrow. We appreciate your accommodating us despite the late hour."

Setter cleared his throat and frowned at Winston.

Winston turned to Andrew Setter, gesturing toward the door. "Thank you for arranging this, Mr. Setter. Mr. Jin can look after us. We'll make sure everything is returned when we finish."

Setter's lips formed a thin line, and he pulled Winston aside. "I know many others are not comfortable having a Chinese man in their office, but he works hard, and I don't have to pay him as much as I would other men. Still, do keep an eye on him."

Winston clenched his jaw as he weighed whether to respond to or ignore Setter's distasteful comments. It pained him to say nothing, but he needed Setter's co-operation. He took a sideways glance at Mr. Jin, who busied himself and seemed not to have overheard.

Setter slid his fingers into his pocket and pulled out his watch. The slowness of his movements suggested he was reconsidering whether to leave the basement. "I am expected at an engagement and wouldn't want to be late." He gave Winston a knowing look before leaving.

After Setter's footsteps had faded, Winston smiled at Jin and motioned for him to continue. "I appreciate your help with this, Mr. Jin. We are looking only for a few names. Should there be others, we will let you know, of course. Can we review the files here?"

"That would be preferable, yes. Files aren't meant to leave this room without a record of their departure."

"You would know if a file were missing?" Miller asked. Winston appreciated that the constable had kept any note of accusation from his tone.

Jin squared his shoulders. "Has someone said a file is missing? It can't be. We take good care here."

Winston cast his gaze around the room. "I've no doubt you do, Mr. Jin. Constable Miller isn't asking about a specific missing file, only inquiring whether you would know if a file were missing."

The clerk scratched behind his ear. "I would only know if I counted them all. Which we do a few times each year. We've never had a file go missing."

Satisfied, Winston smiled. Rather than rewrite the names he needed on the paper Mr. Jin had provided, Winston opened his notebook and showed Jin a page with a list of names: Reginald Sawyer, Arthur Pierce, Caroline Pierce, Caroline Rallston, Abigail Sawyer, and Abigail Rallston. "Now, are you able to retrieve any files with these names?"

Jin walked to the file cabinets and, within minutes, returned to the table with a stack of folders. He pointed at Winston's notebook. "We have accounts for some of these names." Jin pushed the folders at Winston. "You may look."

Winston opened the first one to find two sheets of paper and moved to allow Miller to look over his shoulder. The first page contained details about when an account for Caroline Pierce was opened and a signature he recognized from other documents as belonging to Arthur Pierce. The second contained a summary of deposits into the account. "Were there no withdrawals from this account?" Winston held the document in the air until Jin plucked it from him.

Jin ran his finger down the sheet. "It appears not. Mrs. Pierce was a wealthy woman, according to this. Her account once had fourteen thousand dollars in it, but it is nearly empty now."

Beside Winston, Miller pushed air through pursed lips. "Is there any record of where the money came from? How it was deposited?" He narrowed his eyes and focused on Jin.

"The information we have is what is in the folder. If it's not here, it doesn't exist."

"Good question, Miller," said Winston, turning to Jin. "Thank you. We may need to speak to the clerk who accepted the money. Can you tell from this who that was?"

Jin flipped the page over and extended his finger, pointing to a column of letters. "Each clerk writes his initials when the transaction is complete. Mr. Setter will have to help you find the clerk."

"Thank you, Mr. Jin." Winston leaned forward. "Now, what about the other files you found?"

The second file Jin produced contained information about Abigail Sawyer's accounts. "This is another wealthy woman. Thirteen thousand at one point for her."

Winston smirked. Abigail Sawyer might not be happy about her sister's account being larger. Was it enough to provoke jealousy? "And what about the third one? Who is that for?"

Jin opened the folder. "This account is in the name of Abigail Rallston. It currently has five thousand dollars, most of which looks like someone deposited recently, though the account has been open for over a year."

"Anything for Caroline Rallston?"

Jin shook his head.

Winston considered what that might mean. Had Pierce not had an opportunity to use that name? Which of the sisters was involved with this? Or were they both involved? "Were the other deposits also recent, Mr. Jin? For Caroline Pierce and Abigail Sawyer?" Miller placed the pages beside each other to compare their contents.

The clerk reviewed the files. "Deposits in both accounts within the last month."

"The other accounts, Mr. Jin? Mr. Pierce? Mr. Sawyer?"

Jin pointed to another folder. "The account here for Mr. Pierce. He moved money into Abigail Rallston's account two weeks ago."

"You can tell that he moved the money into her account?"

The clerk's brow furrowed as he examined the documents. "I can see the same amount left his account as was put into her account. He would have had to arrange for the transfer. It wouldn't have happened without his authorization." He pointed to the page. "A similar thing has happened twice before. Money moved from Mr. Pierce's account, then into the Rallston one."

"And what happened the other times?"

"Money was removed from the Rallston account. This doesn't say it was deposited into another account, so it must have been withdrawn as banknotes."

"Would Abigail Rallston have needed to be present to authorize the deposit or the withdrawals?"

Jin shook his head. "No, there isn't any need to tell her when depositing money. Because Mr. Pierce signed to open the account, he could have withdrawn the money without her being present."

"Thank you, Mr. Jin." Winston made a few last notes of amounts, dates, and account names in his notebook. "May I also write down these initials? I'll return to speak with this clerk." The same initials—*SM*—appeared on each page. "Would depositing these amounts trigger any concern?"

Jin shook his head. "I don't know, Detective Winston. Mr. Setter may be able to answer you. I only see the documents after we accept the money."

Miller pointed at the pages. "How does it work? The money is handled upstairs, and the files are down here?"

"It's true." Jin pointed to a pair of pneumatic tubes. "I receive a request for a document in this one and send the information back in the other. The files rarely leave this room, though."

"So you add to the files when a transaction takes place?"

Jin nodded. "Yes. I record the information."

"And you never see the actual customers?"

"There is no need. The upstairs clerk takes the information and sends it to me. Our customers find the service is faster. It was Mr. Setter's solution."

"Very clever," said Winston, rubbing his moustache. "I think we have everything we need, Mr. Jin. I appreciate your time."

"It was a pleasure, Detective."

The policemen waited for Mr. Jin to return the files before following him to the bank's exit, where they shook hands.

Night had settled into the city, and the wind was up. "Where to now, sir?" Miller asked outside the bank.

A chill ran through Winston. "I need my coat before anything else, Miller. I'll never forget it again. You should get home. We'll pick up tomorrow."

Miller thanked Winston and set off toward home. Winston hailed a cab to take him back to the station. On the way, he turned over in his mind what they'd learned at the bank. Pierce had deposited a large sum from his account into one in his sister-in-law's family name two weeks before he died. Why?

When he entered the station, Winston nodded to the desk clerk in response to the man's brief smile. "Chief's looking for you, Jack."

"Thanks. I'll see him now." Winston steeled himself for the conversation.

CHAPTER 33

Jack

CHIEF CONSTABLE PHILPOTT responded to Winston's knock by calling him to enter. Winston gave his uncle a summary of the day, including what he'd learned at the bank. With his elbows resting on the desk and hands steepled, Philpott grew increasingly pale as he listened. "What else have you learned, Jack?" Philpott barely whispered the question.

Seeing his uncle's face, Winston leaned forward. "How involved are you in this, Uncle Lawrence?"

Philpott swallowed and lowered his eyes. "I told you I invested with him. What I have not told you is that I made some introductions for him. And in exchange for those introductions, Pierce paid me a small amount. To thank me."

No man seemed to have been immune to Pierce's enticements. Setting aside his role as investigator for a moment, Winston reached across Philpott's desk and placed his hand on his uncle's arm. "I don't think you should be embarrassed." He wouldn't have attempted the affectionate act with anyone other than the man he had known his entire life. Still, Philpott brushed Winston's hand away.

Why was he so despondent? "How much did you lose?" Winston asked, his voice subdued. He thought of the names Pierce had used for the miner, such a blatant play on their emotions to nudge the men to invest. "By all accounts, Pierce was full of charm, which made it easy for people to trust him. And they wanted the success he promised." He eased himself back into his chair.

"I lost more than I should have, but not so much as to ruin me. Can you keep my name from the case file?" Colour rose in Philpott's cheeks. "I was motivated by his earlier successes." He stroked his full moustache. "But the other men I encouraged. They will have lost because of me." The chief seemed to be torn between sadness and shame.

"You couldn't have known, Uncle."

"Still." He puffed out his chest. "I'm the chief of police, and I can't be seen making this kind of mistake." Philpott focused his gaze on his nephew. Fresh pain flashed across his face. "He told me the miner I was funding was named Ellis."

Sour bile rose in Winston's throat as his brain scrambled to absorb this. The man in the picture Pierce used was too old to be his brother. Pierce had fabricated the story of the miner and his expedition. He had used Winston's missing brother's name to convince Philpott to invest. Still, the name sent a shock through Winston. "Did you think it was Ellis? Did you try to see him?"

Philpott's face fell. "I knew it wasn't possible."

Winston bit the inside of his lip. His uncle wouldn't have known about Pierce's deceit about the miner. "How did you know it wasn't possible, Uncle?"

Philpott drew a long breath. He reached his hand across the desk and took hold of Winston's. "Ellis is dead, son."

Had he been standing, Winston would have collapsed with the impact of his uncle's words. Instead, he sank into the chair as if being crushed by a weight. "Dead?" His voice was barely audible against the shattering of his heart. He had long known there was a possibility that his brother had met with misadventure. "When. . . How?"

Philpott brushed his hand across his face. "This really isn't for me to share with you, Jack. Your parents. . . Your mother. . . She couldn't bring herself to accept it. Your father felt it better to tell everyone. . ." He lowered his eyes. "Your parents told everyone he'd run away. . ."

"Why?" What was Philpott saying? Winston tried to piece together his memory of when Ellis had disappeared. He shoved his hand into his pocket and clasped the rock.

"He killed himself."

Winston's fingers gripped the stone as if to crush it. "No," he said, quietly at first. "No!" This time the word came out with such force that Philpott, who had come around from behind the desk to kneel beside his nephew, gripped the chair to steady himself.

Melodia's words echoed in Winston's mind. "Your parents meant no harm," she'd said.

Philpott pulled Winston's head to rest it against his body, comforting him as one does a child. "I'm sorry. You were young. And you saw the reaction when people thought Pierce had killed himself."

"My family covered up my brother's death. Why? To avoid shame?" Winston's rage pounded against his chest. He pushed away from Philpott, hardly able to look at his uncle. "How could you? How could any of you? I've been searching for him. And all the while, you knew." His body shook as he spat the words. "How could you?" he repeated.

"I'm sorry."

The apology snapped a switch in Winston. He stood. "How did Pierce know?"

"That Ellis was dead? He couldn't have. But it sounds like he did a remarkable job of using the names of people close to his investors to make the opportunity more appealing."

Winston nodded. "That is exactly what he did." To his own ears, his voice sounded disembodied, like it floated up near the ceiling. "I can't be here," he said. "I need to go home."

Jack Winston left his uncle without another word.

*

Winston crossed the threshold of Mrs. Bradley's house replaying his conversation with Philpott in his mind. Ellis had killed himself. His family had lied to him. He clutched his stomach as Philpott's words echoed again. "Your father felt it better," and "Your mother couldn't bring herself to accept it." How could they be so selfish? Let him continue in his fruitless search? And Uncle Lawrence. How could he have kept such a secret?

Mrs. Bradley stood at the bottom of the stairs as Winston climbed toward his sanctuary. He didn't turn when she called his name. Whatever she was asking could be answered another time. His fingers fumbled with the key at his lock, dropping it twice before jamming it into the hole.

Once inside, he leaned against the door and surveyed his belongings in the main sitting room. Above his writing desk, a photograph of his family, taken the day Ellis had given him the rock, taunted him. With two long strides, he crossed to the wall and pulled the frame from its hook. Ellis was too far from the camera to make out the emotion on his face, but Winston recalled his brother's smile, warm and welcoming. He clasped the picture against his chest. How was it possible that he killed himself only a few days later? Winston pushed a tear from his eye and returned the frame with the image facing the wall.

He poured himself a measure of whisky, sat at his desk, and pulled out a sheet of paper.

Dear Mother,

That I am writing this after learning of Ellis's death from Uncle Lawrence fifteen years after it happened—

He struck a line through the sentence and pulled out a fresh sheet of paper.

How could you?

He could never send that. He shook his head and pulled out another piece of paper.

> *Do you ever think about Ellis? Or have you pushed your memories of him aside in the same way that you pushed aside the truth about his death? Did you ever think about telling me the truth when I spoke of going to search for him? When I pored over maps, trying to piece together where he might have gone? What might have happened to him?*

His family had hidden the truth for so long. Did he really think they would reveal their motivations now?

My heart hurts.

Winston reread the words, then crumpled the page and tossed it beside the others in the fire grate. He would never confront his parents. As with so much, the words would remain unspoken.

He hung his head in his hands and sobbed.

※

WINSTON LIFTED HIS head from his writing desk and rubbed his aching neck. What had caused him to stir? He listened for a few moments before he heard it: a quiet knock on his door. He waited until the sound of footsteps receded down the hallway. With a gentle twist of the knob, he cracked the door open enough to see a cup of tea and a roll arranged on a tray. His stomach turned at the smell as his heart warmed at the gesture. He set the tray inside the door and cast his gaze back to where he'd been sleeping.

His furry tongue sucked up the moisture in his mouth. An empty bottle stood beside where his head had been, confirming the source of his fuzziness. The balls of paper in the grate reminded him of the reason for it. Ellis. His parents.

He struck a match and set a ball alight. Destroying that evidence of his night felt important, like turning the page. If only he could burn away the memory of what he'd learned.

With a pounding head, he pulled the journal from his satchel and prepared to pour his feelings onto the page. What would Riley think when she read about Ellis? He warmed up by updating her on Arthur Pierce.

Dear Riley,

Yesterday proved to be a breakthrough in our case. Thomas and I spoke with a few of Pierce's early investors. Each of them confirmed Pierce presented the investment as an opportunity to support a mining expedition led by a specific miner. For each investor, Pierce assigned the miner a name that held significance for them. Often this was their father, but not always. He appealed to their emotions to induce them to invest.

We also discovered that the bank has accounts in the names of Abigail Sawyer, Caroline Pierce, and Abigail Rallston—the sisters' maiden name—and I think this is where Arthur Pierce kept his money, the money he'd taken from investors. I will return to the bank tomorrow to confirm this.

Yet, even with this new information, I am, as yet, still unable to identify who killed him.

He paused and rested his hand on the journal. What could he tell her about his family? How he wasn't sure whether he could continue to work for his uncle? Or continue to work as a detective? This lie had been in front of him for years and he had had no idea. Winston gripped his pen tighter and pushed the thoughts aside. He was a good detective. His family's lies didn't change that. He wrote a brief explanation of what his uncle had told him about Ellis. As the pen moved along the page, his mind calmed.

On a personal note, I learned yesterday that my family has been lying about my brother's death for the past fifteen years. They deceived me, convincing me he'd run away, simply vanished, when in fact he'd taken his own life.

I see parallels in what my family has done with how Pierce gained trust. So much importance is placed on appearances. Pierce gave the appearance of being successful, which helped people believe in him. He invented a miner using names that carried emotional weight for each investor, prompting them to trust the venture. And my family, overly concerned with appearances, manufactured a story to preserve the illusion of perfection my mother has worked so hard to maintain among her society friends. I can't believe my father went along with the deceit willingly. I am most disappointed in my uncle, who, as a policeman, represents honesty. How will I trust him now?

I am in a difficult position: I am forced to continue with my family's lie lest I subject my parents to the shame they dread, or muddy the reputation of my uncle—and the police—by revealing it. Without my knowledge or consent, they have made me a party to this and given me no option but to continue in this lie.

It's been a trying day. I trust you are well.

Jack

Winston set the pen down and hung his head in his hands. He listened to his heartbeat drum in his ears, a steadying rhythm. After a few moments, he raised his head. Enough.

He pushed away from the desk and prepared himself for the day. The tea the maid had brought up had cooled. He left it and managed a few bites of the bun before his stomach soured. The plate clanged against the desk as he set it down roughly, lurching to the bathroom. He glimpsed his sallow reflection as he steadied himself. What would Ellis have looked like at Winston's age? His knuckles whitened as he grasped the door frame. The wave of grief that washed over him left him drained. He shook his head. Focus. He would focus on Pierce.

A quick wash refreshed Winston. He reached for the journal, preparing to return it to his satchel. He flushed at the sight of Riley's handwriting.

Dear Jack,

I cannot express the pain I feel for you after reading your note. I can only imagine how you feel after learning the truth about your brother. It is so disappointing to realize that your parents are not as infallible as you thought and

> to learn such a sad truth about someone you held dear. I'm sorry to hear of your loss, and that you couldn't mourn him when he died. You may feel too raw right now, but in time, you may find a way to understand their decision. What I'm saying is, don't let this drive you further away from your family. We need family. And they need us.

He traced *family* with his finger. She was right: he knew he would eventually forgive his parents. But not yet.

> The information you shared about the bank accounts sounds promising. Do you think the same woman opened the accounts using different names? Was it more likely Arthur Pierce was working with his wife or his sister-in-law?
>
> *Riley*

With Riley's question in mind, Winston left for the station, ready to focus on his case.

CHAPTER 34

Riley

RILEY STARED OUT the window of the bus as it stopped and started on its way to the park. It was the morning after Jules's mom's party, and ordinarily, she would have ridden her bike. But the recent wet weather and temperature drop meant the roads were slicker than usual. Although she didn't mind the ride up and down the hill on the park's one-way road to the tree, she didn't want to risk the descent after the landmark. Besides, being on the bus let her observe the city and its residents. She'd been a people-watcher from way back.

How did Jack observe his neighbours? Public transit thrived in his time, with optimistic city planners laying tracks for the interurban tram and streetcars well before neighbourhoods were built around them. She shook her head at the lack of foresight that saw these tracks ripped up a few decades later to make room for cars.

She shifted her thoughts to the night before. The confrontation with Peter replayed itself in her mind, and her toes curled remembering it.

After the scene with Peter, Johnny had arranged for someone from the RCMP fraud unit to question him. Johnny wouldn't be involved in prosecuting the case because of his relationship with her. Apparently, Peter, even after being grilled by the police, still maintained he hadn't cheated anyone. But Johnny said there was more than enough evidence to charge him with fraud. He felt sure there would be a conviction.

Riley had stayed to comfort her mother. "I didn't know about Peter's misbehaviour, dear," her mom kept repeating. Were her cheeks red from the shame of being deceived, or the shame of almost being caught? Riley had squeezed Johnny's hand as her mom spoke.

"Nancy, it's a bit more than misbehaviour. He stole from people," Johnny said. "I can't guarantee the outcome, but you'll be investigated. The case can't come before me, but if it did, I'd consider how much you knew about the workings of Educoin."

Her mom's reaction had been immediate. She'd stepped away and held her hands in defence. "I didn't know anything about what he was doing. I thought it was all true."

"I understand that," Johnny had said, "But you helped him promote it. I suspect that was part of his plan. Who would suspect someone like you of such a crime?"

"Someone like me?" Her mom's voice had risen.

"Mom, he just means that people like you. They trust you. And that's what Peter used," Riley said. She had kept her voice low, trying to calm her mother as she spoke.

Her mom had looked between Johnny and Riley. Even in the dim outdoor light, Riley could see her mother's eyes were glassy with tears.

Had her mom genuinely liked Peter? She must have. And she must have thought he felt the same. The realization had finally sunk in with Riley last night: her mother was lonely. And she was ready to move on from the loss of Riley's father.

She'd tried to coax her mom to stay a couple of extra days in the city, but she had declined. "I need a few days alone, Riley," she'd said. But she promised to come a few days ahead of Lucy's wedding. "Maybe we can do something, just the three of us," she'd said, clasping Riley's hand in her own. "And maybe I'll be ready to stay in the apartment with you."

Riley teared up again now, remembering that moment and thinking of her mom going off alone, carrying the weight of all that hurt and disappointment. Yes, she was satisfied that they'd thwarted Peter's plan, but she felt for her mom. In her heart, Riley knew why she'd attached herself to him.

She turned her attention back to the window and saw that the bus had arrived in Stanley Park. She disembarked with a handful of others, mostly tourists, judging by the cameras around their necks. Even in cool November, this large urban green space drew visitors. She hitched her backpack on her shoulders and started walking toward the seawall.

She followed the same route she'd run a few days earlier, climbing the steep trail toward the tree. She'd promised herself she'd return here since that first day Jack had written to her about the case.

At the top of the path, she stepped onto the main road of the park. Because it was off-season, she didn't have to contend with droves of tour groups lining up to take pictures. She read the plaques erected to describe the history of the tree. Time had been unkind, though the city's commitment to preserving the tree hadn't wavered. Some residents had formed a society to protect the stump, rallying when it was damaged during a fire. It was even memorialized as a piece of public art displayed near a public transit hub.

Despite being a burned-out shell, the Hollow Tree was incredible. Researchers pegged it as nearly one thousand years old. She placed her hand on the trunk and closed her eyes, willing the tree to share what it had seen.

The tree kept its secrets, and after several minutes, Riley circled the stump with careful steps, inhaling the damp and decay released by each footfall. When a car raced past as she walked behind the tree, she reached out instinctively, letting it support her.

Returning to the front, Riley approached the hollow. She made way for a couple who were leaving. Inside, she spread her arms wide and closed her eyes, almost hearing the echoes of laughter through the generations of people who'd done the same thing in this space. Had Jack taken a spin inside?

A cluster of tourists stood at the opening, and Riley exited into the fine mist. She surveyed the nearby trees, trying to imagine which was the one from which Pierce had been hanged. Had it been a victim of progress in the park? She hadn't expected to find anything useful after so much time, of course. But she allowed a little disappointment to needle its way into her heart because she hadn't been able to summon a connection to Jack in this magical place.

The mist had turned to drizzle, and the temperate rainforest surrounding her sighed in response. With a final glance at the tree, Riley pulled her hood over her head and started toward the beach.

*

At home, Riley opened her laptop and logged in to the newspaper archive to reread the articles she'd found about Caroline Pierce, pausing at the one mentioning the garden. Riley imagined how it would feel to miss someone so much that she donated a garden in his name, as Caroline Pierce had done.

The article didn't include a specific address for the garden but contained the approximate location in the city's West End, which, from her earlier notes, Riley knew was where the Pierce home had been located. As the city grew, its wealthiest residents moved to newer, more exclusive neighbourhoods, but that wouldn't happen for another decade after Pierce died. She scanned a map of the area and couldn't find any reference to it. Where had it been, and what had happened to it? Who was powerful enough to wipe a man from the city's memory?

Riley changed focus to who was responsible for killing Pierce. Surely, to kill someone required intense emotion. She let her mind relax and began a little free-form thinking. She drew a circle and wrote Pierce's name in the middle. Around the circle she drew several smaller ones, each with a line connecting it to Pierce's. Within the smaller circles she wrote names of people Jack had mentioned in the journal: Pierce's wife, Caroline; business partner Reginald Sawyer; sister-in-law Abigail Sawyer; the secretary, Charles Macey. She drew another circle and wrote *clients*. Any of them who lost money might be angry enough to kill him, but did they have access to Pierce? Likely not in the same way those closest to him did.

She pulled out the journal to write him a note.

Dear Jack,

I can't see how anyone would have access to Arthur Pierce in the middle of the night unless they were household or family members.

R.

CHAPTER 35

Jack

THE NEXT MORNING, after he reread Riley's note, Winston thought of the members of Pierce's family and household. Clifford's name hadn't come up in relation to the bank accounts. Did the butler know of the fraud? Perhaps if he'd been a long-time investor or more involved in the business. No, it seemed unlikely he knew the truth behind Pierce.

Next, he revisited the conversations he'd had with Caroline Pierce and Abigail Sawyer. Caroline was the older of the two, but Abigail seemed to dominate her sister. How much of their current dynamic was affected by Mrs. Pierce having just lost her husband? Perhaps little. Abigail Sawyer seemed to have no trouble ordering her husband around and appeared to be equally comfortable issuing commands to Winston. Had she been the same way with Arthur Pierce? He couldn't discount the possibility.

Caroline Pierce, on the other hand, was behaving unlike any widow he had met. Was that because she now had access to her husband's money? A chill passed through him as he considered another possibility. Had she killed her husband to gain that access?

Winston devised a strategy for his day. He'd return to visit Caroline Pierce alone, he'd move on to speak to Abigail Sawyer, and then he'd go on to find the clerk who'd registered the accounts in question at Western Bank. He felt, somehow, that a puzzle piece had fallen into place.

Winston dressed. His hand hovered over Ellis's stone, which sat beside some coins on his dresser. He scooped the coins and dropped them into his pocket. He looked at the rock, polished all these years by his own fingers. Did he want to hold on to this reminder of his family's dishonesty? Or did it serve as a reminder of his job to seek the truth? He considered this as he walked to the Pierce house. The stone remained in his bedroom.

✷

THE PIERCE HOUSE and lands occupied nearly an entire block of the city's West End. A low fence surrounded the grounds, framing the manicured lawn.

He knocked on the door and waited for the butler to open it. Concern flashed across Mr. Clifford's face when he saw Winston. "Detective." He checked behind him and leaned forward. "Have you any news of my investments?"

"I'm afraid I have nothing to share, Mr. Clifford." Winston wasn't yet prepared to speak about what he'd learned at the bank until he understood exactly what it meant. "Before you let Mrs. Pierce know I'm here, if you don't mind, I do have a question for you. How long ago did you invest your money with Mr. Pierce?"

"Just a few months, sir. He offered me a quick return. To thank me for my service. I was expecting it next week."

"Thank you. I will let you know when I can share some news."

"Thank you, Detective." Clifford stood aside and held the door open for Winston to enter. "I will notify Mrs. Pierce."

"Thank you."

The butler showed Winston into the sitting room. "Shall I send in a cup of tea?"

Winston smiled. "If it's no trouble, that would be welcome."

Clifford left Winston alone. While he waited, he searched the shelves. He recognized most of the titles, though few appeared to have been opened. A maid entered the room with a tea service laid for one, including two steaming scones. "Cook's just pulled these from the oven," she explained as she set the tray on the low table. "Mr. Clifford thought you might like them." She turned her head toward the window. "A little comfort on a wet morning."

"Thank you. They smell delicious," Winston said. Their scent caused his mouth to water. After the maid left, he broke a scone in half and was chewing when Caroline Pierce entered. Winston flushed, brushing a crumb from his lip.

"Cook's scones are irresistible, Detective." She eyed the remaining scone. "I admire your restraint not to have had more." She settled into the chesterfield and smoothed the skirts of her dark dress. "Have you news, or are you asking questions today?"

Before he answered, Winston patted the side of his leg and felt for Ellis's stone in his pocket, only to remember where he'd left it. "Both, madam. Do you have an account at Western Bank?"

Caroline Pierce's eyes widened. "An account at the bank? Why would I? Arthur handled all the finances." She clutched a piece of her dress between her thumb and finger. "He gave me whatever I needed, of course, to run the household or purchase clothing. Though I suppose I will have to find someone to handle the accounts for me." She wrinkled her brow, as if the thought had only just occurred to her. "Perhaps Reginald will help with that."

"Rather than do them yourself?" Winston thought of his mother, who knew, to the penny, the amounts in the household accounts. To apply such scrutiny, she needed to know how much money Winston's father earned and added to the accounts monthly.

She shook her head. "I wouldn't know where to start. How do the accounts even work? If I wanted to draw money, for instance."

Her remarks appeared genuine. Perhaps this woman wasn't aware of how much money was in her husband's accounts. "I'm sure someone at the bank would help you, Mrs. Pierce."

Her eyes widened, and she tilted her head as she realized the obviousness of the answer. "Of course they would. Thank you."

Winston leaned forward, bracing himself for the next part of the conversation. "As it is, Mrs. Pierce, I discovered that there is an account in your name at the bank."

"There is?"

"And it's quite a healthy amount. However, I suspect the money in it is ill-gotten and owed to your husband's investors."

Caroline Pierce blanched. "Ill-gotten? What are you saying, Detective Winston? Was my husband—" She swallowed, clenching and unclenching her hand around the fabric of her dress. "Are you suggesting my husband was a criminal?"

Winston rubbed his moustache. "It appears that is the case. I have questions about the source of the funds, though I will have to find answers elsewhere if you are unaware of the account."

"But Arthur assured me—" She looked away.

"What did he assure you?" Winston spoke softly. Mrs. Pierce sat stone-faced, and for a moment he wondered if he'd spoken too quietly and she hadn't heard him. So slowly he almost missed it, her posture changed subtly. Had he not been looking for it, he wouldn't have noticed the slight squaring of her shoulders and tensing of her jaw.

"My family was not wealthy. When our father died, Abigail had to work—mending mostly. But she also found money in other ways." Her gaze focused on her knees. "I never asked how. When I met Arthur, he didn't care about any of that." Caroline Pierce brought her gaze back to Winston. "When we married, we didn't have all this." She waved her hand around the room. "He assured me that his investments were sound. That he had helped others improve their lives." She swallowed. "He pursued different businesses and became successful." She choked on the last word, her eyes pleading. "Was it a lie?"

Though he wanted this woman to know the truth, Winston needed to be sure before he revealed it to her. "I am still piecing it together."

"If he cheated or stole to get this, I want none of it."

Winston put his hand on Mrs. Pierce's. "My intention today was not to upset you, but to learn more about this bank account. I can see you know little more than I do."

She nodded, withdrawing her hand from under Winston's. "You should speak to Reginald. He knows more than he's said."

"You're certain?"

Caroline Pierce retrieved a handkerchief and brought it to her eyes. "I'm certain. Abigail may know more, too." She held Winston's gaze. "Please do not tell her I told you."

"I was already planning to see her, Mrs. Pierce, so there will be no need to betray your confidence." He sipped from his tea and a plan fit itself together in his mind. "If I may, Mrs. Pierce, could I ask you to meet me at the police station this afternoon, two o'clock?"

At this, Mrs. Pierce stood and held her head high. "At the station? I trust Abigail is not in serious trouble. I simply think she knows more about Arthur than she has shared. However, I will do as you ask, Detective Winston." She swept a hand over her hair, tucking a strand into a comb. "Please enjoy the scones and tea. I am afraid other duties require that I not sit any longer with you. I trust you will continue to inform me of anything you think I should know."

Winston accepted his dismissal and the remaining scone, leaving the rest of his tea. He shrugged into his coat and bent to feel for the journal in his satchel. At the next available moment, he would write to Riley about Caroline Pierce's contradictions.

The moment arrived sooner than he expected, as he stopped at a pub, open early to serve breakfast to men working at the nearby port. He ordered a cup of coffee and pulled the journal from his bag.

Dear Riley,

I met this morning with Caroline Pierce, whom I find increasingly full of contradictions. She claimed not to know of the account in her name or her husband's business dealings, yet I cannot believe that a wife would be completely without knowledge of the source of his income. She claimed Arthur provided whatever she needed, but how could she manage the household without some awareness of basic finances?

I am also considering that she is simply acting and that our conversation confirmed suspicions she'd had of her husband. If so, she has chosen to keep her own counsel instead of sharing those suspicions with me. Shame might explain why she has chosen not to reveal more.

Which leads me to wonder how to approach speaking to Abigail and Reginald Sawyer. Their reactions to my questions will confirm whether my theories are correct.

With warmth,

Jack

CHAPTER 36

Riley

RILEY READ JACK'S note in the fluorescent light of the archive room. She'd arrived early to get a head start on her work for the exhibit. Nick wasn't in yet, so she'd stolen a moment to check on Jack's progress.

It sounded like Jack was circling back to Caroline Pierce. The woman seemed a puzzle, for sure. Riley didn't envy him trying to unravel the cues and miscues in her erratic behaviour. Jack badly needed a break in the case, and soon. It was frustrating to have so little she could offer him from her end.

As if to confirm the vacuum of useful information she had at her disposal, Riley's computer screen went dark. She wiggled her mouse to revive it and pulled up the document she'd been working on. She and Nick had a few days to pull all their profiles of the chosen business leaders together and brainstorm ideas for presenting them to the public, designing something both accessible and meaningful. It always seemed like a monumental task at this stage, but it came together, ultimately.

Nick came through the door with his work bag under one arm and a takeout cup of coffee in his other hand. "Whoa, you're early."

Riley pulled a file folder overtop of her journal. "Yep, I really need to churn it out today."

Nick turned to hang his jacket on a hook by the door, and Riley slipped the book into her bag. She'd have to catch up with Jack when he next wrote. For the next few days, she'd be a slave to the exhibit.

CHAPTER 37

Jack

A RED-FACED REGINALD Sawyer answered Winston's knock. "Detective Winston. I wasn't expecting to see you." The man stood close to the door as if to discourage Winston from entering.

Winston ignored this and passed close enough to catch sweat mingling with an earthy soap in Sawyer's scent. "I hope now is a good time anyway, Mr. Sawyer."

Either Sawyer was unaware of how his stance had blocked the entrance or he had recognized Winston would not be deterred. He swung the door wide a moment too late, after Winston had already passed. He quickly shut it. The breeze caused by the movement pushed another waft of Sawyer's scent toward Winston. "It is," he answered at last. "You will have to excuse my appearance, though. I've been moving furniture." Sawyer dabbed his forehead with a handkerchief he'd pulled from his pocket.

It was exertion that was responsible for Sawyer's perspiration. Winston couldn't hide his surprise. "Moving your own furniture?"

"Abigail wanted the chairs rearranged and insisted it happen right now." He looked at Winston. "You haven't a wife, have you?"

"No, I haven't, sir."

"Well then, perhaps you can't appreciate their exacting demands until you have one of your own."

"My mother had high expectations for my father, though I can't recall her ever insisting he move furniture," Winston said. Truth was, he couldn't imagine his mother allowing his father to do so even had he wanted to. She would consider it unthinkable to have him in the state in which Winston had found Sawyer.

"This was the first time Abigail had such a request for me. I am not entirely sure what the urgency was. But, as you will no doubt learn someday, in some matters, you simply do what your wife tells you without question."

Winston looked over Sawyer's shoulder and deeper into the house. "You've completed your tasks now?"

"I have," he said as he patted his forehead with the handkerchief. "Come through and we can speak more privately." Sawyer offered to take Winston's hat and coat.

"Is your butler off?" Winston asked as he handed his garments to Sawyer.

"Our butler?" Sawyer asked. "Oh, he was temporary. We have a maid, but she's off running an errand for my wife. We are not quite in the financial situation that my brother-in-law enjoyed." He clapped Winston on the shoulder.

The informality of the gesture deepened Winston's surprise. This encounter was most unusual. He brushed his hand against his leg, the reflex of feeling for Ellis's rock and realized its absence again.

"At least not yet," Sawyer said. "I trust you're here to fill me in on the progress of the case. Might our fortunes be changing soon?" His eyes widened with anticipation.

"I've uncovered some information, but it might be better to speak with Mrs. Sawyer as well. Is she in?"

"I am here, Detective Winston." Abigail Sawyer's voice came from behind. She stood in the doorway of the newly arranged sitting room, inspecting her husband's work. Seemingly satisfied, she gave Sawyer a curt nod and moved toward a chair. The cut of her dress was similar to the one her sister had been wearing, though of the two, it suited Mrs. Sawyer better. After she'd arranged herself, she motioned for the men to sit.

"Hello again, Mrs. Sawyer. As I was telling your husband, we have learned some interesting information and I thought it best to share it with you directly."

She leaned forward, eyes glistening with the same hope her husband's had. "What have you learned? When will Reginald take over the business?"

Winston shook his head. "While Mrs. Pierce's lawyer has confirmed that Arthur's intention was that Reginald take over, I'm not in the position to say when that should happen." Winston cleared his throat. "Mr. Pierce kept limited records. However, there was reference to several bank accounts in paperwork that we found."

"Several accounts?" Confusion flashed across Reginald Sawyer's face. "Why would he need multiple?"

"I'm trying to understand that. Which is why I was hoping you and your wife might join me at the station today." Seeing the surprise on their faces, he leaned forward. "I am expecting some documents at the station that I'd like to discuss with you. It will be easier to review them there. I hope you understand." He wanted Sawyer, his wife, and Caroline Pierce to be at the station at the same time so he could determine which of them were involved, giving him time to set one more piece of the puzzle into place.

"Both of us?" Sawyer asked. He patted his wife's hand. "I'm not sure how Abigail will be of help, but if that's your request..."

"If you don't mind."

Mrs. Sawyer withdrew her hand from her husband's. "Reginald, remember we are expecting guests for luncheon." She turned to Winston, leaning forward. "Detective Winston, is it terribly urgent? We will, of course, meet you wherever is best for your investigation. Though could we possibly come later today, in the afternoon?"

While the Sawyers had luncheon, he could go to the bank and speak with the clerk who'd registered the accounts. He would ask for a constable to stand watch outside their house to ensure they didn't leave.

"That would be fine, Mrs. Sawyer. I will arrange for a constable to accompany you." The constable would ensure that they arrived at the station as requested.

At this, she blanched. "Is that necessary?"

"Arthur Pierce was murdered, madam. Your husband worked with him. I want to ensure that you are not at risk." He waited for her to nod. "Shall I expect you shortly after two o'clock today?"

"We will be there," answered Reginald. "Abigail, we'll just have to finish luncheon with enough time to get to the police station."

"I appreciate your willingness to assist, Mr. and Mrs. Sawyer. I have no doubt it will help us resolve this case."

"Of course, Detective Winston. We will see you this afternoon." Sawyer stood and followed Winston from the room, leaving his wife behind.

They exchanged goodbyes as Reginald Sawyer handed Winston his hat and coat. For the first time, Winston felt like he was directing the case.

※

ENCOURAGED BY HIS conversation with the Sawyers, Winston nearly ran down the street. The desire to preserve his dignity won out, however, and he settled instead for walking briskly to the nearest streetcar stop. While the streetcar weaved through the city, he considered what he'd learned this morning by speaking to Caroline Pierce and the Sawyers. One of them knew more, and his next task was to get them to reveal it.

The streetcar stopped outside the bank, and Winston disembarked. He was directed to Andrew Setter's office, where Setter stood with a tall man. He was younger than Setter, and his gaze darted between Setter and Winston.

Setter stood straighter when he saw Winston. "Detective Winston. Jin told me you'd asked about the accounts in question and who had set them up. I've invited Stanley McGill to speak to you. He set up the accounts." Winston checked his notebook where he'd written *SM* the night before. His palms grew clammy. McGill could be the key to this.

Setter gave McGill a brief nod. "Detective Winston met me late yesterday and asked to see the account information of some of our customers." He spoke as though assisting Winston had been taxing.

Beads of sweat formed at McGill's hairline, though the room felt comfortable to Winston. The man stood six inches taller than Winston, who, at five feet ten, was tall compared with most men. He put a little space between himself and McGill. Beside him, Winston felt as though he were a child.

As though he sensed Winston's hesitation, McGill lowered his shoulders. "Sorry, Detective. I'm a tall one. My mother always thought I'd be small, and I am the shortest of her four boys, so I suppose she was right. No wonder she fed me extra. Didn't do too badly for it!" The man reached above his head as if to show how much taller he could have been. Suddenly, he coloured. "Listen to me prattling on. I'll do my best to help you. What are you looking for?" He swiped his brow.

Winston smiled, wanting to ease the man's nerves. "Thank you for meeting me, Mr. McGill. I am seeking information on customers who opened accounts with the bank. I understand you help with that?"

McGill nodded. "I do."

"How many customers open accounts with you each week?"

"It depends. I might work with ten customers one day, five the next, and twenty the one after that."

"They're all opening accounts?"

"No, I do more than open their accounts. If they need to withdraw or deposit money or pay another account, I help them do those things."

"Do you remember all your customers?"

McGill shook his head. "Not all of them. I mean, I used to. But we have so many now, I can't keep them all straight."

"Do any stand out?"

"Well, I remember most when I see them, but I might not remember their names."

"I understand. The customers I am asking about are couples, a man and a woman. The accounts are in the women's names."

McGill scratched his head. "I'm usually pretty good at remembering our account holders who are women. We don't have as many of them."

"Do you recall any of these women?" Winston named Caroline Pierce, Abigail Rallston, Abigail Sawyer, and, though they hadn't found an account in the name, Caroline Rallston to test his theory.

The banker's eyes widened at hearing Abigail Rallston's name. "Miss Rallston." He nodded. "Lovely woman." He tapped the side of his nose. "Now that you've said these names together, she reminded me of Abigail Sawyer and Caroline Pierce."

"Why is that? Do they share physical features? Or was it more their mannerisms that were similar?"

"Similar eyes. Friendly eyes."

"Anything else?"

McGill tilted his head. "They were pretty women, all of them. They had similar voices. Soft, gentle."

"Could they have been the same woman?" Winston's voice had risen in pitch with excitement. He drew a breath to calm himself.

McGill shook his head. "I'm certain they weren't."

"You are? Why?" Disappointment flooded Winston.

"They wore different hats."

Winston blinked at the man. Many women had multiple hats. Had this man not noticed that before? "Anything else?"

"One woman was taller than the other, I think."

Height could be adjusted with shoes. And this man was unlikely to have looked at their feet. "What about the men they were with? Do you remember them?"

"They looked like any customer of the bank. Nice suits, well groomed. I didn't pay them much attention."

Winston sighed. "Do you recall which woman you saw last, and when?"

"Mrs. Pierce."

"You're certain?" The detective stepped forward. The clamminess had returned to his palms, and he longed to wipe them on his pants. Decorum forced him to settle for shoving a hand in his pocket as if searching for something. Ellis's rock.

"I am. She was here two weeks ago, maybe. She was inquiring about the balance of the account."

"Alone?"

"Well, yes. A woman only needs her husband or her father to open an account. Once it exists, she does not need his permission to add to or withdraw from the account. But if she were to withdraw a large amount, we would check with the husband to be sure he was aware of it. No harm in her adding to the account."

"And the man who accompanied Miss Rallston. He was her. . .?"

McGill closed his eyes. "Must have been a brother if she wasn't married. He wasn't old enough to be her father."

"You didn't ask?" Winston fought to keep frustration from his voice.

"I'm sure she referred to him as her brother."

Could each account have been opened by the same two people, dressed differently and calling themselves different names each time?

"Would you mind coming to the police station to confirm who you opened accounts for? I have arranged for some people to arrive this afternoon. I'd appreciate your confirming whether you opened accounts for any of them."

McGill blanched. "I'm not sure I can leave here." His gaze flicked to Setter, still standing beside him.

Setter cleared his throat. "While it's unusual, I understand you are assisting with a police investigation."

Relief relaxed McGill's features, though moments later they tightened again. "Why are you investigating these accounts? It's not illegal for a woman to have an account." A hint of fear flashed in McGill's eyes.

"I can't discuss it, but it is for an important case. You're not in any trouble. I just need to confirm the identity of some of the bank's account holders."

Hearing this, McGill stood straighter. "I can help you."

"Very good." Winston pulled out his pocket watch. "It's just gone noon. Please be at the station in ninety minutes. I've asked the others to arrive at two, but if they are early, I'd prefer you were already there."

McGill nodded. "Can I return to my work now?"

"You may. I will see you shortly, Mr. McGill."

"Thank you."

After McGill had closed the door, Setter folded his arms. "I don't really have a choice, do I, Detective?"

"It's better for everyone if you allow Mr. McGill to assist me."

"In that case, use him as you need to." Setter walked toward his desk. "Do you need to speak with any other employees?"

"I don't think so. Mr. Jin was very helpful already. And I expect Mr. McGill's assistance will be equally useful."

"Glad to hear it. At Western Bank, we look out for our customers."

"Thank you, Mr. Setter."

*

WITH A PROMPTNESS Detective Jack Winston appreciated, Stanley McGill stepped into the police station at one thirty. McGill cast his gaze around the room. "I've never been in here," he said. The duty desk occupied much of the space, leaving an area large enough for a few people to stand and a narrow passageway leading to the officers' main area and the chief constable's office. To the side of the duty desk, a door led to the room Winston would use as the interview space to speak with the Sawyers and Mrs. Pierce. "They haven't given you much space, have they?"

Winston looked at the cramped space between the duty desk and the entrance to the main work area. "The force has grown, but not quickly enough to keep pace with the city's population. We have twelve officers now, and the chief constable expects to hire more next year. As you say, it's crowded, and we'll need a larger space soon."

"Who can be a policeman?"

The eagerness in the man's voice surprised Winston. "Are you interested in joining the constabulary, Mr. McGill?"

McGill shrugged. "I don't think so, but I'm not entirely sure that banking is for me either. Do you have any special training?"

"I have been working with the chief constable to create a training program for new constables, and of course, you learn as you go. I could have you speak with Constable Miller, who joined the force relatively recently."

McGill's eyes narrowed as he stepped closer to Winston. "You look like you started not too long ago as well. What does it take to become a detective?"

"I started before Constable Miller. And I believe our present need is for more constables rather than detectives."

"I mean no offence." McGill cleared his throat. "How do you want me to identify who opened the accounts?"

"As I mentioned at the bank, some individuals will meet me here shortly. I was thinking you could stand, much as we are now, to the side of the desk here. I'll send Constable Miller to speak to you so I can greet the visitors when they arrive."

"Can I pretend to report a theft?"

Winston held back a smile. "If you'd like. Three people will arrive, and I'd like you to signal to Constable Miller whether you recognize any of them without revealing that you've observed them. Do you think that's something you can do?"

"Signal how? No pointing?"

"Preferably not. I will bring the people by the desk here so I can take them into this smaller room." Winston nodded toward a door leading from the main entrance.

McGill smoothed his hair, grinning. "How very exciting. Helping the police with an investigation. My mother will be proud." He rocked on his heels.

"Yes, well, perhaps you could seem a little less enthusiastic about being here?"

McGill brought his mouth to a firm line. "Is that better?"

Winston nodded. "Much. Wait here and I'll get Constable Miller."

Minutes later, Winston returned with Miller. He introduced the men and explained what he needed them to do, emphasizing that neither was to reveal why they were standing at the front, other than for Miller to listen to McGill report a crime. "Don't make the crime too dramatic. A robbery is fine. Miller, ask the questions you normally would. You don't need to act as though you were on a stage. Be as natural as possible, especially when the people arrive."

"Should we practise?"

Winston sensed his ruse may not go as well as he planned if he didn't calm McGill's energy. "I don't think there's a need to—"

The door opened and Caroline Pierce entered the station, followed by Reginald and Abigail Sawyer. The constable he'd assigned followed them, and Winston gave him a quick nod of thanks.

Winston stepped forward, pulling his watch from his pocket. Had someone arrived early to wrong-foot Winston?

CHAPTER 38

Jack

"You were expecting to see all of us, Detective?" asked Caroline Pierce. What did he read in her wide eyes? Fear, confusion?

"Yes, I had hoped to ask each of you some questions." He gestured toward the door. "Follow me. We've got a room set up here." Winston walked past the desk where Miller and McGill stood. Miller appeared to take notes as McGill spoke softly. Miller caught Winston's eye and nodded subtly.

Winston talked amiably, recounting the growth of the force. "The constabulary has occupied this space since it was built following the fire in 1886. We were four then and have tripled in size since, and I expect we will see more growth next year. The courthouse is here, as well as the morgue." He indicated the door that led to Doctor Evans' domain.

"Has crime tripled in just over a decade, requiring such a large police force?" Abigail Sawyer's question dripped with distaste.

What could account for this woman's tone? Did she feel threatened, or was she just irritable? "As the city's population increases, so does the opportunity for mischief, it seems, though I couldn't provide specific incident numbers." Winston led the group into the smaller room and closed the door behind him. Moments later, he opened it again. "Apologies. I seem to have left my pencil elsewhere. Please wait here." He exited the room and closed the door, walking toward Miller and McGill.

"Mr. McGill says he recognizes Mrs. Sawyer," Miller whispered.

Beside him, McGill leaned in to whisper, too. "I've never seen the other two before."

"The gentleman was not the one who opened the accounts?" If it wasn't Sawyer, it must have been Pierce.

McGill's head shook with more force. "No. That man was shorter, more athletic looking."

"And the woman?" Winston leaned forward, holding his breath.

"Yes, the one who arrived with the gentleman. When she opened the account, she said it was money she'd received as an inheritance."

"You're certain?" Winston's heart rate picked up. "Is that the only account she opened?"

McGill flushed. "She may have opened another."

"Do you remember which one?"

McGill's finger shook as he pointed to the paper between them. On it, Miller had written the names of the account holders. "I can't say for certain, other than to say she was with another man to open an account." His voice grew in confidence. "I've thought about it since you asked me earlier. She definitely opened one, maybe all the accounts you asked about." McGill pulled several folded papers from his pocket. "I nearly forgot. I brought this." He gave Winston the documents.

"What is it?"

"The registration papers for the accounts. I thought you might want to see them."

Winston unfolded the pages, looked at each, and refolded them, sliding them into his own pocket.

McGill knit his brow. "I'll need those back, Detective."

"You will have them before the end of today." Winston patted his pocket. "Thank you, Mr. McGill. I appreciate your taking the time to step away from the bank and come to the station. You have been a great help. If you wouldn't mind remaining a while longer while I speak to the people in that room?"

McGill's smile spread across his face. "Can I tell my mother now? That I've helped the police?"

"If you must. But you must ask her to keep your confidence."

"What about telling anyone at the bank?"

"Please tell nobody else."

"I won't."

"Thomas, I must return to the interview room. Will you see that Mr. McGill gets a cup of tea?"

Miller set off and Winston returned to the interview room. Inside, Caroline Pierce and Abigail Sawyer sat across from each other. Mrs. Pierce had her hands clasped and resting on the table. Reginald Sawyer stood behind his wife, leaning against the wall. "My apologies." Winston dangled a pencil between his thumb and index finger. "I spoke with you earlier today about accounts at Western Bank. It seems someone has used your names,"—he nodded to the women— "to open them."

Mrs. Pierce shook her head. "I've never stepped inside a bank, Detective Winston."

"I've never brought my wife to the bank," said Reginald Sawyer as his wife nodded.

Winston scratched his chin. "It's interesting you say that, Mr. Sawyer. Someone looking remarkably like your wife is said to have opened the accounts."

"Many women look alike. We wear similar hairstyles, clothing, and some of us have similar names." Abigail Sawyer said, clipping each word. She had mimicked her sister's posture, also placing her hands on the table.

"It's true, Mrs. Sawyer. But you and your sister are two of the more striking women in the city, I would guess. To most men, you're rather memorable."

Mr. Sawyer shot Winston a startled look. "Now, Detective Winston. That is highly inappropriate."

Winston held out the papers McGill had given him. "I've spoken with someone who works at the bank, and he is certain it was your wife for whom he opened accounts. Two are in her name. That information gives me every reason to believe it was her."

Sawyer stepped forward. "I am telling you it wasn't. I haven't opened any accounts for her." His voice shook as he spoke.

"I understand that, and I believe that's true. Which is why I believe that Arthur Pierce opened the accounts for your wife."

"Arthur?" Caroline Pierce inhaled sharply. "Why ever would he do that?"

Abigail Sawyer stared at Winston, her features relaxed and unmoving.

"He also opened an account in your name, Mrs. Pierce."

Colour tinted Caroline Pierce's cheeks, but she was otherwise still. "But I've never been there," she insisted.

Winston considered his next statement. Did he have enough proof he was right? Or was he simply trying to make everything fit? He breathed deeply. "I think your sister pretended to be you."

His statement drew the air from the room.

Pausing for a moment to collect his thoughts, Sawyer placed his hand on his wife's shoulder and glanced at his sister-in-law. Neither woman's gaze left Winston. "Detective, I really must insist. You're upsetting the women."

"Let him speak, Reginald." Abigail Sawyer spoke firmly but quietly to her husband.

"Thank you, Mrs. Sawyer. As I was saying, I think Arthur Pierce pretended to be your husband and opened an account in your name. At some point, you returned to the bank with him, only this time he had asked you to pretend to be your sister, Caroline, so he could open a second account. And I think the two of you returned later so he could open a third account, this time using your unmarried name, Abigail Rallston. Does any of this sound familiar?"

Mrs. Sawyer shrugged from under her husband's grip. "Perhaps you could remind me a little more? Do you have any other details?" Her face remained neutral, though Winston sensed she was trying to assess how much he knew.

"Your family name is Rallston, correct?"

Caroline Pierce adjusted her position, the fabric of her dress rustling as she moved. "Abigail, what is the detective saying? Did you open these accounts? With Arthur? One in my name?"

Abigail Sawyer fixed her eyes on Winston. "You are correct, Detective Winston. Our unmarried name is Rallston."

"Abigail, did you open the accounts?" The pitch of Caroline Pierce's voice rose and her face clouded with confusion. She reached for her sister's arm.

Mrs. Sawyer continued to sit serenely, as if at a church picnic. She began speaking without looking at her sister. "Caro, we can never be too careful. I wanted to make sure I had somewhere to put a little money aside." She patted Reginald's hand. "In case anything should happen. Arthur's tragedy shows we need to be prepared."

Winston pressed on with his questions. "Mrs. Sawyer, I might understand why you would open an account in your name. But what about the others? The one in your sister's name, and the one using your family name?"

"I opened the one in my name." She flicked her fingers. "You yourself said the city was growing. Could it be possible that the other accounts were opened by women who share similar names to ours?"

"You suggested that earlier, Mrs. Sawyer." The closeness of four people in the room was heating the space, though neither woman appeared to notice the cloying warmth. "Did you deposit a large sum into your account? Five thousand dollars?"

Sawyer and Mrs. Pierce inhaled sharply. "Abigail, where did you get that kind of money?" hissed her sister.

Abigail Sawyer brought her hand to her mouth as if surprised. "The bank must have made a mistake. I have only a few dollars in my account." Finally, she appeared flustered.

Winston searched through the pages Setter had given him. "The bank records show such an amount was depostied into your account."

"Then the money has been deposited into my account by accident." Mrs. Sawyer folded her hands on the table.

Winston adopted her pose and leaned forward. "I'd like to think that banks are a little more careful with their customers' money."

"As would I, Detective Winston," said Sawyer, having regained his composure. "But my wife has answered your questions. The account is not hers." Reginald puffed out his chest.

Winston smoothed the pages he had taken from McGill in front of Abigail Sawyer. "Is this your signature?"

"Yes."

"And this?" Winston pointed to the second page.

She glanced at the page. "That looks like my name."

"The first parts of the signatures look nearly identical to yours."

Mrs. Sawyer straightened in her chair. "Anyone could copy my writing."

"This may be true. With a little practice, I'm sure even I could master your style." Winston folded the pages and returned them to his pocket. "But no matter how long I practise, I could never look or walk like you."

A giggle escaped from Mrs. Pierce, who brought her hand to her mouth, her face colouring. Mrs. Sawyer glared at her sister. "Do you think this is funny, sister dear?"

Mrs. Pierce shook her head. "I think this is rather serious." Her cheeks reddened.

"This policeman has accused me of what, exactly? Having multiple bank accounts? I'm not sure what the crime is."

"I'm more curious about the source of the money in the accounts, Mrs. Sawyer," said Winston.

"I already told you. The bank has made a mistake." She pressed her palms onto the table.

Winston pulled another set of pages from his other pocket. "I'm not sure that it did. I have spoken with an employee at the bank who assured me that when you deposited the money, you explained it had come from an inheritance. Whom did you inherit it from?"

"A distant relative."

Caroline Pierce sniffed. "Who only left money to you?"

Doubt crept across Reginald Sawyer's face. "Which relative, Abigail? Who died?" he asked. If this information was new to him, who was behind the masquerade?

Mrs. Sawyer looked from her sister to Winston. She focused her gaze on her sister, narrowing her eyes. "I wanted to spare you, Caroline."

"Spare me what, exactly?"

"Embarrassment. It was Arthur. He insisted I set up the accounts."

"Using different names? Did you ask him why?"

"He wouldn't tell me. I think he was hiding something. And I helped him do it." She brought her hands to her face. "I'm so ashamed." The rapid change in her demeanour surprised Winston.

Sawyer comforted his wife, his face pinched. "You've upset her, Detective. See what you've done?"

"What did he tell you, Abigail?" Caroline Pierce's voice cut through the room. When her sister didn't answer, Mrs. Pierce leaned over the table, putting her face inches away from her sister's. "What did he do?"

"I was to move the money from one account—the one in your name—and put it in the one under my name. I was supposed to do the same with the Abigail Rallston account."

"What was going to happen to the money when you did that?" Winston asked.

"Arthur never said. I was supposed to do it, and then he died. I haven't touched the money." She cocked her head. "But if the money is in my account, does that mean it is mine?"

"I can't answer that." Winston lowered his voice and softened his tone. "Do you know where the money came from?"

She shrugged and wiped her eyes. "He said he was consolidating investments. I never really understood when he spoke about money."

"Why did you help him?"

Mrs. Sawyer shrugged again. "He asked. I thought I was helping you, Caroline."

Winston considered everything he had just heard and stroked his moustache. "To confirm, Mrs. Sawyer, you admit that you opened the accounts, all three of them, with Arthur Pierce."

"Yes." She sat against the back of the chair.

"And you say you did it because he asked."

"Yes."

"Did he ask you to change your appearance when you opened the accounts?"

"What do you mean?"

"The bank employee I spoke with said that when you came to open the second account, you were shorter, and that you had regained your height when you arrived to open the third account. Why would you need to alter your appearance?"

"I don't know what the rules are regarding bank accounts. I thought maybe I couldn't hold so many." The hint of a smile teased her lips. "And who doesn't like to pretend they're someone else?"

Winston held up his hand and counted on his fingers. "You can hold multiple accounts. What you can't do is open them in different names, especially not your own."

Mrs. Pierce drew herself up and leaned forward. "Detective, could this all be a misunderstanding?" She reached for her sister. "Perhaps Abigail didn't understand the banking rules."

"I now have confirmation from a bank representative and your sister that she opened the accounts. She may be unfamiliar with the banking rules, but I'm certain she knows she cannot assume a false identity."

Caroline Pierce swallowed. "And how does this relate to Arthur's murder?"

Winston ran his hands through his hair. Half a theory was forming, but it was too early for him to share it. He needed more proof it was correct. "I believe the money came from his investors. But I'm uncertain why it led to his death."

Reginald Sawyer pulled at the chair his wife was seated in. "Well, with that, Detective, we will be leaving. My wife has explained her ignorance of Arthur's reasons, and we will do what we can to remedy her actions now that we are aware of them. As you say, no crime has been committed."

Winston held up his hand. "Your wife committed fraud by impersonating her sister, Mr. Sawyer. That is a crime."

"Surely not one you will charge her with?" Caroline Pierce's voice rose. "I am not angry with her, and the crime was committed against me."

"The decision is not mine to make, I'm afraid. But I will release you for now. I ask that you not visit any banks until you hear otherwise, however."

Sawyer helped his wife stand. "I can assure you, Detective, that my wife will go nowhere without my knowing." He reached for his sister-in-law and assisted her to her feet. "Good day."

CHAPTER 39

Jack

AFTER HE ESCORTED the Sawyers and Caroline Pierce to the station entrance, Winston returned to the interview room, where he found Constable Miller waiting in the doorway. He motioned for Miller to sit and closed the door behind them. "Abigail Sawyer opened the accounts for Arthur Pierce."

Miller balanced his chair so it leaned on its back legs. "All of them? Did you learn why?"

"No, nor did I learn why Pierce deposited so much into the accounts, though I think we can assume it came from his investors."

"Was he planning an escape?"

Winston leaned forward. He tapped the ledger. "This would be more than enough money to start over."

"With his wife's sister?"

Winston's earlier idea solidified. "The money, once deposited, technically belongs to Abigail."

Miller lurched, and the legs of his chair hit the floor with a thud. "Did Pierce's wife learn about the fraud and her sister's accounts?" He pulled the ledger closer. "Did she kill him because of it?" Miller scratched his temple. "But how? She would have needed help."

Winston heard Miller's questions, but his mind was moving in another direction.

"We've been looking at this wrong, Thomas. I need to work something out. I will see you tomorrow."

※

Winston knocked on the door of his uncle's house. A maid opened the door and led Winston to the sitting room, where a small fire warmed the room. She took Winston's coat and offered him a warm smile. "I have your book, Mr. Winston. That Detective Holmes is a clever fellow."

"I'm glad you enjoyed it," Winston said. "I'll look for another copy. No need for you to return that one to me." She gave him a stiff nod and looked down as Chief Constable Philpott entered the room.

"Jack, has something come up?" Philpott asked. He poured amber liquid into two glasses and handed one to his nephew. "You look like you could use this."

Winston sipped the drink, feeling the burn chase its way down his throat. Winston wasn't yet ready to talk more about Ellis. That would need to wait for another time. He blew out a slow breath. "I'm here regarding the Pierce case."

Winston's tone was clipped, and his uncle nodded.

"We've already spoken about how Arthur Pierce was misleading his investors. Much as you were unaware of his dealings, so was his wife."

Philpott set down his glass. "I'm not sure I'm going to like what you're about to say, Jack."

Winston detected a plea in Philpott's voice. "I doubt it." He explained what he'd learned about the accounts.

Philpott listened, his face growing paler as Winston continued his explanation. "Why three accounts? And why in women's names?"

"I'm unclear on that, sir. I think one account—the last one he opened and the one with the most in it—I wonder if he wasn't preparing to leave town quickly."

"And?"

"If his wife figured out what he was doing, and since the account is in her name, she could take the money for herself. Maybe as compensation for the shame that his secret was about to result in."

"But the money is still in the account?"

Winston rubbed his face, recalling the warmth he'd felt for Caroline Pierce. "If her husband were dead, there would be no reason to move it." As little as he liked the idea, he was going to have to question the woman again.

CHAPTER 40

Jack

As Winston prepared to knock on the door of the Pierces' home the next day, his stomach tightened. This conversation was going to be difficult. The butler opened the door and showed Winston and Miller into the sitting room. Before Clifford set off to find Mrs. Pierce, he asked about the case and his money. "I'm afraid I haven't anything new to share with you, Mr. Clifford," Winston replied.

Clifford accepted Winston's response and left the room. Winston had seen the disappointment in the man's eyes; it was difficult to lose faith in one's employer. With a pang, the pain of the conversation he'd had with Philpott about Ellis returned. Winston was thinking of how powerful an emotion shame was when Caroline Pierce entered the room. She carried herself with confidence and grace, and he quelled the flutter he felt as she greeted him. He was here to find out how much she had really known about her husband's business and had she already learned the truth?

After they'd settled into chairs, Winston began. "You've previously said you knew little of your husband's business."

"That is correct."

"My investigation has led me to believe his business was not what it seemed."

Mrs. Pierce narrowed her eyes. "Not what it seemed?" Confusion pinched her features. Where her sister's reactions were exaggerated, Caroline Pierce's were measured.

"No. He appears to have been paying early investors with the money given to him by later investors. There was, as far as I can tell, no actual investment."

"No investment? There must have been." Her voice faltered. "He spoke of a device... to help with mining." She brought her hand to her mouth.

A maid entered the room and set down a tea tray. Winston waited while she arranged the items. After she had left the room, he continued.

"It looks like the device was a fabrication—it didn't exist. Neither did the expedition he claimed was using it. They were both pure invention, used to promote his scheme."

She held her hand over the tea service, a wisp of steam curling in front of her arm. After a moment, she picked up the teapot and stared at it with intense focus. "What does this mean for me?" she asked when the ritual of pouring was complete. Her voice matched Winston's quiet tone, though fire flickered in her eyes.

"I don't know." Would this woman reveal her part in her husband's death if she grew angry enough?

"Arthur always said he'd protect me, look after me." She plucked at the hem of her sleeve. "He's done this. Left me with nothing." Her voice grew louder with each statement. "When did you learn?"

This question was spoken with such intensity, Winston drew back. "About your involvement?"

The teacup she was holding shattered when it hit the ground. After her hand had released it, the cup seemed suspended in the air before it fell, but Winston's reflexes were too slow to stop it. Beside him, Miller leaned forward. Winston motioned with his hand for the constable to remain seated.

"My involvement? With what?" She held up her hand to prevent the maid—who had appeared almost instantly at the door—from approaching to clear away the mess. The maid bowed her head and shut the door. Neither woman had looked at the other. Mrs. Pierce and her staff knew each other well. Deep loyalty flowed in the household, connecting its members.

"His death. I believe you orchestrated it."

"How? I was here when he died. My maid can confirm this for you." She picked up a pastry from the tray that had accompanied the tea, then set it down. "After you had us at the station yesterday, I thought about the day Arthur died. I think it was Reginald."

Winston wasn't going to be distracted by Mrs. Pierce, but he let her speak, interested in hearing how she would build her argument.

"Reginald and Arthur argued a few nights before Arthur died."

Despite himself, Winston leaned forward. "Yes, you mentioned this earlier."

"It was a minor disagreement, and Arthur assured me they'd resolved it. Now that he's dead, though, I wonder if that wasn't quite the case."

"Do you know what they were arguing about?"

Mrs. Pierce looked away. "I heard Abigail's name. Abigail and Reginald married after us. She was selective in whom she chose." She paused again, letting her gaze fall on the fallen teacup. "I don't think Reginald was my sister's first choice of husbands, but by the time she met him, I think she felt he was her only choice. She didn't want to remain unmarried and had already chased other men away with her intelligence." Her eyes focused over Winston's shoulder as she lost herself in a memory.

"Go on," Winston encouraged, forcing himself to ease back in his chair.

"They seemed happy, but, as I've told you, he's not terribly ambitious. Abigail pushed Reginald to work with my husband. Arthur agreed only because of his fondness for her." She met Winston's eyes. "She and Arthur were very close. It did not bother me, the two of them always with their heads together. I never sensed they shared romantic feelings."

"If you knew your sister and your husband were discussing business, why was it such a surprise to Reginald?"

Mrs. Pierce waved her hand in front of her face. "Reginald is a lovely man, but my sister manipulates him easily. He thought it was his idea to work with Arthur, but Abby planted that seed in his ear and tended it until it grew into his plan."

Winston's mother was good at directing his father and convincing him an idea had been his. Was Caroline Pierce trying to manipulate him in the same way even now? He shook the thought away. "It seems unlikely that Reginald Sawyer would feel strongly enough to want to kill your husband." Winston wanted to test the theory that had formed.

Mrs. Pierce nodded. "I didn't kill my husband, Detective. He may not have been as honest as he should have been, but he was always kind to me. He gave me no reason to want him dead."

"Even if his business wasn't legitimate?"

She looked around the room. "He was finding new ways of doing business."

"You knew?"

"I didn't know the specifics, but a wife can't help but pick up information. We are often ignored, you realize. We rely on the males in our lives for many things, but it also allows us to be invisible."

Winston stared at his notebook. Invisible. He searched her eyes. Sadness had replaced any anger he'd seen earlier. "Do all women feel that way?"

"It's a common sentiment, though it may not be shared by everyone, of course."

Winston rubbed his moustache. "Your sister?"

She nodded. "We spoke of it often. She laughed it off as our trade-off for having so much provided for us."

"She didn't speak of it with anger?"
"Never that I heard. She referred to us as The Overlooked."
Winston stood. He realized now whom he had overlooked.

CHAPTER 41

Jack

WINSTON CAUGHT HIMSELF reaching reflexively to feel again for his brother's stone. He shook his head and knocked on the door.

Shame. His parents had felt it and pretended Ellis hadn't died. Pierce's killer had also felt it. The shame of being deceived. After a maid showed Winston and Miller into the sitting room, Winston positioned himself within view of the house's front door in case the occupants tried to flee. The clock from the front hallway tick-tick-ticked, mocking Winston about the time he'd wasted pursuing false leads.

A swish of fabric signalled that the home's residents had arrived to greet the policemen. "Detective Winston. Constable Miller. It's rather a surprise to see you again." Reginald Sawyer's greeting was warm. "I should think we're becoming regular acquaintances by now."

"We're here to see your wife, Mr. Sawyer."

"Abigail? She stepped out moments ago. Her carriage must have passed you."

A sense of defeat flooded Winston. "How long do you anticipate she will be gone?" Had he let her escape?

Sawyer shrugged. "She didn't say."

Winston stepped forward. "I will send Constable Miller after her. What is your wife's destination?"

Sawyer backed away, searching Winston's face. "It is that urgent?"

"It is." Winston moderated his voice. A gentler approach was needed with this man. "Where has your wife gone?"

"I don't know. She told me she had an errand to run this morning and that she would 'come back for me'."

"Come back for you? Those were her exact words?" Winston's frustration turned to hope. If she was planning to return, she hadn't run off yet.

"I don't recall her exact words, but she suggested she had plans for us this afternoon. She enjoys planning surprises." He ran his hand through his hair. "And after the past few days, I look forward to a surprise."

Winston was certain this surprise was not one Sawyer would enjoy. "It's no matter. I am certain I know where she is." Winston moved toward the door, then turned back to Sawyer. "Perhaps you had better come with us, sir. You said she took your carriage?"

"Yes." Colour had drained from Sawyer's face and beads of sweat had formed at his hairline. "What's wrong, Detective?"

Winston weighed explaining his theory to this man, but decided it would take too long. "We will take a cab."

Winston sent Miller ahead to a busier road to flag down a cab while Sawyer prepared to leave. When Miller returned in a cab, the other men loaded themselves inside and Winston gave the address for the bank.

"Why do you think she has gone to the bank?" Sawyer asked, seated between the policemen.

"Your wife realizes she is nearly caught and is trying to run away. I think she is trying to secure as much money as she can before she does."

"Run away? Why would she do that?"

Winston prepared himself for the reaction his next sentence was likely to bring. "She murdered Arthur Pierce."

Reginald Sawyer inhaled sharply. "How could she have killed Arthur? Hanged him in a tree?" He shook his head. "This is preposterous." He moved as if to open the carriage door. Winston placed a hand on Sawyer's arm but did not stop him. The driver had slowed the horses as they neared their destination. Sawyer's love for his wife and his need to know the meaning of all this would ensure he remained with them.

"We're here. Thomas. . ." Winston looked from Miller to Sawyer, hoping that the constable understood he was to remain by Sawyer's side. Miller lifted his finger to his hat to acknowledge the unspoken instruction.

Winston paid the driver and followed Miller and Sawyer into the bank. After scanning the bank's entrance hall, he approached the first teller with his identification card in his hand. "I'm here on a rather urgent police matter. Do you know if Mrs. Abigail Sawyer, a customer, is here?"

The teller's eyes widened. "Are you Detective Winston?"

Winston tilted his head at the unexpected question. "Yes. How do you know?"

"Here." The teller pushed a slip of paper toward the policeman. Winston unfolded it and read the note. "Clever man," he mumbled. He turned to Sawyer. "Your wife is here." He shook the page in his hand. "Stanley McGill is delaying her as long as possible. Let's go." Winston turned back to the teller. "Can you tell me where I will find Mr. McGill?"

The teller pointed to a door against the rear wall of the bank. "He is back there, sir."

Winston led the way and knocked sharply before opening the door. Abigail Sawyer sat with her back to the door, opposite McGill. She had removed her red hat and placed it on the chair beside her. Several papers were spread on the table between them. She turned to the door, her features pinching when she realized who had interrupted them. "Reginald? What are you doing here?"

"I think a better question is, what are you doing here, Abigail?" asked Sawyer.

She looked past her husband at the two policemen and registered surprise. "And you're here with Detective Winston. Is something the matter?"

At this, Winston stepped past Reginald Sawyer. "Thank you, Mr. McGill. I would appreciate the use of this room for the next little while." Winston turned to Mrs. Sawyer after McGill left the room. "Mrs. Sawyer, you can stop pretending now. I know you killed Arthur Pierce."

Her hand flew to her throat. "What an accusation. How could I have killed Arthur?" She looked between the men in the now crowded room. "Better yet, why would I do that to my sister?"

"Allow me to explain." Winston moved deeper into the room. Out of the corner of his eye, he noticed Miller block the doorway. Reginald Sawyer approached his wife and leaned on the back of the empty chair her hat rested on. "Mrs. Sawyer and Arthur Pierce worked together on his investment scheme. It may have started out as his business, and it may have started as a legitimate one, or maybe it was never honest. The details don't matter right now, except to say that you were partners."

Reginald Sawyer cleared his throat. "I was Arthur's partner. Abigail knows nothing of our work."

Winston gestured for Sawyer to sit down. As her husband moved as instructed, Abigail Sawyer fixed her hat on her head with practised fingers.

Winston positioned himself in the chair opposite the Sawyers and waved for Miller to join them in the fourth chair. "That's what your wife wanted you to think. I believe she was behind much of Pierce's strategy. They were the partners." He pointed to Sawyer. "You were—it seems, unwittingly—simply part of the mask hiding their scheme."

"The mask?"

"They needed you to believe you were involved, and your involvement provided a way for them to conceal their activities. But you were only cover."

Sawyer recoiled. "Abigail? What is he talking about? I had no idea you were working with Arthur."

"Of course you didn't, Reginald dear. That was the point." Mrs. Sawyer's features remained serene, though her words were sharp. "How am I supposed to have killed Arthur, Detective?"

This was the piece Winston wasn't certain of. "The argument Pierce had with the builder?"

She nodded. "I explained to the man that this was an opportunity not to be missed. When he did not receive the return he was expecting from his investment, I sent him to Arthur. It seems he gathered a few other men to exact revenge. He is dangerous to double-cross."

"With some encouragement from you, Mrs. Sawyer?" Winston recalled Otto Jessop's description of seeing red, which must have been the hat she was currently wearing. "You were there, weren't you?"

A subtle movement of her head confirmed this. "I asked him to go for a late-night ride."

"And the builder? He joined you?" Winston asked.

"He met us at the tree with a couple of other men."

"Why, Abigail?" Sawyer's voice was strained.

"Yes, a good question. Why don't you tell us, Mrs. Sawyer?" Winston asked. He let silence fill the room until Reginald coughed and shifted in his chair. Winston threw him a look.

With a sigh, Abigail Sawyer placed her palms on the table. "What do you want to know, Detective?"

"Let's start with how long you and Arthur Pierce had been business partners."

"Since before he married my sister."

Sawyer's eyebrows shot up, but he said nothing.

Winston pressed on. "What caused you to kill Arthur Pierce? Why now?"

Her gaze grew cold, piercing. "He tried to cut me from the partnership. I had more than enough in my accounts."

"What was your role in the partnership?" Winston asked.

"I gathered information. You would be surprised what a woman overhears, especially when others think she is not paying attention. I shared that information with Arthur to use it to encourage people to participate. He had that Macey fellow doing the same thing."

The names of close relatives. She told Pierce what names to call the miner when convincing men to invest. "And when Pierce tried to cut you out, that betrayal was enough to kill him?"

She swallowed. "He wanted to get out. He'd developed a conscience." Her tone was mocking. "Said it was time he became an honest man."

"When did he tell you this?" Miller asked.

"Two days before he died. I needed to move quickly before he unravelled everything." She nodded toward the papers on the desk. "I had hoped to get my money from the bank before they killed Arthur. Had I been faster, I wouldn't be sitting here."

"I need to know who helped you at the tree, Mrs. Sawyer." Winston pushed a piece of paper toward her. "Please write their names down. I'll have Miller find them." He waited while she wrote. "Did you instruct them to hang him at the Hollow Tree?"

"I told them to make it appear as if he took his own life."

Sawyer shuddered. "I can't believe this."

She turned to her husband. "Believe what, dear? That I had Arthur killed? Or that I was working with Arthur on his investment scheme?" Her voice rose. "I'm not surprised at your disbelief. You think so little of women generally. I particularly enjoyed having Arthur lead you along in his 'teachings.' It was simple, really."

"But why?" Sawyer pushed his hands through his hair. "Why do any of this?"

"Why not?" Mrs. Sawyer shrugged. "I was really rather good at it."

Sawyer looked at his wife, eyes growing wide. "How much money?"

"More than enough." She turned her gaze on Winston. "Will my sister be put on the street, Detective? She had nothing to do with this, and I'd rather she didn't suffer because of her husband's greed."

"What about me? Why should I suffer for your greed?"

"Reginald, you benefited from my work. And had you been a little more. . ." She smoothed a stray strand of hair. "Had you been a little more intelligent, you could have been a partner."

He swallowed. "I wanted to be Arthur's partner."

"You could have been mine."

With this, she stared directly in front of her, shoulders straight.

"Mrs. Abigail Sawyer, I am arresting you for murder and financial fraud. You are to come with me now to the police station."

"If I must."

"You must. Constable Miller, please help her."

She shrugged from Miller's grip and he stood by her elbow instead as she walked through the bank, her head high.

CHAPTER 42

Jack

Chief Constable Philpott's cheeks reddened as Winston explained how he had spent the previous two hours. "She told you all this?"

"Much of it, but only after I confronted her. She seemed to realize that she couldn't continue."

"And she is here now? In a cell? And the men she worked with?"

"I had to let one of last night's drunks go to ensure she had her own cell. Miller and another constable collected the men easily enough. They're in the other cell."

Philpott swept his hand across his face, tugging on his moustache. "What about the money? What will happen to it? Will it be returned to the investors?"

Of course, Philpott wanted to know about the money he'd given Pierce. "That is a judge's decision, though I think you'll agree the best outcome would be to return as much as possible to those who lost. Perhaps starting with those who could afford to lose the least."

Philpott nodded. "You may find some men unwilling to come forward."

"If that is the case, perhaps any money that is not returned can be distributed to the other investors," Winston said.

"I'd rather keep my name from the whole thing. If it means my money is not returned, so be it."

Winston closed his eyes, his thoughts returning to Ellis. He did not want his brother's death to come between him and his uncle. "Shame is harmful. The secret—the keeping of it, I mean." He opened his eyes and locked his gaze with his uncle's. "Do you feel better now that you have shared what you know about Ellis? You may feel the same about this, in time."

Philpott held Winston's gaze then reached across his desk for his pen. "Should I contact Bloomington and Steele, the newspaper publishers?"

Winston cocked his head. What was his uncle suggesting?

"I was thinking to discourage publishing anything about this. They were investors too, if I'm not mistaken."

Winston swallowed against the bitter taste in his mouth. This is why Riley could find so little about the case. The newspapers had been stifled. "I don't see the need to cover this story up, sir. But I realize the decision is not mine." Winston spoke slowly, disappointment pressing heavily on his chest. He stood and said, "Caroline Pierce has a right to know."

Philpott waved Winston's comment away. Sensing there was nothing more to say, Winston turned to leave.

"Jack, your mother is expecting to hear from you."

Winston spun around to face his uncle. He took a shallow breath. "Does she know you've told me?"

"She had asked me to tell you when the time was right."

Winston left Philpott seated at his desk without committing to contacting his mother. He would sort out how to respond to his family in his own time. First, he needed to speak to Caroline Pierce.

Constable Miller stood in a doorway of the back of the station, waiting for Winston. "Would you like me to join you, sir?"

"Yes, Thomas, I think I would."

*

THE POLICEMEN RODE in silence, each lost in his thoughts. At the streetcar stop nearest the Pierces' house, Winston cleared his throat and let Miller lead them to their destination. Winston hesitated before he knocked on the door, thinking of the first time he'd done so only a few days earlier.

Caroline Pierce opened the door and showed Miller and Winston into her sitting room. "Clifford is attending to a matter with the horses," she explained when she saw Miller raise an eyebrow, dismissing his unasked question. Concern forced her mouth into a downward turn. It made her look fragile. "Whatever you've come to tell me, Detective, please do it without delay."

Winston waited until she sat. As she moved, he caught a hint of a floral scent. He felt himself colour as he thought of her applying it. He straightened his spine and forced his thoughts back to the reason he sat in her front room. "Mrs. Pierce, I learned today who was behind your husband's death."

Her knuckles turned white as she gripped the sides of her chair. "Reginald?"

"I'm sorry to have to tell you this, madam, but it was your sister."

Several beats passed before she spoke. When she did, her voice was barely a whisper. "Abigail? Why? How?"

"She was involved in your husband's business."

Confusion crossed her face. "What do you mean?"

"Your sister directed your husband's investment scheme. She had been doing so for years. They started small, before they moved to Vancouver. He served as the face of their partnership. She made most of the decisions."

Mrs. Pierce's features darkened as she searched the men's faces. "I don't believe this. Why did she kill my husband if they were partners?"

"She didn't actually hang him, but she instructed the men who did."

"Abigail?" She repeated the name in disbelief.

Winston nodded.

"Where is she now?"

"She is at the station, in the jail."

Caroline Pierce clenched her hands in her lap.

"Are you sure it was her? She got along so well with Arthur. And she is really a gentle person. I can't see her killing or even having someone killed, let alone my husband." Her knuckles were white from the tension in her hands. Winston nodded to Miller, who rose and left the room—in search of tea, Winston hoped.

Winston swallowed and leaned closer to Mrs. Pierce. "She admitted it. I have no doubt it was her."

She pressed her palms into her lap as if she was preparing to stand. Instead, after a shaky breath, she slumped into her chair.

"What of Reginald?"

"He knew nothing of her actions in your husband's death. I am convinced he knew nothing of her business dealings either."

Caroline Pierce cast her gaze around the room. Winston had observed his mother doing the same thing, making a mental tally of the worth of the items in front of her. Books, furniture, art. How much would she lose from her husband's actions? "What will happen to me?"

Winston did not want to see this woman suffer for her husband's crime. Her question didn't surprise him, but her calculation disappointed him. "Their plan caused many people to lose their money. I'd like to see that the investors receive as much as possible of what is owed to them."

"How will you do that?" Her gaze darted to what Winston assumed was the most valuable item in the room, a painting on the wall to her right. "And what will happen to me?"

"I don't know. Your sister has thousands of dollars in her accounts. I expect that money will help their victims recover."

"If it isn't enough, I will sell my assets, however much we can get for this." She passed her arm in front of her in a wide arc. "What about my husband's reputation? Is this all he will be remembered for, this terrible business?"

He couldn't tell her that her husband would be all but forgotten, or that Reginald Sawyer would make the lasting mark in historical records. "Mr. Pierce was involved in defrauding hundreds of men. His reputation is as fabricated as his investment company. I expect a judge might look favourably on your being willing to part with your assets rather than being forced to. But if there's anything left over, I doubt you'll keep it."

"I know Messrs. Bloomington and Steele." She pushed a strand of hair behind her ear. "I will ensure that the men who lost money are repaid, but I will also ensure my husband's name is not tarnished."

"How?"

"Bloomington and Steele were clients of my husband. They will want their reputations preserved, and I will ask them to keep this matter quiet."

Winston had neither the will nor the energy to challenge her. She'd pleaded a complete lack of knowledge of any details of her husband's business when it suited her. Now here she had listed off two of his investors. There was nothing more to be gained from sitting with Caroline Pierce. Winston stood and bade her goodbye.

He found Miller in the kitchen speaking to Mr. Clifford. "I've told him about Mrs. Sawyer," Miller explained.

Clifford's face was ashen. "What will happen, Detective?"

"Your mistress will need support, Clifford. And will appreciate your loyalty. I will recommend that investors be repaid, but ultimately it's not up to me. You may have lost nothing."

Clifford nodded. "Thank you, sir."

Winston and Miller took their leave. On the sidewalk, both hunched against the November wind. "What did you make of her reaction, sir?"

"She'd just found out most of her life has been supported by lies, Miller. That is a difficult thing to learn." He turned up his collar.

"Do you think she'll keep the story from being covered by the press? With so many men who've lost money?"

"If their money is returned, they'll have nothing to complain about, Thomas."

Miller considered this. "What do we do now?"

Winston shook his head. "We do nothing. Our work is done when I hand the chief our report. Go home. Be satisfied with the work you've done on this."

"Are you satisfied, sir?"

"We've solved a murder, Miller. I'm satisfied."

CHAPTER 43

Riley

RILEY GRIPPED THE journal as she read the latest message from Jack.

Dear Riley,

After writing my last note to you, perhaps a little hastily, I realized my mistake. The murderer wasn't Mrs. Pierce but her sister, who had also worked with Arthur Pierce on his scheme.

When I spoke with Mrs. Pierce, she was shocked by the news that her sister was behind her husband's death. And by the news that her husband had spent his life swindling others, including her. I suspect the pain she felt will be shared by all who knew him. I'll use whatever small influence I have to help recover investors' money. Some may not want to be associated with this scandal, while others, for whom the loss is a greater blow, will have no choice.

Thank you once again for your support in this case. Your help has been invaluable. I hope that in collaborating to solve it, we have not altered the future, though I know you take great care to avoid that.

Now I must get on. Today was far more draining than I realized, and I'm looking forward to a warm bath and perhaps a dram of whisky.

Until next time,

J. Winston

Her heart raced. Had they changed the future? Would Reginald Sawyer go on to become a leader of the city, as had been the case before she became involved? She would find out tomorrow when she arrived at the museum. Even if they'd altered the future, surely it was for the better? No. She gave her head a shake. She didn't want that kind of power or responsibility. She would check the archive records to see if the information on file remained unchanged.

CHAPTER 44

Jack

Dear Jack,

I'm happy to report that your solving the case has not altered the newspaper articles or other documents I'd uncovered previously. Reginald Sawyer will continue to become a business leader who focuses on business ethics. No doubt the experience with his wife and Arthur Pierce shapes his future actions.

I enjoyed working on this case with you.

Until next time, keep well.

Sincerely,

Riley

Winston placed his palm on the open journal and smiled. This connection to Riley was a very good thing in his life, and especially right now, he needed good things.

He'd been sipping his tea in Mrs. Bradley's dining room, trying to calm his still-reeling mind, when he'd opened the book to find Riley's message. He pushed aside thoughts of how to deal with his family and looked down at her familiar handwriting. She'd penned this message on the second-to-last page in the book.

"You can always get another from me when you need it." Melodia's words rang in his mind. What had he done with the card she had given him? He rose and climbed the stairs to his rooms.

He found the card, bearing only an address, in the pocket of his jacket. Winston thought it was in the Gastown area of the city, not too far from the constabulary. The idea of exploring the city at his leisure was appealing. He gathered his things and slipped the card into his pocket.

The clouds promised rain, perhaps why the streets were busy for mid-morning. Delivery cart drivers shouted at pedestrians who darted across the street after the streetcar rattled by. People must be anxious to finish their errands before the deluge.

Winston checked the card again and tried to picture the address. It was for an alley, though Winston couldn't remember having walked down it the day he'd arrived from Toronto. For a moment, he watched the crowd and tried to recall the details of that first day in the city. His mind was muddled, no doubt the result of his recent restless nights.

He was still full from breakfast, but he stopped at a pie stand and purchased a pastry. The steaming pie warmed his hand before he handed it to a young boy minding horses. The boy's eyes widened at the gift. As the boy ate, Winston asked if he knew the shop at the address on the card.

The boy gestured over his shoulder with a dirty thumb. "Miss Melodia? She keeps funny hours," he answered between mouthfuls.

"Have you seen her today?"

When the boy nodded, Winston left him to finish his treat.

Even if it had been a bright, sunny day, the alley would have been dark. He turned his collar against a chill that washed through him.

He found the door to Melodia's shop with only the word Supplies painted on it. One would certainly have to know what one was looking for. How had he stumbled into this place before? He realized the shop must be the rear entrance of another on Cordova Street, perhaps a prospecting supplier. Did she rent a small room for her shop? He depressed the handle and let himself into the windowless space.

Upon seeing the narrow room, a memory crystallized for him. It looked almost exactly as it had when he'd last been inside. A table and two chairs occupied the middle of the room, with a low counter set off to the side and running the length of the shop. Behind the counter were shelves of boxes, none of which bore labels.

Melodia stood behind the counter, easing a box into a gap on a shelf. "Ah, Detective. I have been expecting you," she called when she saw him. In her hand was a journal much like the one currently in his satchel. Instinctively, his hand moved to feel for it within the bag.

"Melodia," he said. He was growing more comfortable using her given name, as she'd requested on their first meeting. He recalled the visit to her home that he'd made with Thomas Miller. Nearly every surface had been stacked with books. In contrast, this space was uncluttered, almost empty.

As if sensing his question, she smiled, cradling the book in one arm against her chest. "Some of my clients prefer to visit me at home, while others prefer it here." She drew her free hand in an arc to demonstrate her point. "The man who runs the shop back there kindly lets me this room to thank me for some guidance I gave him." She gestured behind her with her head. "Have you come for another book?"

"I have."

She set the book on the counter and tapped her finger on it. "The first has served you and your little bird well?"

Her question echoed the one she had asked at Arthur Pierce's funeral and confirmed his conclusion that she knew about Riley. "It has." Did she know how well? For a moment, he considered telling her. Would doing so break the connection? He settled on a partial truth. "It helps with my thinking."

She pushed the book toward him. "You know how to get it to your bird?"

As soon as she'd asked, Winston realized that he didn't. "No." At this, his heart began racing. But surely Melodia would not have invited him here if she didn't have a solution. He remembered how Riley had sent him her photograph, and his heart calmed. "She shared a photograph with me once."

"Clever girl." Melodia reached underneath the counter and pulled out two other books. "Tuck the covers of your current journal into this one so the spines face out." She demonstrated with the books, slipping the front and back covers of one into the pages of the other. "Wrap them together, and your bird—your finch—will find them. The new journal must be inside the covers of the old one." She pulled the books apart and slipped them back together again to emphasize her point. "My shop will be here when you need another." She reached for his hand. "As will I, Jack. When you need to talk."

Her gesture triggered another memory from Pierce's funeral. "Your parents meant no harm," she had said, and her hand had been on his arm then, too. The warmth of her hand on his brought him back to the moment. He started to tell her he didn't need to talk about anything, but that was untrue. He didn't need to—couldn't—talk yet.

She read the look on his face and patted his hand. "When you're ready."

Though his mind was swirling, he slid the new book into his satchel, making sure to keep the cover of the old one closed. Wrapping the books together was something he wanted to do alone, back in his rooms. His heart sped up as he imagined Riley finding the bundle. This was going to work. "Thank you," he stammered.

He allowed himself a backward glance toward the shop as he stood in the entrance to the alley. He shook his head when the door appeared to shimmer. His lack of sleep and his hangover conspired to let him see things that weren't there. To be certain, he lifted the flap of his satchel to confirm his journals—the old and the new—were inside.

As he walked toward his rooms and replayed his conversation with Melodia, he returned to two questions. How much did she know about Riley? How had she known about how broken he would be by his family's betrayal? He took a slow, deep breath, knowing he wasn't ready yet to ask them.

*

After leaving Melodia's shop, Jack took his time to walk to Mrs. Bradley's house. He both couldn't wait to see if Melodia's instructions worked and couldn't bear the thought of what would happen if they didn't. The rain finally fell, and he knew it was time to get home.

Once inside, he made a point of being polite to Mrs. Bradley. She hadn't mentioned his rudeness from the other night, but the guilt of it still prickled. Perhaps he would bring her flowers or some other token to quiet his conscience.

In his sitting room, before he removed his coat, he pulled out the new journal from his satchel. The spine crackled as he opened it and fanned the pages against his fingers. He moved it to the back of the writing desk and pulled his old journal from his bag, turning to the final blank page.

Dear Riley,

A few days ago, you asked what we would do when this journal runs out of pages. I realize that I've kept you waiting for an answer. I'm pleased to share that I do have an answer. My acquaintance Melodia Spectre, whom I may have written about previously, revealed to me that it was she who supplied our first journal. I hadn't made the connection, as I had no clear memory of the clerk I'd purchased it from. I have acquired another book from her. She claims she will continue to provide them as long as needed.

As he wrote, Winston felt warmth rise in his chest.

It appears the magic—that is what I will call it—of the journal passes to anything touching its interior pages. I believe this is how you will find the new journal. When I finish writing this, I will nestle the two books together exactly as Melodia has instructed me, and the new one will pass to you, connected to this one, the same way you sent me the photograph.

With hope that this works,

Jack

Winston rubbed his palm across his face. He was unwilling to consider an alternative. He tucked the journals into each other, following Melodia's instructions, and wrapped them together with twine. The result was not the neat bundle he had hoped for, but it looked elegant enough. A shiver of excitement ran through him as he thought of Riley finding the new journal.

He slipped out of his coat and arranged his belongings for the next day. When he could not wait any longer, he returned to his writing desk where the misshapen bundle rested. How would he know that Riley had found both books? Melodia had said nothing about how long it would take, whether he needed to leave it for the night. Winston cursed himself for not thinking to ask the question. His heart pounded in his ears as he slid a finger under the twine. He flipped open the new journal and closed his eyes. After a calming breath, he released a loud sigh.

Dear Jack,

Success!

R.

Read More

FOR A SNEAK peek into Jack and Riley's lives before they met and to receive early notice of upcoming books, visit Sarah's website: https://sarahmstephen.ca/newsletter-book/ to sign up for regular dispatches.

Other books in the Journal Through Time Mysteries:
The Dead of False Creek
Murder in Mount Pleasant (available summer 2023)

He chases crooks in the 19th century. She researches the past in the 21st. When a long-lost necklace is found, can they solve the deaths of the women who wore it last before tragedy strikes again?

Vancouver, 1897. Detective Jack Winston investigates when a necklace disappears and two women who wore it are dead.

Vancouver, 2017. Riley Finch's sister falls ill shortly after wearing a necklace recently found within the walls of an old house.

Unsure where to find answers, Jack and Riley team up again through their journal to uncover the truth behind the deaths. Can the pair solve the crimes in time? *Murder in Mount Pleasant* is the third book in the Journal Through Time historical mystery series. If you like time-bending mysteries, you'll love this twisting tale.

Author's Note

I have so enjoyed continuing Jack and Riley's story. I hope you have enjoyed reading it, and if you did, I hope you'll be excited to learn that there are more mysteries for them to solve.

As I said in the author's note of *The Dead of False Creek*, I have never formally studied history. But I love reading historical fiction. And this is a work of fiction. I've woven in historical details, and I've also taken some liberties to create my own version of history where it suited the story.

Neither am I a financial expert, though I have enjoyed coming up with a financially based crime, spun out of the many stories of fraud reported in the media and Vancouver's unfortunate, ongoing history of playing a significant role in financial misdeeds.

I am thankful for the City of Vancouver Archives, where I spend countless online hours, and the Vancouver Police Museum, where I spend many in-person hours. I used Robert A. J. McDonald's *Making Vancouver* to better understand what life was like in this city of the western frontier. For this book, I also read sections of *Fleecing the Lamb: The Inside Story of the Vancouver Stock Exchange,* by Alison Griffiths and David Cruise. While the stock exchange didn't exist during Winston's time and wasn't central to the story, I wanted to understand the financial mood of the young city, and I appreciate the patience of the BC Securities Commission answering my questions about the history of securities regulations and early frauds in Vancouver.

Receiving kind words from readers of *The Dead of False Creek* has been wonderful. It means so much when someone takes the time to send me a message to let me know they enjoyed it. This is me encouraging you to let an author know when you like what they've written. For me, at least, it is unspeakably meaningful.

If you enjoyed this book, please consider leaving a review or recommending it to a friend. I love hearing your thoughts; you can reach me at sarah@sarahmstephen.ca or follow me on social media to share them.

Warmly,

Sarah M Stephen
Vancouver, 2022

Acknowledgements

This book is the result of many hands. It wouldn't exist without my husband and son encouraging me and putting up with a limited rotation of meals when I needed head space to puzzle over plot. My editor, Janet Fretter, is a firm guide, and knowing that I have her on my side to make sense of my ideas is invaluable. I've said this before, but I cannot thank her enough. My proofreader, Shelley Hudson, is also essential. Any typos are my own. My early readers provided thoughtful insights that strengthened the story. Finally, my parents and siblings, who may be my proudest fans, continue their endless, patient support and louder-than-I'm-sometimes-comfortable-with cheerleading. Thank you.

About the Author

Sarah M Stephen started writing at an early age, first scribbling pages of notes while pretending to be a journalist before she could print. After mastering the alphabet, she moved into poetry and short stories. Following a few successes in grade school (a regional poetry prize) and university (a short story published), she traded her creative tales for corporate ones. A few years ago, she rediscovered her love of words and resumed creative writing. Sarah also co-hosts the *Clued in Mystery* podcast, where listeners can hear about her love of the mystery genre. She lives in Vancouver, Canada, with her family.

Contact Sarah:
Instagram: https://www.instagram.com/sarahmstephenauthor/
Facebook: https://www.facebook.com/sarahmstephenauthor/
Website: https://sarahmstephen.ca/

Printed in Great Britain
by Amazon